DAUNTLESS

DAUNTLESS

VICTORIA DENAULT

HeartEyes Press

For Novid

BOWEN

I'm not sure heaven and hell actually exist, but if they did, I have vague ideas of what my version of each would be. My heaven would be a perpetual warm, balmy, summer night. Like the one at seventeen, when I lied in the tall grass on the hill behind my mother's garden, eating strawberries off the vine, staring at the stars and telling my sister about my first kiss, with a boy. Hell... well, that would be working at Vino and Veritas. Because it seems to be something that, no matter how hard I try, I completely and utterly fail at every single night.

I've only been employed for eight days, and worked four of them, and I'm pretty certain for Tanner, the manager, it's been the worst four days of his career at the wine bar. Tonight, which happens to be a bustling Saturday night, he has me on bar back duties. It's simple, straight-forward work. Make sure the shelves are stocked, the glasses make it back out to the bar after they've been washed, and that the condiments — lemon and lime wedges, olives, and maraschino cherries don't run low. And for the first couple hours, I'm doing fine. Until it's time to change a keg.

I've changed kegs before more than once, at parties in college, and never had an issue. But of course, this isn't a keg at a dorm or in someone's kitchen in high school. This is a professional keg, in a professional establishment, which has a whole bunch of shit I didn't realize need careful consideration when changing a keg. Like the gas and the FOB and the coupler, which it turns out can, on rare occasions, fly off when you don't have a great grip on it, causing beer to spray everywhere, and the coupler to almost take your eye out.

Hell, I say.

This job is hell.

I get everything under control fairly quickly, but I'm drenched in beer. Molly stares at me, her big eyes filled with empathy. You know it's serious when Molly is feeling bad for you. I may not have been here long but one of the first things I learned was that Molly is the resident Calamity Jane. A title you would think I was gunning for on purpose at this point.

"Jesus," Tanner says under his breath when he turns and sees me.

"Everything is fine," I assure him. "Now."

"Except you can't exactly keep working while dripping beer everywhere," Tanner walks up to me and tilts his head. "You have beer foam in your hair."

"Shit," I whisper and touch the side of my head. I yank out the elastic that is trying unsuccessfully to hold my chin length hair back. I sigh and just rub the foam in like it's mousse, because what choice do I have? A few of the customers sitting at the bar are watching me. Most in shock or horror. Tanner notices and gently guides me back into the private storage area. "Can you run upstairs and ask my husband, his name is Jax, to lend you a T-shirt. And maybe a towel."

"Yeah. Sure. Sorry," I say and slink away.

My God, I am not this much of a klutz. What is going on? I immediately head for the stairs, climbing them two at a time because I want to get back to work. I think Tanner is still worried I'm a bit of a slacker because on my very first day my stupid alarm didn't go off and I was late. It's more than a little embarrassing having to tell your boss that you overslept on your first day. Especially when that day starts at seven in the evening. I didn't elaborate further because I thought adding 'I've had insomnia issues ever since my parents were killed in a car accident so sometimes, I fall into coma naps in the afternoon since I don't always sleep at night' would be worse than just being late.

After I knock on the apartment door and introduce myself to Tanner's husband, who is blond and beautiful with a wicked cool accent like the chef at the bar, Jax loans me a plain, dusty gray color T-shirt. It's a little short because I've always had a torso the length of a football field, but it's passable. I rush back down the stairs, stumbling and cracking my ribs on the railing before landing in a heap at the bottom. I let out a string of obscenities at the bruises I'll be sporting for weeks but luckily nothing is broken so I get up and hightail it back into the bar. There's a band playing tonight, which is why it's busier than normal. They haven't played here before, but apparently, they've got a solid fanbase. There's even a line outside.

I love live music, but I doubt I'll get to enjoy it much tonight. I slide back behind the bar with Auden, who gives me a weary smile. "Just cut some lemons," he says and reluctantly hands me a knife. "Carefully."

"Sure thing." I smile back and try not to feel too humiliated. The burly Scot has every right to be weary. Last shift I was opening a bottle of champagne for a customer and the cork blew off and beaned him right in the forehead.

I grab some lemons and tuck myself into a corner on the back of the bar and begin slicing. I manage to cut all the lemons without incident. When I refill Auden's condiment holder, he looks at me like a proud parent when their kid learns to tie his shoes. So yay, and ouch, to that.

Autumn slides up to the bar just as I've decided to tackle loading some clean wine glasses onto the rack they hang from above the bar. Her eyes narrow on my shirt and her round cheeks get rounder as she grins. "That's not your shirt."

"Keen observation, fashion police," I mutter. "Aren't you supposed to be working on the bookstore side?"

"Shift ended and I thought I would stick around and enjoy the show," she says, sliding into the last empty bar stool.

"The band is supposed to be good," I tell her as she pushes her strawberry blonde hair over her shoulders. "They do covers from the seventies and eighties."

"I wasn't talking about the band. You're the show I'm here to watch," Autumn remarks with a glint in her hazel eyes. "I'm sorry I missed whatever new misadventure has caused you to wear someone else's shirt."

I love my only sister, and I know she loves me, but she's annoyingly gleeful about my inability to handle this job. "I wish you were still underage so I could get you kicked out."

"Sorry not sorry," Autumn replies, still smiling brightly. "And Tanner said he would give me a free belated birthday drink."

She waves at Tanner, who is over by the stage talking with a guy from the band. Tanner waves back and pauses long enough to call out to Auden. "Whatever Autumn wants is on me."

Then he goes back to discussing something with the band guy, who I can't help but notice is *very* easy on the eyes. And also, he looks nervous, possibly panicked. He runs a hand through his thick, brown hair and somehow doesn't mess it up. It's got height on top while staying very sleek on the sides. If you put him in a leather jacket, he could be an extra in *Grease*, minus the actual grease. His hair looks silky, not slimy. Even with his thick, straight eyebrows pinched and his blue eyes narrowed, he's really attractive.

Autumn suddenly snaps her fingers in front of me. "Hello! Did you hear me?"

"No," I admit.

"I said what do you recommend?" Autumn repeats what she must have said that I tuned out while staring at the hot guy. "I need a drink, remember?"

"I suggest whatever you drink, you have me make, lass" Auden interjects and smiles. "For all our sakes."

Autumn is giggling now. I ignore her. "Is there an issue with the band?"

"Is that the name of a specialty cocktail?" Autumn kids.

Auden looks over to Tanner and the hot dude. My sister's eyes follow. "Go find out."

"Me? No." I shake my head. "It's not my place."

"Might as well," Auden adds. I think he's just trying to get me to move farther away from him so I don't clock him with anything again. But I do know my way around musical instruments and can set up a drum kit or tune a guitar in my sleep. It might be nice to actually show Tanner I have skills.

I slip out from behind the bar and make my way over to the two of them. The closer I get, the hotter the band dude gets. Those blue eyes are a really great cobalt color and the T-shirt he's wearing with the band name on it — Imposter Syndrome — fits him perfectly, hugging some decent sized biceps and clinging to a very fit waist. His shoulders are broad, and that perfectly high and tousled hair just begs to be held onto during a blow job. I mean, if the guy gave them, but I'd bet money he doesn't. There's a really strong straight boy vibe coming off of him.

"I'll ask Molly, our waitress. She plays in a band so maybe she knows a drummer," I hear Tanner say to the hottie.

"Tanner, I am so sorry. I don't know what else to say, but thanks for trying to save this for us," the guy says and rakes his hair with his hand again.

"Dude, it's saving my night too. You packed this place," Tanner replies and then he notices me standing about a foot away. "Hey, Bowen. Did something else go wrong?"

He doesn't mean it bitingly, so I force myself not to let his words chip away at my ego. "No, I thought maybe you needed help setting up the band or something. It looked like there's an issue."

The band guy tilts his head to look at me. His gaze is intense. I mean, it's probably just the pressure of whatever the situation is, but damn, he gives a good stare. "Not unless you know a drummer who can get here in half an hour or less," Tanner says.

"I might," I say and now they're both staring at me intensely. "I play."

"You play the drums?" Tanner blinks at me in disbelief. "You play, like, *well*?"

Ouch. But I get it. Autumn talked me up to be this excellent, hard worker who could learn anything quickly, which is why he hired me and well, he must have doubts at this point. But I don't. I know I can drum. "I was a music major in college. I mean, I didn't graduate but I wasn't kicked out or anything. I can play drums, guitar, and piano. Proficiently, I swear."

"Can I show you our set list? See what songs you might know?" the hot band guy asks but before I respond my eyes fly to Tanner. I'm his employee, after all.

"If you really think your band member has flaked, I'm more than happy to let you borrow Bowen," Tanner says, and his eyes move back to me. "If you're cool with it."

"Yeah. I love playing." I do love playing, especially more than every job I've had here.

"Cool, let me show you the set list." Hot band dude motions with his hand, and I follow him through the growing crowd to the corner of the stage. He grabs a piece of paper and hands it to me. "I'm Chase by the way. Ashton. I'm the singer."

"Bowen," I reply.

"Yeah, I know." I lift my eyes from the set list, and as we stare at each other, he smirks. It amps up his hotness tenfold. "Tanner said your name."

"Right," I force myself to go back to scanning the song titles. They're all songs I know well, thanks to my parents who loved music. "Here're the ones I'm confident I can pull off."

I point to seven of the ten. Chase's eyebrows shoot to the ceiling. "Really? That many?"

"Yeah. My dad loved nineties grunge and my mom loved seventies and eighties music, so I grew up on a lot of these tunes," I explain. "They're the ones who first taught me how to play."

"The drums?"

"Yeah. And everything else," I shrug. He smiles again. Damn. I like it more than I should.

"Okay, cool, I'm gonna trust you completely," he announces and clasps my shoulder. His hand is strong and warm. "Let me introduce you to the other guys."

The other guys are Grant and Joe and the guy I'm replacing is "Fucking Bennie." At least that's how each of them refer to him. Grant and Joe seem nice enough but they definitely don't seem to have as much faith in me as Chase does. Still, they'd rather take a shot with me than cancel the gig so the next thing I know, I'm settling in behind the drum kit.

I have no idea what I'm getting myself into. These guys could suck. I might end up looking bad by association, but honestly, it can't be worse than how things have gone at Vino and Veritas so far. I take a deep breath and hope for the best.

It turns out to be a pretty great experience. These guys are more than okay. They're pretty freaking great, actually. Chase has a fantastic voice, singing everything from Bon Jovi to the Eagles to Nirvana with ease. And the crowd loves him. He has great banter and a confidence and ease on stage that draws you in and makes you comfortable. We have a couple small mess ups, like I came in late on a song, but everything goes better than expected and I can see Tanner smiling in relief and approval. Feels good to play again, and to not just be a fuck up inside these four walls.

We're short on songs, since there were a few I wasn't sure I could play, so with only three songs to go, Chase grabs an acoustic guitar from the corner of the stage and tells the rest of us to take five. I walk over to the bar with Grant and Joe. Auden gives us fresh bottles of water while Chase starts strumming the chords to a dance song that was popular last year, only he's doing it all slow and with a different cadence and it's really freaking great.

Grant leans into me as he twists the cap off his water. His brown eyes are kind so I know he means no harm when he says, "He's showing off now."

Autumn wanders over to stand beside me and clutches my arm. "It is so awesome seeing you play again."

I look down at her and try to deflect the words and the relief in her eyes. "Beats the hell out of a beer shower."

Everyone claps when Chase is done, and I give him an impressed smile as I get back on stage. He winks at me. If I didn't know better, I would think it was flirting. The rest of the gig flies by and ends in a roaring round of applause. As I step behind the bar again, Tanner gives me the first real smile I think I've seen since my first shift. "You did great!"

"He did," Chase adds. I turn and see he followed me back to the bar. "I honestly can't think of a way to thank you for saving our asses."

"Don't worry about it. I had a great time," I reply, and his smile is making me smile and it feels a little like flirting again. But then a woman with short, dirty blonde hair and high cheek bones appears behind him and latches onto his arm.

"Chase! You were fantastic," she coos.

"Thanks again," Chase tells me and then he nods at Tanner and disappears into the crowd with the pretty blonde lady who is likely his girlfriend. I'd be lying if I said I wasn't just a wee bit disappointed.

"Can you clear some empty glasses off the tables, Bowen?" Tanner asks, looking nervous. I nod, and he hands me a tray.

I make my way through the crowd, being extra careful with the tray as I load it with empty wine and pint glasses. Suddenly, as I think I've forged a clear path to the bar, Autumn appears in front of me and I have to come to an abrupt stop. The glasses teeter and I panic, but luckily, I don't drop anything. "Autumn! For crying out loud, do not ruin what is turning into the best shift I've had so far."

"Did you see who your hot band buddy just walked away with?" she asks, a frown turning down her mouth. It looks incredibly unnatural on her. She inherited our mom's bright sunshine-y attitude and rarely finds reason to frown. I picture the woman who curled herself into Chase in my head again. She does seem vaguely familiar and the way Autumn is glaring impatiently at me, I should definitely know who she is.

"Umm… she run a rival Etsy store?" I ask, thinking this has to do with her side hustle selling hemp jewelry online. But her frown only deepens. "Someone from high school who used to tease you about your weight?"

Kids were brutal to her in high school.

"Ugh." Autumn rolls her eyes. "It was Lacey Baldwin. How did you not recognize her? Her face is plastered everywhere!"

Yep. Now that she's said the name out loud, I see it. "She looked different. She wasn't in a pantsuit and she looked like a normal person."

I scoot around my sister, eyes glued to the tray, and continue to the bar. Autumn follows along behind me. I slip behind the bar and Tanner takes the tray of dirty dishes from me. "Not one casualty," he says in awe and my ego takes another kick to the nuts. "I'll get these washed. Auden says you're good with the condiments. Can you refill the olives and cut some limes?"

I nod and get to work. "Autumn, you should go home. You have finals soon."

"Yeah. I know," Autumn says tersely. She hates when I parent her. The only thing that makes her angrier is our older brother Woody doing it. To be fair, she kind of is the most grown-up person of the three of us. "You know, if your boy band singer is related to our arch nemesis, you can't play with them again."

"First of all, I haven't been asked to play with them again," I reply as I open a jar of olives and begin transferring them into the condiment container we keep on the bar. "Second of all, they look nothing alike, so I doubt they're related. He might be dating her though."

Autumn snorts at that. She does that a lot when she thinks people are idiots. It's somehow more adorable than offensive. "Okay well, that's even worse." The freckles that pepper her ski jump nose form one giant freckle for a second as she wrinkles it. Then she almost jumps as a thought slams into her brain. "Oh wait! Maybe he knows campaign secrets. You should play with them again so you can pump him for information that could help Woody."

Our brother is running for mayor and Lacey Baldwin is also running for mayor. This is why Autumn is talking like this. And also because she recently marathoned *House of Cards* as research when my brother decided to run in the emergency election. "Woody needs a miracle, not a double agent," I mutter.

Autumn sighs in defeat and gives up on the silly idea. "Anyway, you sounded great up there. It's good to hear you play again."

"No big deal," I reply casually, but it kind of is a big deal to her because she thinks I haven't played since I quit school. I have, just not often and never when she's around. "See you in the morning."

"Okay." Autumn smiles and makes her way to the door, like so many others are doing. Now that the band is done, the evening is winding down for everyone. I glance over at the stage. Chase is there packing up the equipment, but Lacey, our brother's main opponent for mayor, is nowhere to be seen now.

I'm so busy concentrating on not screwing anything up, the next time I glance at the stage it's bare. Chase is gone and I'm bummed I didn't get to say good-bye. Molly walks over and asks Auden for two Shipley ciders for her table then she passes me a napkin. I'm about to ask her why when I see something scrawled on it.

Bowen

Band likes to unwind at my place after shows. Stop by after work.

187 Church Buzz 3.

Chase.

I thank Molly and tuck the napkin into the back pocket of my jeans. And then I narrowly miss cutting my thumb off as I start slicing limes again. I curse myself and concentrate on work and not the hot straight dude with the amazing voice.

"To a great set!" Joe says as he raises the fresh beer I just handed him into the air.

"To a fucking amazing set," Grant adds, lifting his glass.

I lift the glass of Merlot I poured for myself. "To the bar back with rhythm who saved our asses."

Rhythm, a smokin' hot body, and a hell of a set of bedroom eyes, I add to myself. Bowen Whitlock grew up to be one great looking guy. Not to mention talented as fuck. And he saved our asses tonight without even blinking, which I am still amazed by.

We clink our drinks and all take a sip. My eyes move through the loft to the front door. I wonder if he'll show? Grant moves to the living room area and Joe follows, so I follow them both. "What was his name again?" Joe asks as he sinks into my black velvet couch. "Bryan?"

"Bowen," I correct as I sit on the oversized leather ottoman by the fire and Grant puts his ass in one of the club chairs. "Bowen Whitlock."

"Whitlock?" Joe's dark eyes narrow. "Why do I know that name?"

"There's a Whitlock running for mayor," Grant says. "The farmer dude whose parents were killed a few winters ago."

"Five winters ago. And yeah, Bowen's his younger brother," I add and sip my wine. "I was at the funeral, but I don't think he remembers."

"Why?" Grant wants to know.

"I was in college and my grandfather went to pay his respects and asked me to go with him," I explain. "He didn't know the family. It was a political move. He thought it would look good since he was an assemblyman for the state and the accident made the news and everything. It was an election year after all."

I see the sour look I know I'm sporting reflected back at me in the faces of my bandmates. Joe shakes his head. "Man, your family sucks."

"That they do," I agree without hesitation. Joe and Grant have both known me long enough to be able to make those statements. Grant went to boarding school with me when I was a teenager and Joe was my roommate freshman year here in Vermont. I've never held back any of the horrible truths of life as a member of a political family. They know this hobby—as my father calls it—has been a key component in helping me cope with my family obligations since I graduated college. "Anyway, I don't think Bowen recognized me. I met him for all of five seconds on the worst day of his life."

Joe takes a long swig from his beer. "Well, hopefully we get to play again at Vino and Veritas. I had a blast."

"Yeah. I think Tanner would book us again, but I also think we should find a new drummer before that," I say, studying their faces to see how they react to that. Bennie has been in the band since it formed. He didn't go to Moo U with me and Joe, but he's from Burlington. He went to Harvard with Grant and then moved back home to take over his family's construction business. Only, it's been years and his dad hasn't given him the reins yet. "Bennie just isn't reliable."

"I agree," Joe says without pause. "He was late to our last gig, and he bailed on practice a few times, including last week."

Grant looks conflicted, which is fair. He's the one who brought Bennie into the fold. I don't mean to put their friendship in the line of fire, but I guess I should have thought of that before I fooled around with Bennie. I don't know for sure but I'm betting that's why he ghosted us tonight. "Yeah. I don't think we really have a choice."

"That's why I invited Bowen over for drinks when he gets off work," I say. It's a half-truth, but Grant and Joe don't need to know that right now. "I figured we could see how we vibe with him since he didn't really get to talk much at the bar. And then if it feels right, we could ask him to join."

"This is all happening really fast," Grant says and scratches his head. "I mean I'm not against it, but let's get to know him better and see how it goes."

"Fair enough," I say as Joe nods and shrugs at the same time, as if to say whatever.

Joe is really easy going which is how we stayed so close all through college and now well into our adult lives. He's never intrusive, doesn't have strong opinions. He's like Switzerland in human form. Also, he didn't blink twice when I told him I fooled around with a guy and I liked it during the first semester of college. I don't trust that information with many people, but I knew I could trust Joe.

A loud buzz echoes through the loft and I jump up a little too quickly and make my way to the door. If Joe or Grant took note of my enthusiasm, they don't say anything. They start a conversation about the upcoming NHL playoffs, ignoring me completely. I don't even ask who it is, I just say, "Take the elevator to the third floor." Then I hit the button that unlocks the door to the lobby of the building.

I lean against the wall and sip my wine and wait for Bowen. Joe calls out, "Alexa play the playlist After Gigs"

"Playing your playlist After Gigs," Alexa replies dutifully.

The apartment fills with the first chords of a Nirvana tune. We created this playlist, together, drunk, and add to it after every gig, also while drunk. So sometimes I'm pleasantly surprised by what's on it. The elevator lists open and Bowen blinks, confused. "Wait… I'm *in* your apartment?"

"Yeah. I have the top two floors," I tell him as he tentatively steps off the elevator and the doors slide closed behind him.

"And the roof!" Grant calls out and gives Bowen a welcoming wave. Bowen nods hello back.

"And the private rooftop," I confirm. "It's a loft."

"Cool," he says slowly, like he isn't sure he means it. I try not to take it personally. I've been to the house he grew up in because that's where the wake was for his parents. It's a lovely two story farmhouse. Quintessential old Vermont. My loft is far from quintessential old Vermont. It kind of looks more like classic New York. Bowen walks further into the large, open space, and his eyes slowly scan the room, taking in the charcoal gray polished concrete floors and the velvet and leather furniture and the thick wood beams and powder coated black metal railing that skirts the stairs that lead to the bedroom.

He doesn't look impressed so much as intrigued, which is fine. My loft wasn't bought to impress anyone. It was bought to piss off my parents. My dad mostly. "Glad you came. Can I get you a beer? Wine?"

"Beer is good, thanks," Bowen gives me a small, relaxed smile. "Good tune."

"How'd you get into music?" I ask as I walk past the oversized island, which is also my dining table, to the fridge to fetch his beer. He follows along behind me, eyes still scanning every surface and corner. He even tilts his head up to take in the floor to ceiling windows on the wall that faces the front of the building.

"My mom was raised by a Laurel Canyon hippie. Used to sing at jam sessions Grandma would hold at her house every Sunday. My dad was more about the grunge and nineties alt rock scene. He grew up in Seattle. He not only played guitar, he started building them too."

"Cool," I reply as I hand him his beer. "How did a California love child and a Seattle grunge guy end up in Vermont?"

"They met at a college party in Northern California, decided to form a band and play gigs and busk in the street together for tuition and beer money. They fell in love. My dad's parents didn't approve of the band thing, or my hippie mom, so they decided to run away together and become farmers." Bowen says it like it's the simplest, most common tale in the universe instead of one of the most unique ones I've heard in a long time, maybe ever. "I'm sure there was more to it than that, but that's the gist of it."

He holds my gaze for a moment without saying anything. His eyes are a really cool mix of amber and moss green. He's got a hint of a smile on his face, and I swear he's flirting with me, which makes me happier than it should. I can't be the guy who costs us two drummers... can I? He puts the beer to his lips, eyes never leaving mine, and takes a sip. "Thanks for the beer."

He turns and walks over to Grant and Joe. I follow behind and make a mental note to put an ad on Craigslist for a drummer tomorrow. Because if this guy is interested in playing with more than my drum kit, I'm not saying no. Before I can sit down across from Bowen, who dropped down on the couch next to Joe, the buzzer goes again.

"Must be the girls," Grant grins as I get up to let them in. I swear I see Bowen's face fall a little, and I take that as a good sign. If he's disappointed women are coming to the party, it's likely because he thinks I invited him for more than just a band bonding thing, but I didn't invite them at all.

Monica, Andrea, Colleen and Becky saunter into the loft as soon as the elevator doors slide open. Grant and I work with Monica, so she came to the show. He also has a thing for Monica's friend Becky, which is why he invited them here and I guess they decided to bring friends who were also at the gig. I realize, looking at Bowen, who is surveying the scene unfolding in front of him, that it looks like a set-up. Four guys and four girls. I probably should have thought of that when Grant asked if he could invite them. Oops. Nothing I can't fix later, I hope.

I play the happy host, pouring drinks for everyone, chatting, laughing at stories. After I introduce him, Bowen slides right into the middle of everything, like he's not the new guy. He chats with Grant about hockey, debates the best local burger place with Joe, and gets into a long debate about a Netflix show with Monica. But he doesn't talk to me much. He's not rude or anything, just distant. I'm hoping it's because he thinks I'm straight and he misread the situation, but to be honest, I have no idea if he's gay. Even though Vino and Veritas is gay-friendly, it's not exactly an employment requirement. And when I met him as a kid, which he still shows no indication he remembers, I just saw a devastated college kid. His sexual orientation wasn't even a consideration at the time, obviously.

"How do you all know each other?" Bowen asks me as I peel away from the group to pour more wine and he follows me to the kitchen for a fresh beer.

"I went to college with Joe. Grant and I have been friends since we were sixteen and we work together with Monica," I say as I hand him another beer. "At a local marketing and public relations firm."

"Oh. Cool." He seems genuinely impressed.

"Thought I was just some dead-beat musician?" I ask with a smirk so he knows I'm kidding.

"I thought you were a talented musician," he replies with ease, like he's not giving me a compliment just stating the obvious, which my ego likes even more. Then his eyes dart around the loft again. "And then I thought you were some kind of mafia king pin on the side."

"Part-time mafia man, full-time cover band member?" I laugh so hard I lean on the island. "In Vermont?"

"Could happen." He shrugs and laughs with me. "What firm you with?"

"It's called Dauntless. It's on the first floor of this building."

His eyes light up and an impressed smile hits his very kissable lips. I have a feeling that it's quite the feat to get a reaction out of Bowen. He's one of those guys who is so mellow he probably doesn't react to much. All night he's given nothing more than a casual smile or a jovial but relaxed laugh, no matter what ridiculous things my friends have managed to say. "Is that the company that's done some freebie stuff for a couple places that are struggling to stay afloat?"

"We offer seminars and free one-on-one consults sometimes, yeah," I say and I'm trying not to look too proud, because I don't do it for my ego.

"You're the firm that helped the music shop with learning how to do social media ads," he says. "I went to college with Barry, the owner, and he said he's increased his private lessons, and his sales, and is finally in the black again."

"Really? Good for Barry!"

"The owner is a great guy for doing that. Or girl," Bowen muses as I watch way too closely as he lifts the beer bottle to his lips. I'm a lips guy. Weird, I know. But I like a good wide mouth with an enticing smile and lips that are symmetrical. Bowen checks all those boxes. I can't help but picture other things between them, besides the beer bottle.

"Thank you," I say.

Bowen pauses, the beer bottle hovering near his bottom lip before he drops it, and cocks his head. The ends of his long blond hair skimming his shoulder because of the angle. "You own it?"

"Yep." I sip my wine. "You didn't think it was odd I live above my place of employment?"

Bowen shrugs. "Thought maybe you liked a short commute."

I laugh but it's interrupted by a pesky bandmate.

"Dude, I gotta head out," Joe says as he stands up. Andrea, Monica, and Colleen stand up at the same time. "We're gonna all group Uber it together."

"Okay." I wave. "Text me tomorrow about practice."

"Where do you practice?" Bowen asks as Joe starts toward the door.

"Here," I reply. "You should come next time. Jam with us a little more."

I don't wait for a response, I just walk over to the door to see my guests off and leave him there to think about it. Ten minutes later Bowen is in a club chair, across from where Grant and Becky are sitting on the couch, and I settle into the other club chair. "You guys serious about the band thing?"

"About you swinging by a practice?" Grant asks, and Bowen nods. "We may need you again. Our regular guy is a flake."

"You had a good time, right?" I ask.

"I did." Bowen nods. He pulls his leg up so his left ankle is resting on his right knee. "I'd be interested in checking out a practice but as for filling in... I can't give up shifts at V and V because my family needs the extra cash right now, so I'm not exactly available either."

"Well, lucky for you we don't take the band too seriously," Grant explains to him. "We all work full-time so we usually do one gig a month. Maybe two in summers when there's festivals and stuff."

"Can I think about it?"

"Sure thing," I reply and Grant nods.

"What do you farm?" Grant wants to know and to be honest, I'm curious too. I have no idea. It could be anything. Although my mom's side of the family has been in Vermont for several generations, not a one has ever been a farmer.

"Hemp."

Grant blinks in surprise and I don't blame him. We were both expecting apples or corn or even beef or dairy. Bowen has a small smile on that perfect mouth, like he was expecting that reaction. "That's marijuana, right?"

"No." Bowen shakes his head and then runs his fingers through his hair to settle it down. "Same species of plant but hemp contains less than point three percent THC which is tetrahydrocannabinol."

"Ah… the good stuff," I say and that makes the smile on his face grow.

"The good stuff."

"So why grow hemp and not the good stuff."

"Hemp's a profitable crop that's not hard to grow," Bowen says. "We sell it to clothing manufacturers and to oil companies for example. With marijuana being legal, it's also a great crop to grow and we would love to expand into that as well. But the paperwork and red tape is a bitch and unfortunately permits are few and far between. At the moment."

I'm actually really interested in this — in him. He's got a way of talking about it that makes it even more fascinating than it probably is. And the little caveat he ended on — at the moment — I find particularly intriguing. It's like he knows something we don't. "You can, however, keep four marijuana plants at home, for personal use only."

"You can?" Grant is shocked. "Anyone can?"

"Anyone." Bowen smiles and shifts on the couch, pulling a cigarette pack out of the pocket of his scruffy jeans. He flips the top and taps it against his palm and two perfectly rolled joints appear. "Even a hemp farmer."

"Now there's a nice way to end an evening." Becky smiles.

"Also, I need to go find me four marijuana plants this weekend," Grant grins. "For my flower box."

I laugh. "You don't have a flower box."

"I will by the end of the weekend," Grant quips. I feel Bowen staring at me, so I slide my eyes his way. He's still got the cigarette pack on his knee. He looks down at it and back at me.

"Let's move this party up to the roof," I suggest. "If you're willing to share."

"Least I can do," Bowen replies as we all stand up. "You guys gave me the best night I've had in a long time."

He reaches for his coat, but as I walk by to lead the way to the roof deck, I put my hand on top of his and squeeze. "You don't need a coat."

"It's cold tonight," Bowen argues.

"Not in the hot tub," Becky explains and starts pulling her hair up with an elastic that was around her wrist.

Grant is already climbing the stairs, Becky right behind him.

Bowen lets go of his jacket but still doesn't look certain. "I don't have a suit."

"Lucky for you house policy says underwear is allowed in the hot tub," I reply and then I grin. "And so are birthday suits. Your call."

I wink, head for the stairs, and am more than a little thrilled when he's right behind me and not running out the door.

3

___

BOWEN

___

Maybe I shouldn't smoke tonight because this guy is already a trip. To say I'm fascinated by Chase Ashton would be an understatement. I barely know him but every little piece of information that gets revealed tonight just makes him more interesting. And appealing. I am no longer betting on the fact he's straight. At least not unequivocally. No straight dude has ever winked at me the way Chase has tonight.

I follow along behind him, up the metal and glass staircase, to the second floor of this beyond impressive loft. The entire floor seems to be his bedroom. There's a king-sized bed against the far wall with a thick wood frame. The wall across from it, above a simple desk, displays a variety of guitars from electric to acoustic. I stop to admire them. There's what looks like a huge bathroom and a walk-in closet, and at the end of the room, a spiral staircase with a glass hatch door at the top. Grant leads the way and opens it. I'm the last up behind Chase and I take a minute to enjoy the view of his ass as he climbs in front of me.

The roof is flat and square, a corner of it covered in fake grass with two outdoor couches and a chair around a coffee table. The other corner holds the hot tub. There's a metal railing that resembles the one that leads to his second floor, skirting the perimeter of the entire area. Chase pulls off the hot tub cover and Grant pulls his shirt over his head and Becky quickly does the same with her sweater, leaving her in a dark purple bra.

"Light it up, Bowen," Grant says.

I stick a joint in my mouth and do what I'm told while the two of them strip to their underwear. As I pull the lighter from my pocket Chase also starts undressing. Becky, with her dark purple bra and black panties, thankfully, is the first in the hot tub. Grant gets in after her, wearing dark blue cotton boxers with French Bulldogs all over them. I hand Chase the lit joint and he steps out of his pants. He's wearing white boxer briefs. White, bound to be see through when drenched, boxer briefs. He hasn't even gotten in the water yet and I'm already fantasizing about him getting out of it.

"Forgot the lights," Chase says as he gets in the tub. "Bowen, can you flip the switch by the stairs?"

I nod and when I do it, fairy lights along the railing illuminate the area. I yank my shirt off over my head while toeing out of my sneakers and then reach for my belt. Grant and Becky are sitting next to each other talking animatedly about something, Chase is next to Grant, staring straight at me, the joint in between his lips.

I climb into the massive hot tub at the same time Chase exhales and hands me the joint. Grant starts talking about their set lists, and we figure out what songs I would have to learn and which ones I might want to add to the list while Becky tries to convince us to cover "Girls Just Wanna Have Fun" by Cyndi Lauper. I mention some Nirvana songs and Chase grins. "Is that what the hair is about?"

He reaches over and actually touches my hair, his fingertips skimming it and kind of brushing it back from my cheek a little. "An homage to Kurt Cobain?"

I let out a soundless laugh and try not to let the spark I felt at his touch make it all the way to my balls. I do not need to get turned on right now, not more than I already am. "It's more about being too lazy to get a haircut."

"Lazy works for you," Chase murmurs.

Grant yawns after one last toke, and hands the joint back to Chase. It's such perfect timing I would have thought it was staged if I didn't know better. Wait... do I know better? He gets out of the Jacuzzi. "I'm outta here. That joint made me sleepy and I'm going to take advantage."

Becky follows him. "Can I still sleep at yours tonight, Grant?"

"Of course. I have a very comfy couch." Grant grins at us and then turns back to Becky who is gathering her clothes. "Or an even comfier king-sized bed we could share."

Becky smiles back at him like that's the offer she was hoping for but doesn't say anything. Grant walks over to the coffee table and flips up the top. Turns out it's storage for towels. He hands one to Becky, wraps one around his waist, takes out two more and puts them down on the edge of the hot tub. "See you tomorrow, Chase. Hope to see you at practice, Bowen. But if not, thanks anyway for filling in tonight."

"You okay to drive?" I can't help but ask.

"I live stumbling distance from here," Grant replies.

"And stumble he does. On multiple occasions," Chase notes and chuckles.

With a wave, Grant and Becky disappear down the stairwell. Now, with just Chase and me, the hot tub somehow feels like it's gotten warmer. He's watching me intently as he takes one more inhale of the joint. It's basically done now, so when he passes it back to me, I shake my head. He stubs it out on the side of the tub and pulls himself up, out of the water, to lean over the side and drop it into a half empty beer bottle Grant left behind. There's enough light out here to see the full, round curve of his ass through his soaking, now translucent boxer briefs. Then, he turns around before sinking below the water so I get an up-close and personal view of the outline of his not totally soft dick. But it's just a fleeting glance before he sits back down.

"I'm a bit of an exhibitionist," he says, and our eyes meet. He knows I checked him out. He doesn't mind, though. "I actually prefer to be in here naked, but I didn't want to scare off our potential new bandmate."

"I don't scare easily," I say, and he smiles. It's a *really* good smile.

"I should tell you, we've met before," Chase says and it's the last thing I expect to hear.

Say what, now?

I cock my head. "I feel like I would have remembered that."

"You were dealing with a lot," Chase replies and suddenly all that warmth I was feeling is fading. Fast. "My grandfather is… was Ned McDaniels."

"The politician dude?" I ask. "The one who showed up at my mom and dad's funeral?"

"Yeah."

I blink and stare at him even harder now, and I can see the quiet, lankier, younger guy in the navy-blue coat and suit. Both he and his grandfather were wearing polished leather dress shoes. I remember staring at their feet as they stood in front of me, wondering how they'd made their way through the snowy cemetery in those stupid shoes. Ned, an assemblyman or something, had approached us right after our parents were lowered into the ground and the pastor had said the final prayer. He offered me, Woody, and Autumn his sincerest condolences. The words didn't really sound all that sincere coming out of Ned McDaniels' mouth, especially when he went on to ask if we would be so kind to shake his hand for the photographer. Chase was the one who sounded sincere when he told his grandfather, "I think we should just go." And then I looked up and saw his cheeks burning with embarrassment. "I'm really sorry."

I blink and focus on the face in front of me now, not the younger one attached to that memory. "Oh."

"Yeah." Chase looks far less confident than he has all night. "I didn't want to mention it at the bar. There really wasn't time and I thought maybe if you knew, you'd have decided not to play with us."

"Nah," I say easily. "And if I can't join the band more regularly it won't be because of that either."

"I'm still embarrassed about how that went down," Chase admits. "Everyone in my family has trouble doing anything without a political agenda. I hate it."

"Everyone?" I shift a little, to get one of the jets to hit a spot on my lower back that has been aching a little since I started working at Vino and Veritas and standing on my feet hours at a time. The move brings me a couple inches closer to Chase.

"Ned is my mother's dad, and he was a Vermont assemblyman. My dad is a senator for Rhode Island. My brother works in the District Attorney's office in Rhode Island and wants to run for mayor of our hometown there next year," I explain. "So yeah. Feels like everyone."

"And you?"

"Never," Chase says flatly and with certainty. Then he lowers his voice and slides a little closer. "But don't tell my parents that. At least not yet."

I don't know why he added *not yet*. I would ask him but I'm concentrating on the feel of his knee which is now brushing up against mine. The moonlight and the fairy lights are putting a glow onto his handsome profile that I can't help but enjoy. Is this guy into me? "Anyway, I'm still ashamed of that moment."

"Don't be," I reply, my voice suddenly heavy and thick. "I barely remembered it. I try not to remember much from that time, which is likely why I didn't recognize you."

"I get that." His hand is lying on top of mine suddenly, on the bench in the small space between our hips. I turn my head a little so I can see more of his face. His mouth relaxes, no smile anymore, and it's so close to mine. I feel his fingers slip in between mine and curl in so he's kind of holding my hand. My eyes drop to the water, as if I need to visually confirm he really did that. Of course, I can't see our hands because the bubbling water makes it impossible, so I look back up. He's still staring at me with those impossibly blue eyes, without a care in the world. Like he has no idea how straight I thought he was.

Now I have the confidence to make my own move. My eyes still on his, I move my hand — the one he's resting his hand on top of — lifting it off the bench in between us and dropping it on his thigh.

Chase doesn't blink, or smile as my palm settles over his leg, just above his knee. If anything, his expression darkens a little, but in a way that makes my cock start to grow. And then he leans closer, the tip of his nose grazes my cheekbone and his exhale brushes my mouth. I know his lips are next and my eyes close with the anticipation. And then... an instrumental version of "Hotel California" fills the air.

"Fuck!" I curse and immediately start to get out of the hot tub to retrieve my phone from the back pocket of my jeans. "I have to answer that. It's one of my siblings."

Chase nods but doesn't hide the disappointment creasing his face either. I guess most grown ass men don't leap out of hot tubs a second before a first kiss to chat with their brother. But my parents died in a car crash and so if one of us is not home at night, when we should be, we call and have promised to always answer. If someone had called my parents, maybe we would have been able to get an ambulance to them sooner. Maybe… I yank my phone out of the pocket of my pants and as I drip water on the rooftop, say hello.

"Where are you? V and V closed hours ago," Woody asks. He doesn't sound groggy so he's likely not at home to notice my bedroom door was open and my bed is empty. "But your car is still parked where you left it before your shift."

"You're in town?"

"Yeah. Was at the campaign office strategizing," Woody replies. "And by strategizing, I mean panicking about how to get more people interested in me. I'm trailing in the latest polls."

"Yeah. Sorry," I say and man it's freezing when you're soaking wet on a roof in the middle of the night. I have my back to Chase and the hot tub, but I can hear water sloshing, so I think he's getting out too.

"So where are you? Can I hitch a ride home? I cycled into town this morning and don't want to ride home in the dark," Woody explains. "I was gonna call a cab but then saw your car. And every penny counts."

I glance over my shoulder and see Chase standing there holding a towel out to me. He's taken one too but draped it over his shoulders. His very white, very wet, very see-through boxer-briefs are not covered up in the slightest. And shit, yeah. He is definitely half hard. And well endowed. God damnit.

"Bo! Hello?"

"Yeah. I'm at a party but it's winding down. I'll meet you there in ten," I reply and hang up. I take the towel and wrap it around my shoulders. Then I force my eyes to stay on Chase's face, which is no easy feat. "My brother needs a lift back to our farm."

"Shit," he says.

"Yeah. Shit," I agree as my eyes slide down and I blatantly check him out. At this point, I feel like I have nothing left to lose. I want to make it crystal clear that I'm interested, even if I don't have time to act on it. If I somehow misread everything on an epic level, and my ogling his junk is offensive, then I'd rather find out now. Before I decide whether I'm going to play in his band. Because I'll gladly join a band full of straight dudes or even bi-curious ones, but not homophobic ones, so his reaction here is critical.

When my eyes make it back to his face, he's smiling a smile that exudes confidence, ease, and anything but fear or anger. "Let's go downstairs to change," Chase announces and bends to grab his clothes. As I do the same he adds, "If we stay up here in this cold night air, that view your enjoying will all but disappear."

I almost cough. Yeah. He's definitely not straight.

I follow him down the stairs and as his feet hit the wood floor of his bedroom, he tosses his clothes onto his bed and turns very abruptly to face me. I'm still on the last step, which makes me slightly taller than him. He looks up at me, his blue eyes that seemed so light in the bar are as dark as Lake Champlain at midnight now. "I wish you could stay a little longer."

"I do too," I admit. He steps closer and his hands come up. All ten of his fingertips land on my torso, splayed out across my ribs like he's bracing me, or about to push me backwards or something. Honestly, I don't care what he does next, I just love the shiver of lust that fills me at the feel of his skin against mine. He does neither though. Instead, he lets his fingertips slip down my wet stomach, across my abs, his two index fingers tracing the trail of dark blond hair that leads down past the waistband of my underwear. But sadly, the journey ends at the elastic barrier and he tips his head up to meet my eyes. "We should get you some dry underwear."

And then he's gone. Moving away from me so quickly that my cock jerks in protest, or to run away with him. Probably the latter. I step off the bottom stair and dry myself off as best I can while waiting for Chase to reappear from the walk-in closet he went into.

I'm pulling my T-shirt – well, actually Jax's T-shirt – over my head when Chase reappears. The towel he had around his neck is now wrapped around his waist. He stops near the foot of the bed and tosses something at me. I catch the black fabric easily. "They're clean, I swear, and better than driving home in cold, damp underwear."

I hold up the boxer-briefs. "Thanks. My brother would probably want to know why the crotch of my pants were drenched."

"No one needs to know," he says quietly. "Anyway, I'll let you change in private."

Despite his words he doesn't move. And honestly, if he stays in this room while I take off my underwear, I'll end up bailing on my brother, I know it. And I shouldn't. But yet, I'm walking over to stand in front of him anyway. We're chest-to-chest. His is still wet, water droplets cling to the smattering of dark hair across his pecs. I know it's dampening the shirt I just put on, but fuck it. "I'm glad you invited me."

"I'm glad you came," Chase replies. "I just wish you could have come too."

The double entendre rocks me in the best possible way. And now I'm pretty sure no one in this room is just half hard anymore. I have never had a night like this, and I may never have one again. I've learned life can turn on a dime, and not to put things off because tomorrow may never come. So, I tilt my head and bring my lips to his. He responds immediately with the shameless confidence he has shown in everything tonight from his stage presence to his party-hosting skills.

His mouth opens as both hands reach up and grab my face, fingers tangling in the hair by my temples. He parts his lips and my tongue is met eagerly by his own, creating a tornado of desire that swirls through me. When I slip my arms around his waist and grab his ass, he pushes his hips into mine and our cocks brush, barely. The wet fabric of my underwear and the thick terry cloth of his towel are my worst enemies right now. I have half the urge to yank that towel off him but honestly, the kiss is so consuming that I just let it take over. Chase's mouth moves with passion, and his tongue with abandon. He's so dominant and wildly needy at the same time, I'm fucking swooning. And when it ends, I almost whimper.

"Wish this could be more," he pants, stepping away from me, because we both need distance or this *will* be more.

"So do I," I admit. "Maybe next time?"

"I don't really..." Chase pauses and stops walking backwards, coming to a stop just in front of the open bathroom door. His smile flickers, almost disappearing, before it comes back as strong as ever. "Never say never."

He seems... not quite insincere but something equally as unwelcome. But I don't have time to figure out why. Woody will call again if I'm late.

"I'll let you get changed," Chase says, and his wide, strong hands reach for the front of his towel. It drops to the ground. He's not wearing those wet white boxer briefs anymore. He's not wearing anything but a mighty fine hard on. "I need a shower. Is it okay if I let you show yourself out?"

"Yeah. I'll manage," I say and a little groan of regret escapes as well. I feel like this is the end of something before it even began. Fuck Woody's constant, unwavering pledge to save the environment. If he didn't give a shit, he would own a car and would have driven himself into town today. That's how much I want this guy. For the first time in my life, I'm annoyed with my brother for caring about global warming.

With a final smile, Chase disappears into the bathroom. I drop my wet briefs and put on his dry ones, shoving my aching, hard cock inside as I whisper, "Sorry buddy."

I finish dressing and as I hear the shower water running, I make my way downstairs. As I'm grabbing my coat I notice a pen and notebook on a small table by the window. There's yet another acoustic guitar in the corner. Alexa is still playing. Now it's Foo Fighters. I grab the pen and flip open the notebook. It's filled with neatly printed… poetry? No. Lyrics. Song lyrics. Original, I think because I don't recognize any of them, but they're beautiful. I feel like I've suddenly intruded, so I flip to the very back, to the last blank page, and quickly scrawl my name and phone number.

I'm not looking for a relationship. I never am. It's not that I don't want one, I do. I've just got so much going on right now that I don't have time to find one. But maybe one just found me? And yeah, they want me to play in the band again, and know they can find me at the bar, but I want Chase to know he can reach out whenever. For whatever.

I carefully tear the page from the back of the book and walk over and leave it on his kitchen island before heading out the door. Because that kiss is worth repeating.

BOWEN

"You know you could always ask to work on the book side," Autumn is suggesting as the Vermont scenery flies by outside the car. Spring has definitely sprung and everything is turning from brown to green — the fields, the trees, the bushes. My mom used to say that was part of what convinced her to move to Vermont from California before we were born, the ability to watch nature change. California, she used to quip, had two seasons, smog and fire.

"Books are your thing," I remind her.

"Well, serving definitely isn't your thing," Autumn surmises and a devious little smile plays on her lips. She's speaking the truth, not teasing, but the smile says she takes a wee bit of delight in it just the same. "And neither is bar back. Or bartender."

"I could probably do that pretty well, but Tanner's afraid to try me out," I reply as the houses on either side of the car grow closer together, signifying we're on the edge of Burlington.

"I'd say he isn't afraid, he's just… cautious."

"Thanks Autumn. That's so much better." I roll my eyes.

"It's so weird," Autumn announces, and now all the delight is gone from her face and she looks honestly perplexed and a little sympathetic. "You're great at everything I can think of. You rock every task on the farm. You balance our house budget without blinking and fix most of the farm equipment all by yourself. You say books aren't your thing, but you were minoring in literature in college. And look how easily you stepped in to play with that band last week. You didn't even practice with them and you did great. But every task at V and V you are a total failure at."

"Again, thanks for your insight," I reply but I'm caught on one small tidbit of her little speech. It's been a week since Imposter Syndrome played at the bar. And I haven't heard from or seen Chase Ashton once.

Guess that kiss wasn't worth repeating for him. That stings more than it should. More than it has with the other, few and far between, hook-ups I've had in recent years. Autumn snaps her fingers in front of my face. I swat her hand away gently. "Driving here!"

"Then stop day dreaming," she replies. "I asked you a question and you didn't answer."

"What did you ask me?"

"How it felt to be playing again."

"Good," I murmur and steal a glance her way to find her frowning. Autumn is the opposite of me. Whereas I am the water-off-a-duck's-back guy, Autumn spends every waking moment excited about something. Today, if I don't give her a more insightful response, this will be the next thing she gets passionate about. "Great, actually. I've missed it more than I realized."

"You could go back to school and finish that music degree," Autumn suggests and that makes me frown, so she elaborates. "I mean not right now, but in a year or two, when everything else is more settled. When Woody is mayor and we have a permit for marijuana crops and I've graduated and am running the Whitlock empire."

"Empire?" I laugh. "Mom and Dad would be in hysterics, and possibly horrified, at the idea of a Whitlock Empire."

"Nah. Their hippie hearts would be fine with it because I'd make it so successful they could retire and Dad could just build guitars and Mom could just make jewelry all day," Autumn lamented. "No farming for them anymore. Just crafts and music."

Damn, I wish this imaginary picture she's painted could happen. They deserved that. I give my head a shake. "Well, I hate to break this to you but Whitlock Empire or not, my schooling days are over. I actually don't mind either. I like working full-time on the farm. I just don't like having to work part-time at the bar. But I'm grateful to

Harrison and Tanner for helping us out. God, Woody better win this so it's worth it."

"He will." Autumn doesn't sound as confident as I wish she did. But I also wish I didn't need her, or anyone else, to bolster my confidence.

I pull into an empty parking spot a block away from Vino and Veritas and turn off the car. Autumn unbuckles her seatbelt. "Woody has that interview with the local news station today. He's been practicing what he wants to say so hopefully it goes well."

"Fingers crossed," I say as we get out of the car. My brother would be a good mayor. This isn't just about us getting the zoning for marijuana farming in Burlington. He cares a lot about this city, and he wants to see it do well on every front. He's also smarter than he looks and smarter than he sounds. Woody used to have a stutter as a kid and he got over it with speech therapy, mostly. But he talks slowly and with big pauses when he's stressed or nervous so he doesn't stumble over his words. It can make him look a little dim, if you don't know him. And the voters of Burlington, for the most part, don't.

We walk together the half a block in silence, Autumn's texting someone on her phone and giggling. "Is that Briar or Jeremy?"

"Briar," Autumn says about one of her co-workers at the bookstore that she has become close friends with. "Telling me a story about the most recent way Jeremy embarrassed his boyfriend Aaron. But in a good way."

"There's a good way to be embarrassed?" I question.

"Yeah, like not the way you embarrass yourself at the bar," Autumn retorts and her devious grin is back.

This time it makes me smile too, until I look up to see if we've got the light to cross the street and I find myself staring right at Lacey Baldwin's confident, reassuring smile. "It's official. She's bought every advertising space in Burlington."

Autumn's golden eyes follow my stare and she swears under her breath when she sees the giant poster at the bus shelter across the street. "I know I read somewhere her family used to farm, but I didn't realize until now they must have a tree farm. Money trees. How the hell does she afford all this advertising?"

I shrug because I don't know but also, it doesn't matter. Fact is, she can afford it and we can't. Even after we mortgaged the farm —

the only thing we have — we only have enough money for one poorly placed mural-type advertisement that the Caruso farm let us put on the side of their barn. It was located by the interstate, but half blocked by trees depending on which way you were driving. We also had a radio ad, which wasn't the best because, like I said earlier, Woody isn't well spoken.

"We need to work on him about the posters and the flyers for people's mailboxes," Autumn tells me as we cross the street. "I understand and support his concerns about the environmental impact, but the fact is, he needs more visibility."

I nod in agreement, but I also know Woody won't be easily swayed. Man, he needs to win this. I can't work two jobs forever and if it does come to that, it definitely can't be this one, I think, as we make our way down the alley to the back joint entrance. When we get inside, Autumn heads left into the bookstore and I turn right, heading down the hall. Joss, the chef who was hired to expand the menu almost a year ago, is the first person I see. He gives me a nod. "Bowen. You here to try and wreck the place again?"

"Ha ha." I smile.

"You know I'm just taking the piss, mate." Joss gives me a friendly smile. "I hear you were great with the band last week."

Again, *last week*. Another reminder of how long Chase has had my phone number and not called it. I push down the bad feelings and nod. "Just wanted to prove to you all I'm not a total disaster."

"You'll find your grove here too," Joss assures me as I keep walking past the kitchen and into the bar. It's still an hour until the doors are open to customers so I expect to only see Tanner and whoever else is working tonight, but there's more than just staff in the bar.

Chase Ashton is sitting on the last stool at the bar, swirling a glass of red wine, while Tanner leans on the bar in front of him. They've both got intense looks on their faces and if I didn't know Tanner had recently eloped with the love of his life, Jax, I would have a twinge of jealousy at how they're leaning into each other. But that would be ridiculous because Chase isn't mine and who he leans into isn't my business. "Earthy. With a few darker notes. Sensual."

"I thought the same thing," Tanner replies.

I feel a nudge on my shoulder and look down to see Murph

standing beside me. He's a fellow employee and must be the bartender tonight. I've only worked with him once before, but I kind of already knew him through my sister. He's unabashedly unique, always upbeat, and seems undaunted by my fuck-ups so far. "Sounds like they could be discussing your performance, huh?"

"What?"

"Oh please," Murph winks. "I was here the night you played with him and his band. You were meant to be a Rockstar, new guy. And so was your singer over there. Stage presence was through the roof."

"He's not *my* singer." *Or he would have called.*

Murph shrugs. "You know what I mean."

He slips past me to enter the room I've been too busy eavesdropping from the doorway to enter myself. "Happy Thursday everyone!"

"Hey Murph," Tanner replies and when he glances up. He sees me lurking and adds, "Ah. The guy I was looking for."

Chase's eyes meet mine and he gives me that same confident smile that I found so appealing the other night. I walk over to them. Chase sips the wine he was swirling, and I realize, as I come to a stop just a stool away from Chase, that Tanner is holding his own glass. He wasn't leaning into Chase, he was leaning into his own glass that was on the bar. "Rich. Not a wine I'd drink a whole bottle of in one sitting."

"Yeah, I said the same thing to Jax when I discovered it in a bar in Cornwall," Tanner sips it again. "But I fully admit I'm not an expert wine guy, which is why I wanted your opinion. Do you think it would go well with a dessert from our new menu?"

Chase nods. His eyes move from the glass he's just put down on the bar to me. Tanner turns to face me too, but his gaze is cool compared to Chase's. "Chase popped in to talk about the potential for more band gigs."

"Okay," I say awkwardly. "Just let me know where you want me tonight and I'll get out of your hair."

"Well, actually I need you in this conversation," Tanner replies and I wish I could be happy about that. Any chance to hang out with Chase is what I want, but it's not what he wants or he would have called. "Chase mentioned he needs a replacement for his drummer and that you were thinking about it."

"I was, but this job is my first priority," I reply, and I don't know if

I should be irked by Chase telling my boss about this. I mean, he seems to be friends with Tanner, and I don't think he did it to get me in any kind of trouble. But Tanner is frustrated enough with my blundering, maybe he'll use this as an excuse to let me go and the band gig isn't stable enough to provide the income I need to help with the mortgage payments.

"Yeah I don't doubt that." Tanner empties his wine glass into the sink and looks almost sad he didn't finish his tasting sample, and then he looks back up at me. "But I wanted to offer to move your shifts around. I can always schedule you on weekday nights, which frees up weekends for any gig you guys might do."

I blink, shocked at how easy going he's being about this, but then my battered ego figures out his plan. Weeknights are considerably slower than weekends. Which means, less babysitting the problem child — AKA me — and less chance I can screw up as much. More opportunity to train me in a slower pace. Still, all of this is actually appealing to me. "We make about sixty bucks each for a gig. Sometimes more," Chase tells me. "Last year we did a wedding and it was two-fifty each. We're going to try and get more of those this summer."

Why does this guy want me so badly when he clearly doesn't want me so badly? Am I the only dude in Burlington, besides the guy who flaked on them, who can play drums? They're both staring at me expectantly and as weird as it may end up being working with Chase after that kiss, I find myself nodding. Because it really did feel great making music again. I've missed it a lot. "Sure. I mean, if you're sure you can swing it, schedule-wise, Tanner, then I can do the band stuff too."

Chase's grin is anything but casual now. It's ecstatic. "Great! I'll tell Grant and Joe. They'll be thrilled. And don't worry, we won't interfere with your job. We've got other commitments too."

I nod and then Murph pipes in, "Bo, can you make sure the kegs don't need changing? And if they do, I brought an extra shirt just for you. It's got a pink unicorn on the front."

Tanner shakes his head, laughing. Chase just smiles, but he looks confused. I'm not about to elaborate. I just nod at Murph and shuffle off to do what he asked.

Four hours later, the rush of the after-work crowd is in full swing. Murph is great behind the bar, he's graceful and fast and always wearing a smile. He's not even distracted by his boyfriend, Jason, who is sitting at the bar. I figured out in the first five minutes of my first shift with Murph that he is head-over-heels in love with Jason and not afraid to show it. I haven't had a serious relationship, at least not one I could admit to in public, and I feel like if I was as in love as Murph is, it would be hard to focus when he was in a room. Hell, I'm distracted by Chase, who hasn't left the bar yet, and he isn't even interested in me let alone in love with me.

"Oh, man, I have to tinkle and there're three orders left to fill," Murph huffs quietly to me. "Can you run and get Tanner to cover me for a second?"

I walk over and look at the drink orders. Two ciders and a gin and tonic. "I can do these."

Murph blinks, his happy-go-lucky expression disappearing for a second before it comes back. "You're right. It's a few quick and easy orders. It's fine. I can hold it."

"Murph. Honestly," I say my voice low so no one hears me trying to plead my case. "If you had any other bar back tonight, wouldn't you let them cover for you?"

"Yes." Murph says guiltily and now I feel like shit. I mean, the guy is a literal ray of sunshine and wouldn't hurt a soul and I'm making him feel guilty when I deserve the caution he's taking. But the thing is, Chase hasn't moved from that spot at the end of the bar. He's had another glass of wine and ordered a burger and is now finishing up a cider. And I want to do something other than restock glasses and cut lemon wedges. Because he's been watching me most of the night. "Okay. I'll be like two minutes."

"Take three," I say as he starts to walk away. "And wash your hands."

"Of course!" Murph gasps at me like I just accused him of murder. I wink. He laughs. Jason, his partner sitting two seats over from Chase, just smirks at us and shakes his head.

I grab a pint glass to pour the first cider. "Should we all duck and cover?"

I glance over at Jason. Apparently Murph has shared my misadventures. "I think you're safe, but I make no promises."

I see Chase eavesdropping, so I turn to him. "I've hit some bumps my few weeks here. But I swear, I'm not a total screw-up. Normally."

"I've seen you play drums, remember?" Chase says, sipping his drink. "I know that."

I nod and reach for the next glass to fill. Molly picks up the ciders, which are poured without spilling a drop, and plops them on her tray. "Be back for the G and T."

I reach for the glass for the gin and tonic and bend to scoop some ice into the glass. Chase lurches over the bar and wraps his hand around my forearm. "Stop!"

Our eyes lock. He looks nervous. "I'm just scooping up some ice for the drink."

"Never put a glass into the ice trough," Chase warns. "Use the scoop. Always. If the glass breaks or chips in there, which can happen, then you have to empty the whole thing. All the ice is useless."

Oh. Shit. That makes total sense and I can't believe I'm too stupid to think of it. I feel my cheeks redden, like a tool. Chase slides back down onto his bar stool, letting go of my arm, and I quickly put the glass on the bar top and use the metal scoop that's right there. Crisis averted. Chase just probably saved my job because that would have been a big mistake on a busy night like tonight, and I've had too many little ones to forgive a big one. I finish making the drink and as Molly puts it on her tray Murph bounces back. He surveys the bar area and smiles. "All good?"

"Yeah. Can I run to the bathroom now?" I ask. I don't even have to go, I just want to get away from Chase and Jason and anyone who witnessed my near screw-up. But mostly Chase.

"Yeah, in fact, take fifteen," Murph says and looks out over the crowd which is shifting. The drinks groups are starting to thin out and so we'll likely have a lull in a minute. "You're overdue for a break."

I mumble a thanks and without looking back, I head off, making my way out of the bar and to the street. I have no place in particular to go, I just want some fresh air. I walk past the windows on the bookstore side, and around the corner, where I stop and lean against the brick wall. "Bowen."

My name is called just as I was about to close my eyes. I turn and see Chase walking towards me. "Hey."

He walks over all casual, calm, and confident. Three C words I used to be familiar with before I started working here. He smiles. "You're beating yourself up, aren't you? Over an averted disaster?"

"I take my job very seriously." It's not exactly an answer.

He stops directly in front of me and runs a hand through his hair. It's ridiculously perfect despite him raking his fingers through it. The man is *so* fucking hot. I've never really thought about my 'type' much before. Now I feel like I could write it down. It's old money confidence meets bold sexual curiosity, wrapped in a sculpted body with devil may care hair and eyes of the purest blue. Unfortunately, that type seems to know he deserves more than a poor farm boy who can't scoop ice without a tutorial.

"I get it." Chase breaks the tense silence between us. "You're new and no one told you the little details. Seriously, crisis was averted. Unlike when I did it at my cousin's engagement party."

"You bartended at your cousin's engagement party?"

Chase shakes his head and that confident smile I find so attractive slips a little. "No. I got rightfully smashed at my cousin's engagement party. Was annoyed at the length of time it was taking to get my seventh scotch on the rocks and slipped behind the bar to do it myself."

"Oh." I cringe for him. That makes his smile grow stronger.

"Yeah. Dunked my crystal tumbler into the ice trough and it broke." Chase shakes his head slowly. "Best part? It was being held on a boat. A yacht. But a yacht without another way to get ice so the whole damn vessel had to cruise back to the dock and someone had to run off and fetch bags of ice from the gas station"

"Oh man."

Chase shoves both hands in the front pocket of his suit pants. He obviously came right to Vino and Veritas from work because I don't know why else he would be dressed so formally. Marketing and PR firm owners wear suits, right? Anyway, he looks even hotter in a suit than he did in jeans and a T-shirt on stage last week. The man clearly doesn't have a bad look. And now he's trying to make me feel better with tales of his own shortcomings. Which makes him pretty fucking awesome. "Thanks for saving me from the same fate."

Chase shrugs and his eyes twinkle in the glow of the nearby streetlamp. "Even if you'd done it, your fate wouldn't have been as bad. That happened almost two years ago and there hasn't been a family event since where my aunt hasn't brought it up."

"Sorry."

He shrugs. "You don't look like a guy who would let that bother him."

"Neither do you," I counter.

Chase's blue eyes drop to his dress shoes. They look like they cost more than the eleven-year-old car I drive. "I won't care, eventually."

A silence settles over us and I pull my phone out of my back pocket and double check the time. "I don't want to leave Murph hanging for too long."

"Thanks for not leaving us hanging," Chase says. "The band."

"That's hardly a chore. I love playing and getting paid for it will be great," I say and realize we're both making this way more awkward that it has to be, so I decide to just say it. "And don't worry about the other night. I get it was, like, a mistake or a one-off or whatever. No worries."

I push myself off the wall in order to make my way back to the bar but he takes a quick step to his right so he's blocking my path. And he's close enough that I can smell his cologne, which smells as rich and sensual as his loft looked. "I should have called you."

"Not if you didn't want to."

"I wanted to." Chase's eyes are suddenly everywhere but my face. He's looking to his left, his right, and over both my shoulders, before his gaze lands on my face again. The three Cs he's been exuding since he met me — confident, calm, casual — are replaced with a different C. Concern. And suddenly my only boyfriend, Trevor's face, dances through my memory. "It's just I'm kind of a one-night stand guy. More than once becomes a thing and I don't do things... relationships. I mean I would but can't because... I don't really know if—"

"You're not out."

"I am. Mostly. Sort of." Chase sighs and tilts his head to the side. "It's complicated."

"Yeah," I nod. "I know it can be. But I've got a lot going on with my brother and his campaign, this job, and the farm. So complicated isn't really my thing."

"Fair enough," Chase says but he isn't hiding the disappointment in his voice. "I figured with the band thing now too, it's probably best if we keep it simple."

"Sounds like a plan." A shitty one, but life can be that way sometimes. I give him a smile filled with as much disappointment as his voice was. "Well now you can use my number to text me about band practice. So at least I didn't waste a perfectly good piece of paper."

"Yeah. True." I move past him, almost having to step off the sidewalk to do it. Chase has such broad shoulders but a lean, narrow waist. I'm bummed I won't get to see more of it. Even if I play with the band, it'll be better to avoid the hot tub after parties going forward. He pivots and follows along beside me. "I parked this way."

I nod. The air around us is cool and crisp and as sobering as the conversation. "I don't want you to think that it wasn't… that I didn't enjoy the other night. If your brother hadn't called, I'd have been open to a lot more than that kiss."

"You don't have to placate me. I don't have a wounded ego or anything," I reply and give him a sideways smile. "I'm fairly confident my kissing skills are much better than my bartending ones."

Chase laughs. "I definitely don't think I have to give you tips. It's all I've thought about for a week."

My step slows a little. I mean, sure I don't need his praise, but it's still very nice to hear. "Me too."

We're a step away from Vino and Veritas, right in front of the alley next to the side of the building. The door is at the other side, past the front window. So why am I slowing down now? Because Chase is slowing down too. And his eyes are on me as his tongue slips out and wets his bottom lip. For some reason, that makes my legs feel heavy. I stop when he does. He tilts his head toward the other side of the road. "I'm parked over there."

"Okay. Have a good night."

Neither of us moves.

"Bo! We're getting slammed again!" Molly is suddenly calling to me from the open front door.

"At least something is getting slammed," I mutter. It's a juvenile joke but it gets me one of those sexy smirks Chase seems to be an expert at. "Night Chase."

"Night Bowen."

5

CHASE

I open the door to the law office at exactly three minutes to ten. I am not going to be late but you bet your ass I'm not spending a minute longer than I have to with these people. My family. The receptionist greets me with a genuine smile. "They're all in the conference room. I know you know the way."

"I do," I reply. "Thanks Jeremy."

"Do you want me to slip some bourbon into your coffee?" he asks and gives me a sympathetic smile. "I can do that for you. It'll take the edge off."

"I appreciate the thought, but I'll muddle through without it." I smile back. As much as I hate meeting every month with my family, I do like the law firm my grandfather picked to oversee his affairs after his death. It lacks the corporate, uptight vibe he always had. It's simple, down-to-earth, and very Vermont.

I make my way to the back of the building and into the conference room. Just as Jeremy said, my family is all present and accounted for. Well, all the members that need to be, which is my father Charles, my mother's sister Hilda, my brother Colin, and my cousin Amy. We are the group that my grandfather, former Vermont Assemblyman Ned McDaniels, declared in his will would run the charitable foundation he wanted created in his name.

"Hi all," I say simply and take a seat across from my brother at the long table. Unlike everyone else in the room, I'm not wearing a suit.

Both my brother and father are in suits, with ties. My aunt Hilda is in a crisp off-white linen pantsuit and Amy is in a similar one in a muted gray color. I wear suits to work almost every day but today, I threw on a pair of jeans, a wrinkled dress shirt I didn't bother to tuck in, and a blazer. Just to piss them all off. Judging by the scowl on my dad's face and the way my aunt Hilda's eyes sweep over me while her brows pinch together, it's working. Amy just rolls her eyes while Colin shakes his head.

"Do you need me to purchase you an iron for your housewarming gift?" Aunt Hilda asks curtly.

"I've been in the loft for two years now," I remind her. "And you sent me a juicer."

She makes a sound in the back of her throat. "Good thing I didn't get you an ice machine. You would have wrecked that by now."

And there it is.

Colin decides it's his turn to lambaste me. "Do they not have dry cleaners in Vermont?"

He acts like he's never set foot in the state when we used to spend a month every summer at our grandparents' estate less than a ten-minute drive from this very building. "Is Iris joining us for this or should we just start?"

"She's joining," my father says. "Your mother wanted a word with her first."

"Mom is here?"

He shakes his head and then reaches up to smooth his silver hair — what's left of it. His bald spot gets bigger every time I see him. "She called."

"Still sticking to that whole 'will never step foot in Vermont again' oath," Colin mutters and Aunt Hilda looks visibly pained.

My grandfather may have willed a good sum of his wealth to create a charity, but he was not charitable with his own family. He and my mother had a falling out when I was ten and my beloved grandmother died. Grandma Bette was the glue that held our family together and when she died, he also disowned my uncle Matt, his only son, for "his immoral life choices." This is why the trustees to oversee this charity do not include two of his three children. Aunt Hilda is the only one of his children he kept a relationship with, so here we are. And despite not talking to my mom for over a decade, he always kept in contact with my dad. I thought it was just to keep tabs on Colin and me, but it turns out the two were actual friends.

The rest of the will is more or less settled, but there's been some haggling over the house he owned when he died. It's the only thing he left to my mother and my uncle. And Uncle Matt, being the "immoral" heathen he was, chose to stay in Costa Rica where he taught yoga at a resort with my aunt Lori who was ten years older than him and had two kids older than me, and let my mom handle it. That was likely what she was discussing on the phone with Iris, who has just marched into the boardroom, in her long green skirt, powder pink sweater, and green crocs. She's followed by Peter Landry, a new addition to her firm, who will be taking over our business completely once she feels he's ready to handle the blood bath. "Sorry! Sorry! But Donna and Mike, as you all probably know, have accepted an offer on Mr. McDaniels' home."

"I didn't know," Aunt Hilda says sharply, and her eyes scan our faces with a scowl.

I lift my hands. "First I'm hearing of it."

Iris clears her throat and sits at the head of the table, with Peter taking the chair to her left. They both place laptops on the conference table and open them. Jeremy walks in with a pitcher of water and some glasses. He also offers everyone coffee and when I ask for one with sugar but no milk, he catches my eye and mouths the word 'bourbon?' I smirk but shake my head.

"So, with the house settled, all we have left to settle with the family part of the will is Chase's trust," Aunt Hilda says as she crosses her arms and leans back in her seat, her pale eyes narrowing on me. "If all the requirements are met."

"Well, the non-negotiable requirement would be his age," Iris says, opening a folder and then her laptop. "And that happens in…"

"Seven months, fourteen days, and roughly eleven hours," I respond and grin when all eyes in the room turn to me.

"As I've said before, this morality clause is… well, vague enough that I would have a hard time holding it up in court," Iris says, and she levels her keen brown eyes on me.

"But I will take it to court if it means upholding Ned's wishes," Dad warns.

"Yes. You've made that abundantly clear," Amy snaps.

Peter looks at all of us like we're the Manson Family but then quickly refocuses on his laptop screen. Poor guy.

I think he's still horrified that for Colin, Amy, and me to receive our inheritances, Grandpa Ned said we needed to prove a strong moral character and be living a life that would uphold his religious and ethical values.

"Well, we can discuss that in seven months, fourteen days, and eleven hours," Iris tells everyone. "For now, we're here to concentrate on the charity. You've all decided what we'll do with the first year's budget?"

And that's when the inevitable happens. We all start throwing out our ideas, talking over each other. Our words are all muddled and Iris looks positively horrified, but she shouldn't. She's been working with us for months so this shouldn't surprise her. She lifts both hands and raises her voice. "Okay! One at a time!"

Jeremy wanders back in and quickly places down all the coffees. "I wish I had said yes to the bourbon," I mumble, and he pats my shoulder sympathetically.

"I think we need a scholarship, obviously," Dad says, talking over Aunt Hilda who was trying to explain her idea. "Ned was a fan of education. A scholarship for a political science student at the local school, also his alma mater, is perfect."

"Something that directly benefits this city would be better," Aunt Hilda interrupts. "I mean, there's a billion scholarships. But what about a community center, where people can come and take programs or put on cultural events that benefit the locals."

"I was thinking of something to do with farming," Amy says. "After all, that's the backbone of Vermont, and the industry as a whole is struggling."

Dad and my brother roll their eyes. Aunt Hilda just frowns, like being reminded that Vermont is predominantly a working class, agricultural state is somehow inconvenient. Peter looks over his laptop at me. "Chase? What do you think?"

"I like the community center idea, but Burlington already has one of those. I volunteer there once a week," I tell him, and I guess my family too, since I doubt they know. "And the farming idea definitely has potential. I know there's a lot of need. I'd like to investigate that further. But I was thinking I'd like some kind of youth program that grants funds and guidance to young entrepreneurs. Not all kids want to go to college and not all can. There's a lot that could be learned to help young ambitious people with great ideas, but no resources to get their businesses off the ground. My company already offers free seminars on marketing and public relations, but a lot more could be done. Grants, loans, partnerships."

No one says anything at first, and the only person smiling is Iris so I know, when my family does speak, it's not going to be positive. My brother sets the tone. "Is this just a way for you to access Granddad's cash before your inheritance kicks in? Because that's what it sounds like."

"I knew you'd say something stupid like that," I reply, and he scowls back at me.

"Well, I mean, none of *our* ideas involved the money going to us," Amy says, and Colin gives her a thankful look.

"I'm sorry but doesn't your husband's family own one of the largest dairy farms in Vermont?" I snap and instantly regret it.

"I never said they would take a hand-out!" Amy barks.

"I actually do things for this community already. I volunteer. I'm on the Chamber of Commerce." I hate that I can't stop letting them get to me. "What do you all do to help this town?"

"None of us are still trying to earn Granddad's' money," Colin shoots back. "We don't have to pretend to care."

I grind my teeth. Amy received her inheritance two months ago, which was almost a year after her twenty-eighth birthday. I know she was *this close* to having it denied. My father and aunt decide if we've met the requirements, and my dad was adamant that Amy did not. His proof was the daughter Amy gave birth to seven months after her wedding. Amy and Aunt Hilda swore the baby was premature. But Dad wasn't buying it because she weighed six pounds and seven ounces. If we aren't deemed to meet the requirements, the funds are supposed to be moved into the charity, but of course Amy and Aunt Hilda fought him. Iris refused to let it go to court, forcing them to battle it out with multiple meetings in this office. Eventually Aunt Hilda got a doctor to give a sworn statement and Dad gave up. Amy got her money. But he still comments on the kid's early arrival every chance he gets. He literally calls her preemie-Lily instead of just Lily every time he sees her.

"I actually like helping the local businesses," I reply but I know it's futile. Nobody believes me, except maybe Iris and Peter who are both smiling at me sympathetically.

"So, I see the purpose of this meeting is to pick, not because you picked already," Iris doesn't bother to contain her sigh. "Jeremy! We're going to need more coffee. And maybe some of the bourbon you keep in your desk."

Two hours later I'm in the elevator with Dad and Colin, leaving the office of Sprysky and Gentry and I am completely exhausted, mentally. But at least we have a focus. At Iris's suggestion we kind of melded Amy's idea and mine and we're going with a fund for local farms to help them expand their businesses. There will be money designated for things like equipment upgrades but also classes to expand their reach and visibility within the community. I volunteered to run that side of things, with Aunt Hilda overseeing things, and my dad and Colin and Amy are going to handle the funding requests for equipment.

"So local boy, know any farms that may need new equipment or tutorials on Instagram?" Colin asks, smirking. I have never been close to my only brother, and it used to bug me. It actually hurt me a lot as kids, but now... well he's just some guy I have to deal with, like an annoying co-worker.

"I don't know a farm that couldn't use a boost," I reply, ignoring his digs. "There's an apple farm locally that is run by a family called the Adler's. They're struggling."

"The Adler kid plays for the Moo U hockey team, right? He's really good," my dad surmises.

"And there's a hemp farm that is looking to expand into marijuana production."

Colin's head snaps up at that and his usual cocky expression slides off his face, replaced by shock. "You want us to fund a grow-op?"

"Cannabis is legal in Vermont, Colin. It's a legitimate farming industry and also, like I said, right now they produce hemp which isn't the same thing," I don't know why I brought up Bowen's farm.

The truth is I don't know many local farms. I knew of the Adler farm because a guy named Ben Adler came to one of my seminars wanting to advertise their baked goods. I was just suggesting anything I could think of, and I think of Bowen a lot so…

"What's the name of the farm?" Dad asks, turning to look up at me with a scowl. "It isn't Whitlock, is it?"

"It is."

"Ha. No fucking way."

"Colin, language," Dad barks.

"You know Dad is very close friends with Murray Baldwin, Chase," Colin explains. "And you're friendly with Lacey, who is also running for mayor. Against this Whitlock dude."

"What does that have to do with farming?"

"It's a conflict of interest," Dad says curtly, making it clear the subject is now closed.

The elevator doors open and we jostle awkwardly as we all try to exit at the very same moment. I sigh and let them both pass before me. Colin isn't done being Colin, so he waits, whereas Dad is briskly striding towards the door. "You still in that little garage band of yours?"

"Imposter Syndrome. And yeah." There is no point elaborating further.

"Play recently?" Colin asks and I start to feel a tingle at the back of my neck. He's baiting me. "Around town?"

"You guys have a long drive back to Rhode Island," I reply instead of answering the question. "You should get going."

"Are you still honestly doing that band thing? You don't even have original music. What's the point?" Dad usually doesn't listen when we speak, especially to each other, but of course he decides to break that pattern now.

"I have original music," I reply and shove my hand in my jeans so he can't see they're balled into fists. I hate giving them any indication that their constant disapproval gets to me. "I just don't play it with the guys. People like hearing songs they know. Cover bands are popular and it's an easy outlet. It's a hobby, Dad. Have you honestly never had one of those?"

I can't think of one thing my father has done in my life that wasn't work-related. Even having his two sons and marrying my mother may have actually been politically motivated. She was from a political family and we were created to follow in his footsteps. Colin has started that journey. My father hinted heavily that I should be on the path already as well.

"I don't have time for a hobby," Dad replies with a condescending frown. "And if you had the career ambition your brother and I do, you wouldn't have it either. You'd be running for mayor instead of Lacey Baldwin. I told you the current mayor was going to retire and call a snap election months before he even announced it. You had time to prepare."

"Speaking of time, wow! It's getting late!" I exclaim without looking at my phone or a watch or any other time piece. "I have to get going. I have hobby practice. I mean band practice."

"On a weekday? Before five?" Dad looks positively horrified.

"I took the day off work because I didn't know how long this would take," I reply calmly. "And I'm the boss Dad, I can do that."

He frowns. I have so many of his features, including his blue eyes, but I hope to hell I don't have as many wrinkles around them when I'm fifty as he does. I'm trying hard to avoid a career, and life, that makes me scowl as much. I turn to make my way down the sidewalk, towards my loft. But Colin, dear brother that he is, isn't done yet. "Let me know if you ever play a bar that isn't…. *Con Plumas.*"

"What the fuck does that mean?" I turn back to face him, the words coming out in a growl because I'm pretty certain whatever it means, it's not pleasant.

"Lacey said you played that gay bar a few weeks ago," Colin says, his voice dropping to a stage whisper on the word gay, and my blood instantly starts boiling in my veins. "*Con plumas* is Spanish. It means with feathers. I was just trying to be discreet."

"That makes no sense. If you're going to be a homophobic jackass at least have it make sense," I spit out and turn to leave.

"Chase!" My dad bellows my name so loudly people on the sidewalk passing by turn and look but I keep walking. I don't stop until I reach the corner and then I don't have a choice because there's traffic and I don't have the light.

"Son," my father's voice startles me. I didn't expect him to follow me.

I look at him and pull my sunglasses down from on top of my

head because I don't want him to read a single emotion that he might be able to see in my eyes. He sighs. "Colin was out of line."

Well, that's unexpected. "Yes. He was. And wrong."

"Incredibly tasteless," Dad agrees, and I have to work to keep my jaw from dropping. This is not the man who I came out to—well, sort of came out to—in college who insisted I was just confused because my liberal school was brainwashing me, and it would pass. I would grow out of it. Could he have actually grown as a person, into someone who will accept me as I am? "I'll make sure he knows it on the ride back home. In fact, this just confirms what I have been debating for a long time now."

"What's that?" I ask and ignore the fact that the light has changed, and I could walk away right now.

"That Colin desperately needs a coach. Someone who can help him learn what is acceptable and unacceptable behavior for a potential political candidate," he explains, shaking his head and looking at me like this is the actual problem with Colin's behavior. "Those people are a huge and growing demographic and if you're going to succeed in this world nowadays you have to appear to be an ally or get, what do they call it? Cancelled?"

He couldn't say that more begrudgingly if he tried and it turns all those stupid feelings of hope I had seconds ago into little jagged rocks in my gut. Dad blinks. My disappointment must be visible on my face, even with the Ray-Bans I just put on. "What I'm saying is I have no issue with your band playing in gay bars. Lacey was smart to go and watch you too, because it shows that population they can vote for her."

"Or maybe she just wanted to support a talented friend," I mutter. "I have to go Dad."

"You weren't there for anything else, right?" he asks bluntly. "I mean, we've talked about it and you've said you're not really gay. You like girls still, mostly, too, right?"

"We are not having this conversation again," I tell him and cross the street even though I no longer have the light. Luckily, Burlington isn't exactly New York when it comes to traffic so I'm not putting my life at great risk. And I'd take a jaywalking ticket over trying to explain what bisexual means to my dad again.

The walk back to my place is short. The sun is shining and the sky is cloudless and I would normally enjoy the gentle spring breeze and the sun warming my skin but, as always, spending time with my family has created a cloud inside me that eclipses any goodness in the world around me. But then I turn the corner, and my building comes into view, and standing outside of it are three people. Joe, Grant, and Bowen. They're in a semi-circle, facing each other, talking about something. Everyone is smiling. Bowen lifts his head, the wind blowing his long hair across his cheek. As he brushes it away, he catches sight of me and he smiles. And that cloud inside me starts to dissipate.

BOWEN

We spend two hours jamming in the loft. Turns out the drum kit that they brought to Vino and Veritas for their gig is Chase's and lives in the corner of his massive living room normally. Those guitars he has on his walls are also used by the band and well, basically, Chase owns all the equipment and musical instruments. The session goes great. Amazing, if I do say so myself. I have to work a little on "Come as You Are" and "Summer of Sixty-Nine" which means I'll have to dust off the old drum kit at home, but I'm actually looking forward to it.

"I can't believe your neighbors let you have band practice in your living room," I say to Chase, and he shrugs as he puts down his guitar.

"I own the building."

"What?" I try to do the mental math on that. I mean, it's not a huge building. Narrow, four stories. He occupies the first floor with his business and the top two with his home so that means he isn't paying additional mortgages or rent elsewhere, but still. It's downtown. Church Street. Prime real estate. It wasn't cheap.

"Well technically I don't own it. It was part of my grandfather's assets. And before he died he promised I could use it, for free, if I stayed in Vermont and opened a business he approved of. So I did, like a good boy," Chase grins. "Grant rents the loft in between the office and this one, so he doesn't complain about noise."

"I have had to jab a broom handle into the ceiling some nights when there isn't practice," Grant says and laughs as Chase shrugs sheepishly. I realize Grant wasn't exaggerating when he said he could stumble home the other night.

I don't know what to say to that, so I say nothing. The dude is rich. I don't think I've ever met someone as rich as him before. Joe hands Chase his guitar and claps him on the shoulder, then turns to me. "Good session today. We'll be ready for that gig next Saturday. Now I have to go grade papers."

He sighs and heads towards the elevator. Grant grabs his coat off one of the stools at the kitchen island. "I have to head downstairs and put the finishing touches on a presentation for tomorrow."

"The outerwear company?" Chase asks and Grant nods. "Need me for that?"

"No, man, I think we're on track," Grant says as he shrugs into his coat and starts toward the elevator as the doors open and Joe gets on. "I'll call if there's a red flag. Otherwise, the pitch will be waiting for you when you get in tomorrow."

"Awesome." Chase nods as Joe holds the elevator for Grant to step in. As soon as he does, the doors swish closed, leaving me alone with Chase.

He walks over to the fridge and pulls out a beer and holds it up. "One for the road?"

I nod. "If you're having one, yeah. Okay."

"I'm having a glass of red," Chase replies and plucks up a bottle from the corner of the counter. "Opened it last night but didn't finish it and I hate leaving an open bottle too long."

"Okay. I'll try a glass of that then."

Chase cocks one of his eyebrows as the corner of his mouth quirks too. "You don't seem like a wine guy."

"Well, so far I haven't been," I confess and walk over to the kitchen. "When I was in high school, my boyfriend stole a bottle from his mom's collection and it tasted like someone crushed gooseberries into vinegar. I had a pounding headache for two days after we drank it. But I'm always open to trying something twice."

"You haven't tried wine since high school?"

I nod. "It was truly not a good hangover. And once I discovered beer and cider, I didn't see the point in trying it again."

"You work at a wine bar," Chase reminds me, and he looks incredibly bewildered and maybe a little amused as I shrug. "And you had a boyfriend in high school?"

"Yeah. I came out when I was seventeen after I kissed my first guy, who went on to be my first boyfriend. That lasted half of senior year and my first year in college," I reply and watch his hands as they uncork the wine and grab the stems of two glasses hanging upside down under one of his kitchen cabinets. He has great hands. It's a weird thing to notice but I always notice hands. His fingers are long and wide, but he moves them — over the microphone stand or the bottle of wine or the stem of the wine glass — with a grace and elegance you wouldn't expect. His nails are clean and short. His skin, smooth with only a barely noticeable dusting of fine light hair on his knuckles. Lighter than the chestnut hair on his head that I'm so obsessed with.

Chase pours the first glass of wine and slides it toward me, his hand on the base. I take it by the stem, and as he moves his hand away, his fingers brush my knuckles and I feel a jolt so intense I actually look down to see if there was an actual spark. "I didn't know I was into guys until I was almost done with college."

"You didn't know?" I repeat his words and he smiles sheepishly.

"I didn't let myself confirm that I liked guys," he rephrases and finishes pouring his own glass of wine. "Swirl it around a second, let it get some air."

I swirl the wine. He does too, those very blue eyes concentrating hard on the liquid as it circles the wine glass. "Why did you wait so long?"

It's not my business, but I ask anyway. If I had to guess, I'd say it's also the reason he's still in the closet. Chase stops swirling his wine, so I stop, and then he leans across the island between us and gently taps his glass to mine in a cheers. "Because I was doing fine with women. I didn't think I needed to complicate my life further."

I sip the wine. He does too, but his eyes are firmly glued to me, waiting for my reaction to his answer and the wine, I'm guessing. "It's nice," I reply. "Not at all gooseberries and vinegar."

Chase lets out a small chuff of laughter at that. He grabs the bottle and walks around the island, toward the living room. "Come on, let's sit down."

I follow. He takes one end of the couch and I take the other. He leans forward and puts the bottle on the coffee table and then grabs a remote. I wonder for a second if he's going to turn on the television, but instead the fireplace roars to life. His eyes find mine again. "I have never thought of my sexuality as a complication."

"You're extremely lucky."

"Yeah," I agree and take another sip of wine. "My parents didn't even blink when I told them I liked Trevor in *that* way. I think one guy in my entire life has tried to make me feel bad about it. That's it."

"Who?"

"Trevor."

Chase's eyes widen. "The boyfriend?"

"He wasn't out and didn't intend to be," I explain, trying to sound like it doesn't matter, because it doesn't anymore. But boy, it used to matter. I can still feel the sting if I think about it too much. "I thought he was just scared and needed time, so I gave him plenty. Too much. I finally ended it when he didn't show up to support me when my parents died because he was worried people would get the wrong idea."

"You mean the right idea," Chase mutters and sighs. "That's brutal. I'm sorry."

"Thanks." I shake my head and push away the memory. "Anyway, I am who I am and I like me. I know my sexuality isn't something I should feel bad about."

"I know that too, by the way," Chase replies, and I can hear the tinge of defensiveness in his tone. He pauses and sips his wine. His eyes move to the flames dancing in the gas fireplace. "I don't feel bad about the fact I'm into men."

"Then why are you in the closet?" Again, none of my fucking business, but I'm dying to know. Chase is like something I know I shouldn't want but I do anyway. If he explains it to me, maybe I'll want him less.

"I'm not totally in the closet. I've told my parents I'm bi," Chase explains. "Grant and Joe know that too."

"But are you bi or gay?"

"Does it matter?"

"To me, no," I reply easily. "I'm attracted to you either way. Hell, I was attracted to you when I thought you were straight."

He smiles slyly and that feeling in my groin, that tingling tightness I get when something really turns me on, starts to happen. I wish it didn't because I'm still not going to do anything about it.

"I'm gay," Chase says firmly. "In college my girlfriend wanted a threesome with me and a guy on my swim team. He was game. I obliged and he and I probably had way more fun than her."

Ah. Swim team. That explains the broad shoulders, trim waist, and lean but well developed muscles.

"Anyway, I thought I could ease my highly religious, conservative parents into my truth with baby steps. So, I went home for the weekend and told them I thought I was bisexual. And well, let's just say, unlike your parents, they blinked."

"Sorry."

"Me too, but to be honest I wasn't the least bit surprised." Chase scratches his head, ruffling that thick, glossy hair I want to touch so badly. "Anyway, I haven't bothered to clarify things for them because we've all agreed to just not talk about it at all. Don't ask, don't tell."

"Well, you said your dad is a politician and that's a very political way to handle it."

"The marketing guy in me actually has to give him credit for being so on brand," Chase quips and reaches for the wine bottle. He tops off my glass and then his own. "The marketing guy in me is also very interested in your campaign strategy for your brother."

"Ah well, strategy is a very lofty word." I sink back into the lush velvet of the couch because it gives me an extra couple of inches of distance from him and I kind of need it. The wine is making me relaxed and the intimate conversation we just had is making me want to be close to him physically too. I'm glad he's changed the subject. "At first we thought we could rely on word of mouth and some meet and greets, but that didn't work so we gathered up some cash and bought advertising on the side of a barn."

"Where?"

"Near the last exit on 91." Chase doesn't even try to hide his bewilderment at that. "I know, not the best location. Anyway, we hired this campaign manager. The same one that got our current mayor elected so we thought it was a sure bet but turns out all her ideas cost a ton of money. And we don't have a ton. Also, Woody is an environmentalist. I mean our whole family recycles and has a compost and we actually sat down and tracked the carbon footprint of our farm and our lives. But Woody is by far the most intense about it. He's vowed to never have kids because the planet is overpopulated, he only rides a bike or walks or takes city transit and only lets us own one car between us. And he's against stuff like flyers and posters and things that all the other candidates are using."

Chase is listening intently. His expression has changed from that vulnerable, sexy guy who I play in a band with to this focused businessman guy. "Okay. Well, being an environmentalist will get him votes for sure. But you have to tell people about it. Have you?"

"I'm sure Woody brings it up," I reply but to be honest, I don't think he's gone into much detail about it in interviews. I've been working so much I'm not sure. "And it's a whole section on his website. A lot of his plans for the city involve improving its carbon footprint."

Chase nods and scrubs his hand over the stubble on his chin, lost in thought. "So you have a website. That's good. Have you optimized it correctly? What about Facebook ads? Does he have a Twitter account? A Facebook page?"

"Autumn set up the website on one of those free places, so I'll have to ask her what optimizing is and if it was included," I explain and his face falls. "And I don't think we're running ads and he has a Twitter. He's had it for years. But he doesn't use it."

"Oh man, you guys need to run some Facebook ads and get him on Twitter talking with locals," Chase advises. He stands up, putting his wine glass on the coffee table, and climbs the stairs to his bedroom two at a time. I sit there, frozen, wondering what's happening but before I can ask, he's on his way back down the stairs holding some papers. He hands them to me. "Take this. It's a booklet I give out when I do a free, one-day course on social media advertising. There's a whole section on there about Facebook ads. It's just the basics, but even one basic ad is better than none. Give it to whomever you think should run the ads. It's key that he gets more visibility."

"Thanks, Chase." I look at the papers and then back up to him. He's settled on the couch again, but not in the other corner. He's kind of in the middle, closer to me. "I saw you talking with Lacey Baldwin the night of the show."

He nods and refills his wine glass. "We're friends through those pesky parents I told you about."

"So why are you helping her competition. I mean, I'm not trying to look a gift *course* in the mouth here, but I'm curious."

"Ha! Cute pun. Witty, hot, and talented. Triple threat," he replies and winks. Fuck that is hot. "Because despite knowing her, I don't have a dog in this fight. I think she'd probably make a decent mayor, but it sounds like your brother would too. And he's got one clear advantage over Lacey in my opinion."

"That is?"

"That I want to kiss his brother again."

Well, shit. I think he just made me blush. Either that or this wine is warming my cheeks, but I doubt it. "I like that reason more than I should."

Chase shifts on the sofa, draping an arm across the back, his fingertips brushing the back of my shirt by my shoulder. I feel another ripple of electricity. I can't remember the last time I was this turned on by a guy. "Look, I can't do the whole boyfriend thing, but I can give someone a really good time. And I can be a bandmate and friend after the fact. I don't get weird."

Now I'm the one shifting my position, turning to face him, with my back against the arm of the sofa. I reach out with one hand and put my almost empty wine glass on the coffee table next to his and then lay my arm across his on the back of the couch. I shouldn't, but I can't resist. I've had a couple of hook-ups with no strings attached and they were fine. They served their purpose, they got me off. I *do* want more than that, but if I can't have more with Chase, should I deny myself what I can have? Plus, if I fool around with him now, maybe that sexual tension that distracts me when we're in the same room will disappear. That would be helpful. Playing drums while fighting a hard on and the urge to make-out with your lead singer will get old fast.

Chase's mouth quirks up in a smirk. "Who's winning the battle in that head of yours? The devil or the angel?"

I smile sheepishly and let my fingers curl around his forearm near his elbow. His skin is warm and supple. "Which one has me making out with you again? Because that's the one currently winning."

We both lean forward at the same time and before I can even close my eyes, our lips crash together. This is a different kiss than the first one. That one tested the waters. This one is a cannon ball into the deep end. This one is even more needy, somehow. Chase is still forceful and confident in the way his tongue sweeps into my mouth, but now he's also greedy and impatient. And before I know it, I'm on my back and he's on top of me. I slide my hands into that hair I've been fantasizing about and it's even more silky than I imagined. I curl my fingers around the ends and tug, pulling his head back and his lips off mine. He doesn't go without a fight, gently biting my bottom lip before allowing me access to his neck. I kiss and suck my way from his collarbone to his jaw. He smells delicious, woodsy and crisp at the same time. I drop my right leg off the couch to make better space for his body between my legs and he takes full advantage of the room, grinding his hips into mine, his hard-on pressing into my own.

We make out and kiss and lick each other for a long time. So long that my balls are aching and my whole body feels hotter than the flames in the fireplace. "There's way too much clothing in the way."

The weight of Chase's body is suddenly gone, as is his mouth, and I look up to see him sitting between my legs unbuttoning his shirt. He hastily shrugs out of it, balling it up and tossing it to the floor, and then his hands are shoving my own shirt up and undoing my belt. He gets my belt undone, and I pull myself up and lift my shirt over my head. Before my head is even free of the fabric, I feel his tongue against my left nipple and I groan. That makes him bite and white-hot lust runs like an electrical current from his teeth to my balls.

I want to reach for his belt. I want to tug his pants off. I want to kiss him again, long and deep, and fuck him with my tongue the way I also want to fuck him with my cock, but Chase is determined to control this. And who am I to argue? He moves his mouth to my other nipple and growls. "Lift your hips."

When I obey, he yanks my pants and underwear down to my knees. My bare ass meets the smooth velvet as his hands crawl up my thighs and his teeth nip my sensitive flesh. "I want you to fuck my mouth."

I like a man who knows what he wants. "Kiss me first."

He finds his way back to my mouth. The bare skin against bare skin, chest-to-chest, is enough to make me groan but then he presses his hand palm down onto my cock between us and groaning is unavoidable. "You're thick," he whispers against my lips, sounding a little surprised. I get it. My frame is lean and almost wiry so the thickness and length of my cock surprises men.

My hands want to get his pants off too, so I can take another look at what is wedged up against my thigh. That first glimpse when he dropped his towel wasn't nearly enough. I manage to only get his jeans over his ass cheeks when his fingers curl around my shaft and he starts stroking me. Then I'm suddenly in quicksand, being sucked down by my desire and unable to do anything else but let it consume me. He kisses my neck, my collarbone, my shoulder, and his lips dance across my nipple again before continuing their descent. I shove my fingers into his hair as his tongue gives my head a long, slow lick. My pre-cum glistens against his lips in the light from the fire.

It's been four months since my last hook-up, but that feels like four years all of a sudden and this… this is going to be something special. I know it instantly, from just that one slow pass of his tongue. Chase's lips circle my tip and then move lower as he takes me into his mouth at a teasingly slow pace, centimeter by centimeter, his tongue swirling and swirling over my shaft and Jesus, I am dying the best possible death right now.

I arch my back, tipping my head back onto the arm of the couch and fisting his hair between my fingers. I bend and wiggle my knee until I get my right leg free of my pants and underwear and drop my foot to the floor. He pulls his mouth off my cock just long enough to reposition himself in the vacant space between my legs and repeats his first request. "Fuck my mouth, Bowen."

And then, when his lips hit my tip, I do what he wants. I start pushing myself in and out of his mouth. I'm careful and measured at first, making sure to keep my thrusts gentle and not too swift but his tongue is doing such magical work and there's this perfect amount of suck and pressure… and then I make the mistake of opening my eyes and looking at him.

His eyes are open, darkened with desire and staring right at me. "You're fucking magic," I whisper. "You suck my cock like you were born for it."

I push my hips up again and he bears down, taking me right to the back of his throat and that's it. I can't play it cool a second longer. I hold the back of his head and pump faster and harder and he moans in approval against my shaft and my balls tighten. I somehow find enough common sense to warn him. "Gonna come."

That doesn't make him move away. I'm so lost I can't keep my pace, so he starts sucking and licking faster, I'm gone before I even know it. I come with the force of a rocket blasting off into space. My eyes snap shut, my mouth drops open, my voice catches in my throat garbling whatever words were trying to escape. Chase swallows every last drop that spills from my body. When everything stops tingling, and my heart stops trying to crack my rib cage wide open, my eyes find him. He's leaning back against the other side of the couch, head tilted back, pumping his own cock with abandon. I pull myself off the couch, push his thighs apart, and kneel between them. In a raspy whisper I tell him, "My turn."

7

CHASE

Carter hands me the samples and Auden watches us with his arms folded over his broad chest. I glance at him and smile. He half smiles back. "Don't know why he didn't just ask me directly."

"Maybe because you scare the hell out of him?" Carter, Auden's boyfriend and business partner in Imprescott Designs, replies with a wink. Auden rolls his eyes. "Don't you scowl at him all the time since he nailed you in the face with that champagne cork?"

"It hurt."

"Honestly, Auden, he doesn't even know I'm here," I explain, trying to make sure there's no extra tension for Bowen when they work together again. "I asked him about his brother's campaign the other night after band practice and he said Woody wouldn't do posters so I thought this would be a good solution."

Carter walks over and pats Auden on his shoulder. "Maybe don't be so scary."

Carter kisses Auden's cheek and I look away. I'm not uncomfortable with their affection. I'm jealous. I wonder if I'll ever be able to be that open with my sexuality. I promised myself that as soon as that inheritance is in my bank account, I'll be out and proud. But sometimes I worry I've been hiding myself for so long that I'll just keep doing it out of habit. And then I worry that by the time this charade ends, I won't have someone I can kiss on the cheek in front of my friends.

"Chase?" Auden says, and I realize I've been staring off into space.

"Yeah. Sorry." I clear my throat. "I'm going to head out. I'm sure Bowen's brother will get back to you with one of these options. Thanks again for the samples."

I tuck the paper into my messenger bag. Carter shakes my hand. "I think he's got some good ideas, even if he seems a little rough around the edges in his interviews."

"Yeah." I nod but the truth is, I've been ignoring the election coverage. My business takes up most of my free time and the rest of it I spend on music. Also, I just assumed I would vote for Lacey since she's a family friend. Now, I realize, I have stronger ties to her opponent. Because Lacey wasn't the one to give me the best blow job of my life.

I give them both a final wave and head out of the press shop, making my way toward my office. It's a bit of an ominous looking day with gray clouds hovering low in the sky. The air is heavy, like rain is imminent and I didn't bring an umbrella so I should probably pick up the pace, but I don't. The sooner I get back to the office, the sooner I have to concentrate on work, and I'd rather walk slowly and reminisce about the other night.

Screwing around with Bowen was supposed to be like it always is with my hook-ups — quick and simple gratification. I always make it clear that I'm a one and done guy. I never explain why and no one has ever asked. And it hasn't been a hardship to walk away after even the most satisfying hook-up. I've always felt like once was enough. It got me off and I moved on until the urge came again. And when it did, it was never for someone I'd already been with. But for the last three nights since we hooked up, Bowen Whitlock is all I think about.

The way his mouth tastes, the feel of his long, silky hair tickling my thighs as he bobbed up and down on my cock. The little confident smirk on his lips after I came. The way he wiped his thumb across his bottom lip and then pushed my hair back off my forehead and planted a kiss on it as I floated back to earth post-orgasm. As soon as he got dressed and headed out the door, I wanted to drag him back in and do more. I thought maybe the feeling would ease with a few days distance, but it hasn't. I'm positively itching to see him again.

I open the door to Dauntless and the receptionist smiles at me. "Grant has news for you."

"Thanks, Betty," I say, and she nods her gray head. Betty is sixty-six. She's a retired communications professor from Moo U. She was one of my favorite teachers when I went there. I ran into her a couple weeks after I opened Dauntless, and she told me how much she hated retirement and how she wanted something to do part-time. I offered her a job consulting with us, which she also does, but she says she prefers answering the phones and making coffee because it's simple and she likes taking care of us. She works three days a week and an intern manages the front desk the other two.

I make my way down the main hall. I opted against open concept for Dauntless because I hated it at all the firms I did internships at. It felt like working in a fishbowl and wasn't conducive to creativity. Instead, everyone here has their own office off the main hall with glass walls with retractable blinds. At the end of the hall is a long conference room and at the front, by Betty's desk, is a kitchen. My office is the first on the left and Grant's is across from mine. He's got his blinds up and is sitting behind his desk. He gets up when he sees me.

He's smiling as he enters my office. "We got the account."

"Really?"

"We barely made it back to the car after the meeting and I got the email. They signed the contract," Grant says proudly. I get up, grab him by the shoulders, and pull him into a bro-hug.

"You're a fucking king," I declare, and he laughs.

"The monthly hashtag contest was your idea," Grant tells me. "They loved it."

"I'm sure it wasn't just that," I reply and walk back over to sit behind my desk. I figure he'll go back to his office but instead he walks over and closes my door.

"Uh-oh," I say as I lower myself into my chair and start to roll up the sleeves on my button down. "That was only the good news, right? There's bad?"

Grant sighs. "Yeah, but it's not work-related. Hence the privacy."

My brow furrows. Grant rubs his chin and his brown eyes look conflicted. "Bennie reached out."

"What does our *ex*-drummer want?" I emphasize the ex part,

trying not to sound nervous. If he wants his job back and Grant and Joe want to give it to him, then I'll have no excuse to see Bowen again.

Grant puts his hands on his hips, his suit jacket opening. "He wanted to explain to me it isn't us, it's you he can't work with anymore."

Grant's eyes hold my stare for a long second. Long enough to make me look away sheepishly, which confirms what I'm sure Bennie already told him. "Chase, I thought you had rules."

"I do. One and done." I sigh and lean back in my chair. "It was a weak moment. I swear I told him it wasn't going to be a thing. It was just one night. And he said that was fine."

"Of course it wasn't fine, Chase. He has a crush on you. Joe and I both told you that a long time ago." Grant frowns like I'm the obstinate child who was told not to touch the stove because it was hot, and then I touched the stove. He shakes his head and scratches his beard again. "People with crushes don't usually get over it after they have sex. Unless the sex was bad."

"I don't do bad sex," I reply, and Grant almost laughs at that. Almost. "I don't do sex at all, but when I do it'll be great. It was just a couple of blow jobs."

"Okay Romeo, well whatever the details, you fucked us all out of a good drummer," Grant replies, losing his smile.

"But Bennie was always flaky. He was late for practice all the time. He didn't play half the songs as well as Bowen does," I argue but he doesn't seem less annoyed by those facts.

"Bennie is a nice guy. You hurt him." Grant holds up a hand to stop me from arguing. "I know you didn't do it on purpose. I know that you don't exactly get how feelings work because you haven't been allowed to actually have them. But either way, the damage is done. I'm not saying I want him back in the band, but it would be nice if you could at least try to mend the friendship."

"I can try." Grant seems happy with that and opens the door to my office. But before he can step through it and cross the hall to go back to his own office, he pauses and glances at me over his shoulder.

"Can you make a new rule?" he asks. "No nakedness with bandmates unless it's in the hot tub. Platonically?"

I just stare at him. He blinks. Then he blinks again, and I can literally see the light bulb flicker on behind his brown eyes. "Are you fucking kidding me?"

"It was just once and Bowen is totally cool with it. I swear to God," I tell him in a whisper so no one in the office will overhear if they walk by. "I was very clear. Clearer than I've ever been. And he gets it. I swear."

"I hope so," Grant warns. "Because I just booked another wedding, for double the price we did the last one for because it's a last-minute thing, their band bailed, and it would be fabulous if we had a drummer for it."

He leaves, closing the door behind him.

***

Later that night, I order another Crianza from Murph and try really hard to keep my eyes from wandering over to where Bowen is serving a couple in a booth. This is my fourth glass of Spanish wine. I'm full-on tipsy with drunk on my horizon. It isn't normal for me to get hammered on a weeknight, but I had to come in here to tell Bowen about the paper options and the wedding gig. And then Tanner mentioned they'd finally gotten another shipment of the Spanish red I like so much, so I decided to have a glass. And then Bowen offered to buy me another one. And then… well, sticking around and chatting with him in between customers felt like a much more enjoyable option than going home and watching TV or working on a new song. Which is crazy because I love working on my own music. I can spend a whole weekend holed up at home doing just that and not get bored. But I'd rather be here stealing snippets of conversation with Bowen.

Bowen appears next to me and puts his tray with two empty pint glasses and some cash on the counter beside me. His eyes land on Murph. "Last customer of the night, I'm guessing."

Murph leans on the bar top and grins. "I don't want to jinx anything but Bowen, it looks like you've made it through your first catastrophe-free shift."

Bowen turns to look back at the tables. The couple is putting on their jackets and heading for the door. Besides me, Murph, and Bowen, the only other people left in the bar are the owner Harrison and his husband Finn. Bowen's head swivels back and he's almost smiling, but then he knocks on the sleek wood bar top. "Knock on wood, you may be correct."

"This one here must be your lucky charm." Murph tilts his head to me, grinning, before taking the empty glasses off Bowen's tray and walking towards the kitchen. "You wanna start wiping down the tables, please?"

"Sure thing." Bowen nods and grabs a rag from behind the bar.

Now, with Murph gone, and Harrison and Finn ignoring everything but each other in the back corner booth, I allow myself to stare at Bowen. He's busy, bent over one of the tables, scrubbing away. His shirt is lifting at the waist just a little so I can see the smooth skin of his lower back. His butt is pressed into his jeans and God damn it's a great ass. His triceps and biceps flex as he rubs down the table, a couple strands of his golden hair escape the elastic he's using to try and hold it back at the base of his neck. That neck that felt so fucking good under my lips. What I wouldn't do to walk up behind him right now and kiss the back of that neck of his while he's bent over and have my cock slide right in between…

He moves to another table and glances my way. I'm busted. He doesn't seem to mind. He just smiles his sexy, lazy smile and continues his chores. I reach for my wine glass but it's already empty again. I really can't indulge in another one. Then I'll have crossed into the totally drunk zone and I'll have to work hungover tomorrow. I hate working hungover. So I should just go home… alone… but a few more minutes ogling Bowen's ass will at least give me some prime masturbation material.

Someone clears their throat. My head snaps around and I find Murph watching me. Busted again. And this *isn't* okay. Murph doesn't know I'm gay and can't know. I stand up and dig my wallet out of my messenger bag on the stool beside me. "I was just wondering what kind of cleaner you guys use here? Because I'm looking for a new… disinfectant. Something organic or like environmentally friendly."

Oh my God, do I really expect Murph to believe this? I almost want to laugh out loud at my own shitty excuse. Murph is gracious enough not to laugh though. "I think it's just a water, lemon, and vinegar solution. I can ask Harrison if you want. Or Tanner tomorrow."

"Nah. I'll ask him next time I see him, no worries." I hand him a couple of bills and grab my bag. "I'll see ya around, Murph."

Bowen is standing up now, done with wiping the tables. He lifts his forearm to his forehead to brush his hair back and starts to walk over to me. "Thanks again for the paper samples. Such a brilliant idea."

"And don't forget to ask Auden about the vegetable-based inks he can use," I reply and grab my suit jacket from the little hook it's been hanging on under the bar. I opt to drop it over my arm instead of putting it on. "I'll see ya at the next practice."

"Yeah. Wouldn't miss it." Bowen nods and his smile feels intimate now, but maybe I'm just drunk.

"You know, I can handle the rest of the clean-up," Murph announces. "It was a really easy night. There isn't much more to do. Why don't you head out Bowen?"

"Really?"

"Sure." Murph nods. "I feel like not spilling drinks or breaking glasses for the last eight hours must have taken a lot out of you. Go home, rest up. You're on again tomorrow night, aren't you?"

Bowen nods and laughs. "I'm going to take you up on this, but not because I'm exhausted from not fucking up. But because I didn't sleep well last night and could use the extra Zs."

"Mmm...hmm." That doesn't sound like Murph believes his co-worker but then he smiles again. "Go. See ya tomorrow."

"Thanks." Bowen turns to me. "Wanna walk with me? I parked not far from your place."

"Sure," I say casually but for some drunken reason inside I'm cheering like my team just won the Stanley Cup. Hell, like *I* did. "Wouldn't want to leave you alone on the mean streets of Burlington."

Bowen and Murph both laugh. "Meet you out front."

I nod and head out the door. Murph waves as I go. Bowen appears a couple minutes later, holding the paper samples I gave him and wearing a khaki jacket over his T-shirt. His hair is finally free of the elastic, which wasn't really containing it anyway. "Hey."

"Hey."

We start to walk down Church Street, side-by-side, hands in our pockets. Bowen has the paper tucked under his arm and he glances down at it and back up at me. "I may actually be able to sell him on the idea of paper promotional materials now."

"Good. Happy to help," I say. "Keep me posted on how it goes."

"I will."

There's a rumble of thunder in the distance. The storm that's been threatening to start all day may finally be ready to make an appearance. Either that or it's the universe warning me to back off.

"Did you really get a shit night's sleep last night?" I ask because I'm scrambling to say anything other than 'come home with me and let's fuck around again.'

"I don't sleep well in general. It's why I have the weed." He pulls his little metal container out of his pocket and then promptly sticks it back in.

"It really works, huh?"

"It can. For lots of things from insomnia to anxiety and panic attacks to muscle and joint pain, even helps with nausea for chemo patients," Bowen explains. I've read some stuff about the benefits of marijuana, but Bowen seems to have read a hell of a lot more. "Vermont wants to keep growing to smaller sized farms, which is great, but for the zoning they're leaving it up to mayors and city councils to decide and my brother is the only candidate who has an ethical, feasible zoning plan for it."

"Lacey doesn't?"

"Lacey doesn't want it within the city at all," Bowen says. "The other candidate has a plan with so few permits available that we simply wouldn't be able to keep up the supply. Retailers would have to be bringing in product from farms outside the area. Why throw that money at non-local farmers when we could be giving it to local ones?"

He has a really valid point. My grandfather, God rest his cold and judgmental soul, would agree with him. For all his faults he really did want his hometown to prosper and thrive. "You know, there's a charitable foundation in my grandfather's name and one of our first initiatives will be to give funding donations to local farmers for equipment and stuff. So, if you need anything like that for the hemp farm or to transition to a marijuana farm, you should check it out."

"We're good," Bowen says quietly, his eyes on the dark street in front of us. "Thanks though, for thinking of us."

I feel like I said something wrong. I don't want to make him feel like I think he's not running his farm right or like I'm an arrogant rich kid offering him my pocket change. "Sorry. That might have come out wrong. I don't wanna seem like some douchebag Daddy Warbucks or anything."

"Daddy Warbucks?"

"*Annie*."

He cocks his head, the moonlight glinting off his pale hair. "The movie?"

"Yeah, the movie too I guess, but I was thinking of the musical," I reply. "My mom took me to see it on Broadway when I was really young and I freaking loved it."

He laughs and then leans into me and whispers. "Are you sure no one has figured out you're gay?"

I laugh too and use my shoulder to give his shoulder a little push. "Fuck off. Musicals are good shit. Well, they can be. But they can also suck. Anyway *Annie*, for a seven-year-old who already dug music, didn't suck."

"You have an artist's soul," Bowen murmurs after we've walked half a block in comfortable silence. "I noticed some of the lyrics in your notebook when I grabbed a piece of paper to leave my phone number that first night. They're good. You should play some of them at gigs."

"Nah. No way, not until I get some formal training," I say it before I can think to filter myself. Must be all the red wine. Shit.

"You intend on getting formal training?"

I shrug. "I've thought about maybe taking a few classes at the University."

Or an entire degree.

We stop in front of my loft and I glance down the street. "Where are you parked?"

"Back by V and V." He grins. "I just wanted to walk you home. You had a lot of red wine."

"I did," I admit and pull my keys out of my pocket. "So much that I think I should probably invite you in."

"For what? A beer or a wine?" Bowen asks.

There's another rumble of thunder and this time it isn't so distant. It's close and loud and angry. Bowen tips his head up to the sky and I take a step closer to him and then stop myself. God I want to kiss him. He drops his head and tips his chin up ever so slightly so our eyes can meet. I've got an inch on him, maybe two, but I'm six-two so he's not exactly tiny.

"So, what are you offering?" he asks again. "Beer or wine?"

"Neither," I reply.

Lighting illuminates us for a split second. Just long enough for him to see the lust in my eyes. "You said you don't do repeats."

I shrug. "There's a first time for everything."

Thunder booms, so loud I can feel it in my bones like when I'm standing too close to an amp on stage.

"I should say no."

The sky opens up and the first big, fat rain drops start to slap our jackets and our faces. Bowen blinks. I shove my key in the door and yank it open, reaching back to grab his arm and pulling him in with me. If he's going to turn me down, he might as well do it in dryness. I reach for the light in the stairwell, but he bats my hand away. And then I feel his hands on my hips and he whispers three words before his lips crash down on mine. "Ah, fuck it."

BOWEN

Some part of me knows I shouldn't be here. I've done the whole closeted relationship before and it ended badly. I swore after Trevor I wouldn't ever do that again. And I don't intend to, I remind myself as my lips crash onto his and my hands find their way to his ass. I'm not the one with the one-and-done rule. That's him. I can fuck around with him twice and still walk away.

Chase fists his hands around my jacket and yanks me toward the elevator. Blindly, with our mouths still pressed together and his tongue greedily sweeping across mine, he manages to hit the button. The elevator opens and as soon as we're inside and he's hit the button for his floor, I press him into the back wall and dare to open my eyes. I break our kiss, making sure to tug his bottom lip between my teeth as I do, and push my cock against his hip. His reaction to the feel of my erection is everything I could ever want. His eyes open at the same time his mouth does and one of his hands leaves my jacket to grip my ass and pull me into him again.

"So, one and done?" I pant against the shell of his ear, biting his lobe, which makes him shiver.

"Twice is nice," Chase replies, his words coming out in ragged gulps. And then a devilishly sheepish smile hits those lips of his that feel so good around my cock, and he shrugs. "I'm not in the mood for logic tonight."

"What are you in the mood for?"

The elevator opens into his loft. "Let me show you."

Our clothes are like breadcrumbs, dropping in a haphazard line across the loft and up the stairs until we're face-to-face at the end of his massive bed, both buck naked. I'm excited we made it to the bed this time. Gives me more ways to work him out of my system. Because this has got to be it for us. Trevor always had an excuse for why no one could know about us and I put up with way too many of them. Not again.

His hands move over my shoulders and down my chest and towards my stomach. "You are in incredible shape."

"Farming," I say because it's literally my only real exercise besides fucking up at the bar. I step into him, his hands falling away as I pull him flush against me. He lets out a little murmur of a groan. "And you? Marketing and PR isn't exactly a physical career. You still swim?"

"I do," he whispers, his lips ghosting my collarbone. "After I teach."

"You teach swimming?" I ask but honestly, I don't care. All I care about is the feel of his ass under my palms and the way his cock is pressing against my hip.

"Aquafit," he murmurs. "At the community center."

A visual of Chase, in swim trunks, buff body on display, bouncing around in front of a pool full of little old ladies has a laugh exploding from me before I can stop it. He pulls back and smirks at me like he was expecting it. "Sorry, but I've been to the rec center and it's all seniors all the time. And aquafit? Like water aerobics?"

"It's great for seniors and like you said, that's who goes there," he replies as his hands begin moving again, sliding over my bare ass to my hips. "I waive my teaching fee so anyone can come, regardless of income."

"That's unbelievably generous of you. I've never fucked an aquafit instructor before, much less a generous one," I whisper and then before he can answer, I push him back on the bed.

I crawl over him. When my hands are planted just above his shoulders, I dip down and capture his mouth in a kiss. It's all tongues and teeth and grows even more wild when I drop my hips onto his and our erections press together. Chase's hands reach up and tangle in my hair. I can't stop rolling my hips because the friction is so fucking good. But then he tugs on my hair, pulling our mouths apart just enough to speak. "I…. I umm… can't sleep with you."

Everything in my body kind of freezes. There is no way I misinterpreted him. He wants me. I want him. I'm confused and so I just blink a lot, but I nod. Because I'm not an asshole. If he's changing his mind, I'll respect it. I start to lift myself off him, but he isn't letting go of my head. His hands are still buried in my hair. His eyes look dark and conflicted. "I just don't… I don't have condoms in the house."

"Oh." I relax a little. "I thought you were changing your mind about me."

He pushes his hips up, his cock still as hard as stone pokes my belly. "My mind and my dick are one hundred and ten percent Team Bowen. No take-backs."

"So… we get creative." I smile and slowly he begins to smile back. "I like creative."

I kiss him again and for a long, luxurious time we just make-out and grind together. It's making me feel like a wide-eyed, heart-open teenager again and it's wildly addictive. Finally I can't handle it anymore and I move off his body, lying next to him on the huge and incredibly comfortable bed. Chase runs a hand over my shoulder and down my arm. "I want to suck you off again."

"I am not turning that down," I reply but stop him when he tries to slide down the bed to my aching cock. "But first, I want to do something to you…"

"Okay." He doesn't look like it's okay. He suddenly looks very cautious. It hits me, like a freight train, that this guy is closeted, which may mean he's also very inexperienced. His blow job skills say otherwise but then again that might be the extent of his explorations. I really want to be the one to change that and I hope that doesn't make me an asshole. It's not just that he's gorgeous and charming and I'm lonelier than I realized. It's because I really actually like him, at least what I know of him.

"You have any lube?"

He nods. "Night table."

I roll onto my belly and reach across the space he vacated on the bed. I open the sleek wood drawer and there's the lube and also a couple toys, including a vibrating prostate massager. Chase isn't as inexperienced as I thought and my dick gets harder thinking about him using it. And then it gets impossibly hard thinking about me using it *on* him. But judging by the look that passed over his face earlier, that's not going to happen tonight. So I only grab the lube.

I pull myself to a sitting position, my back against his massive headboard, and wiggle my finger at him. "Come here. You're too far away."

He gets closer, but that look of concern is inching its way back onto his face. I cup the side of his face and pull him in for another kiss, but I keep it light. "Lie down and let me enjoy you. And if you don't enjoy it like I know I will be just say it. No harm, no foul."

He presses his mouth to mine. I kiss him back, trying to make him more promises with my mouth. He starts to relax, and slowly but surely he ends up on his back and, when I'm sure the hesitation is gone from his face I lower my mouth to his cock. Chase's dick is slightly longer than mine but a little less thick. He's cut, so I take just that perfect mushroom tip into my mouth, his pre-cum coating my tongue as it swirls over him. He lets out a small moan. "Don't stop."

"Touch yourself," I tell him, my voice so deep I almost don't recognize it. I flip open the top on the lube as I watch him fist his cock and give it a slow tug. He reaches up with his other hand and tucks it under his head, his eyes watching my every move but with curiosity now, not concern. I hold my own cock and squeeze some lube onto it.

"You're going to… get yourself off?" he questions. His hand is doing just that as he talks and, fuck it's creating a fire in my belly. I pay careful attention to his rhythm and pressure so I can mimic it with my mouth in a minute.

"Yeah," I smile. "Or you can do it while I do it to you."

His eyebrows raise but his lips do too. "I like that idea."

He sits up and reaches for me but instead of letting him pull me down to lie on the bed, I sit beside him and pull on him to come over to me. "Straddle my legs."

He hesitates but does it. "Closer." I squirt some more lube into my palm and then wrap my hand around his cock. His eyelids flutter and he inches even closer to me so our cocks are almost touching. "Grab me."

He does. I squeeze him and start to move my fist around him. His head tips back and he gives my cock a few tugs as well. But I'm losing him to the sensations I'm creating and I'm okay with that. I hope it only gets worse, actually. I take my free hand and with two fingers, I swipe up some of the lube on my own cock. Then, I move my hand to his ass cheeks. He doesn't notice or he doesn't mind. I'm pumping him in a nice, strong rhythm now and he's making noises in his throat with every tug that is so fucking hot. My fingers slip between his cheeks. "What… are you…"

"Pretend I'm that toy I saw in your drawer," I whisper, and my fingers breach his entrance.

"Bowen."

"Just say stop if you want me to stop," I remind him, and he bends at the waist. The motion almost moves his erection out of my reach, but it also pushes my fingers deeper into his hole. Just two, but for him I have a feeling it's the first two that don't belong to him. I lean forward so that I can work his cock better and our foreheads touch. "Say it."

"Don't stop," he pants. "I don't want you to stop."

I move my fingers in and almost out in sync with my hand on his cock. He's groaning and panting and then he says my name. It's this guttural needy sound and it makes my own cock jerk and throb. His hands hold my face and he kisses me, sort of, he's so far gone it's just really lips crushing lips, but damn if it isn't hot as hell. He somehow finds my dick again and starts rubbing me. It's frantic and uneven but I'm already so turned on, it's enough. I curl my fingers just a little inside him and he moans into my mouth and comes. I follow, my release mixing with his on my chest and belly.

He drops his head to my shoulder as my own tips back against his headboard and I let myself absorb this perfect moment. Everything with this guy is pretty fucking great, and as my orgasm high wanes, I realize what a problem that is. We can't be anything. Even tonight was a stolen moment. "You okay?"

He nods. "I am more than okay. *That* was so much more than okay."

I smile. "I agree. But you broke your own rules tonight. I let you, but they aren't my rules, so I don't have regrets."

"I don't either," Chase replies and lifts his head, kissing the side of my neck as he pulls away. He stands up and walks into the bathroom. I watch him go and then look for something to clean up with. I'm covered in our mess.

I hear the shower come on, and Chase's naked body and just been fucked hair, which looks as good as his perfectly styled hair, steps into the open door. "My shower is big enough for two. Never had two in it, but tonight is about trying new things, apparently."

I was right. He hadn't had ass play with a partner before. I get off the bed and join him in the shower, which of course ends up with us fooling around a little bit more. Just some kissing and fondling. I make sure to keep it PG, and I can tell he's doing the same. But my memory is storing everything about this moment, the warm water sliding over his taut body, the desire in his light blue eyes, the sleek luxurious feel of gray slate shower floor under my feet. Because this moment is going in the spank bank for future use. I have a feeling I'm going to be jerking off to thoughts of Chase for a very long time.

We're drying off when my phone starts going off. First, I can hear it ringing. Then it's alerting me to a video call. Then there're a bunch of pings which must be an influx of texts. With each sound my anxiety climbs to a new level. "Shit." I wrap the towel around my waist and rush out of his bathroom.

I follow our trail of clothes until I find my pants at the top of the stairs and dig into the back pocket to get to my phone. Chase wanders out of the bathroom and stands at the foot of the bed, watching me as he rubs the towel over his wet hair. "You have heard of voicemail, right?"

"Yeah, I don't do that," I mutter and open up my phone. It's Autumn. *All* of it is Autumn. I scroll through the texts and each breath I take gets deeper and deeper as I read. Because she's okay. It isn't a life or death situation, so the anxiety vise that had started to compress my chest releases. "It's my sister. My brother did a TV interview today. She says it wasn't great."

That's an understatement. Autumn used words like disaster. Nightmare. And political suicide. Her last text is simply a link. I click it as Chase comes to stand beside me. It's my brother Woody, wearing a blazer and a button-down shirt that definitely needs an iron. He's got on a stupid bow tie too. I don't know why he thinks those are a good idea. The reporter is off-camera. She holds her mic out. "So you think that people need marijuana in Vermont?"

"I think it's a viable industry," Woody replies. "We need to tr-treat it as su-such."

Shit. He stops to clear his throat. That's what he does to regroup, mentally, when his stutter gets away from him. It's a nervous response. He smiles. It's a tense smile if you know him, but if you don't, it might appear annoyed or fake. Or both. The reporter asks another question. "So, this election is about creating grow-ops for you."

"Supporting a new, growing farming industry," Woody replies and I sigh in relief he didn't stutter over that. I'm about to ponder why Autumn thinks this is so bad when it happens.

The reporter asks, "Do you smoke drugs, Mr. Whitlock?"

"What?"

"Do you smoke drugs?"

"Marijuana is a medical aid for everything from cancer to insomnia to anxiety," Woody shoots back. I hear Chase groan behind me.

"So do you have a medical condition that you think requires drugs?"

"I… we…. It's... I don't think it has to just be for medical reasons but—"

"So, you smoke it for fun?"

"I didn't say I smoke or take anything," Woody looks like his bow tie is suddenly way too tight.

"You haven't said you don't."

"I don't."

"Would you take a drug test then?"

"Okay, thank you for your questions." Finally that bumbling idiot we're paying to run his campaign steps in. "We have to go."

The clip ends. I'm stupid enough to scroll through the comments, briefly. Chase is reading them along with me. It's all a varying degree of negative. From 'Why is this dude so shifty' to 'I'm not voting for a drug dealer'.

"Why didn't he just say yes? He uses marijuana. It's legal," I question, not expecting Chase to have an answer but he does.

"It's an un-winnable question," Chase explains. "If he admits to using, the rightwing voters will consider him a junkie, even though it's not the same thing and it's legal. For them it will never be acceptable. And the centrist ones will think he's been doing it since before it was legal, which makes him untrustworthy. The lefties will support an honest answer, but a lot of them are youthful and cynical and doubt the electoral system so much at this point, they don't vote.

"Oh." I feel like a fool with how little I know. And I feel panic because we gambled our parents' legacy on this and we are so out of our element. Chase squeezes my shoulder before he walks to his closet.

"This alone won't sink him, but damage control will be required," Chase explains. "He's going to need a follow-up statement on his website. Something that says he's not against being drug tested for illegal substances because he doesn't consume illegal substances. He doesn't, right?"

"No. He doesn't," I reply and start to pull on my clothes, the pieces within reach anyway, like my underwear and my jeans.

Chase smiles. It's so reassuring and confident. "So put up the statement and then link something much more detailed on the pros of marijuana farming, and make sure there's numbers in it. Fiscal numbers. Righties need the numbers. And make sure there's environmental and sustainability statistics. Lefties need those details."

"We have that on the site already. It's really good. I think."

"I'll read it over tomorrow, and tell you my thoughts. If you want."

"I want," I reply and give him a timid smile. He is so sure of himself, and I feel like a bit of a kid around him. More than I should considering he's only maybe two or three years older than me. But listening to him talk right now, it feels like he's ten years older and so much more intelligent than me. I'm not dumb, but... I feel it right now.

"Great. I'll text you with my thoughts. But get that statement up first thing, okay?" I nod as Chase emerges from his walk-in closet in a pair of black pajama bottoms and a vintage Nirvana T-shirt that's so worn it's almost see-through. His damn hair is every which way and I wish I could stick around to see it dry, but...

"I'm going to head home and make sure this gets done. And also calm Autumn down who will be calling me again any second, still freaking out," I explain and start down the stairs. He follows me. "I had a really good time, in case that wasn't clear."

"So did I," Chase admits and when we reach the ground floor, I pick up my shirt which is in a puddle by the door. "You're going to make it hard not to try for a three-peat."

When my head emerges from my shirt, I find him directly in front of me, looking gorgeous and available. But he isn't. "As much as I love that idea — and I really do love it — you and I aren't on the same page," I remind him. "And another round will make it really hard for me to convince myself you're a random hook-up."

"Yeah. I can see that."

"And I don't date guys who aren't out."

His eyes drop from mine and his mouth flattens into a line. I feel comforted by that because it means he likes me. *Really* likes me. And maybe he was considering dating me. Which is flattering. I have little to offer someone as put together and successful as Chase. Especially since everything I own may be gone if my brother's campaign doesn't change course soon.

"Well, I don't date anyone," Chase says, and his voice is uncharacteristically solemn. He reaches between us and brushes my hair back from my cheek. "I should add that if I could date someone, I'd definitely be trying to date you."

"And if you were out, I'd be more than willing to swipe right," I say and my joke gets me a smile, but it's hollow.

And then I kiss him. And he kisses me back.

It's sweeter and softer than any kiss we've shared.

Probably because it's a good-bye kiss.

9

CHASE

The day is dragging. I hate long, boring weekends, and I haven't had one since I was… well, I can't remember the last time I was so bored I was annoyed. I don't have a lot of downtime, so I usually find really enjoyable ways to fill it. I mess around with new music, I go out with Grant and Joe, I work on new lyrics. I listen to music, read, marathon something on Netflix and work out. But today… nothing brings me relief from my mood. I close my notebook and toss it onto the coffee table, moving my guitar from my lap and standing up. I walk over to the windows and stare outside. It's a great spring day. Sunny and warm. People are everywhere outside, smiling and enjoying life. Why can't I? Even at brunch this morning with Joe and Grant at the Maple Factory, after teaching an aquafit class that went really well, I couldn't enjoy myself. I kept wondering if Bowen had worked last night. If he was working today. If one of the many gay customers at Vino and Veritas had hit on him yet. If they had, was he interested?

Fuck. When did I become this guy? I have never thought twice about a hook-up. But Bowen is in my head all the time. Maybe it's because we haven't seen each other since that last mind-blowing session. Grant and Joe have been too busy for a band practice, so we skipped this week. I did text him once, to tell him the statement he put up on Woody's campaign website worked, but to add a few more fiscal numbers to the marijuana farming section. He texted back with a thank you and told me he owed me a glass of wine next time I was in the bar. But I haven't gone to the bar this week. Seeing him is all I want but also feels overwhelmingly like a bad idea. I mean, I know me. I'm nothing if not self-aware and one drink will lead to a bottle and that will give me just the excuse I need to proposition him again. And he doesn't want me. Not right now. I can't give him what he wants.

And I hate me for that.

I walk through the kitchen, grabbing my keys off the island where I tossed them when I came home from breakfast with the guys, and punch the elevator button harder than required. Once I'm outside, I throw on my shades and start to walk. I have absolutely no destination in mind. I just need to do something other than everything I have been doing. Because none of that is making me feel better. I find myself at the lake. The farmer's market is just about to close up, but I grab some apples from Adler's Apples and some goat cheese from the booth next to them and then some veggies from a booth down the way. I decide to grab some flowers at the last minute too. Sometimes I like to give some to Betty to brighten her day and her desk. After all, it's the first thing people see when they come to my business.

But today, I take too long deciding between pink or purple tulips and I hear my name from a familiar voice. "Hey, cousin!"

I turn and there's my cousin Amy. She's pushing a stroller with her daughter in it. Next to her is another familiar face, Lacey Baldwin. "I was just telling Amy here how much fun your show was the other week."

"Thanks!" I lean in and give them each a hug and a friendly kiss on the cheek. It's more of an air kiss. It's such a Waspy thing to do, but my family wouldn't have any culture if it didn't have Wasp.

"And I was just telling her not to bring that up to your father the next time she sees him," Amy smiles, but it doesn't reach her eyes. It's not that she doesn't like me. She wouldn't warn Lacey to avoid the topic of my music with my dad if she hated me. She'd want to shake that hornet's nest. She does like me, as much as she likes anyone in her family, which is hardly at all. I get it. I wish I didn't, but I do. "But then again, with the future mayor on your side maybe you'll get so many gigs you won't even need your inheritance. Then you can become a Godless, morally bankrupt musician full-time."

I laugh, because she's quoting my grandfather directly. He said that once. About the Backstreet Boys when Amy asked for tickets to their show for her sixteenth birthday. "You have to want more in life than to waste your birthday watching Godless, morally bankrupt musicians gyrate their pelvises."

That's when my brother had pointed out that Backstreet Boys aren't musicians. They don't play instruments and the tirade got worse. Amy never did get tickets to the show. I bend down to ruffle the downy hair of my second cousin, Lily Edwina Briggs. She giggles. "I have no intention of forfeiting my inheritance."

"Then always use condoms," Amy mutters under her breath. Our eyes meet and she swiftly changes the subject. "Lacey here has a problem she was telling me about. One that I think you can actually fix."

Trepidation makes my heart quicken a little. I hope this isn't election advice or marketing help because I already gave that to Lacey's opponent and I, quite frankly, don't want to work against Bowen's brother. Lacey looks uncomfortable, her hazel eyes darting around, unable to look at me. "It's not a big thing. But you would fit the bill. I mean, of course it would be a friend date. I just…. It's hard to get them to take me seriously as a young candidate and then you add in being a woman… and then single. Well, single puts me over the edge into unvote-able territory, according to my father and his advisors."

"Burlington is full of free love and liberal hippies and you think they care whether you're single or not?" I ask, confused, still not sure what we're talking about, exactly.

"My dad keeps reminding me my slim lead wouldn't be so slim if I was male and not single," Lacey confesses. "I won't fix the first problem, but I can pretend I've taken care of the second."

"Luckily that farmer dude gave you some breathing room, with his pro-drug agenda," Amy pipes in, clearly referring to Woody Whitlock.

"He talked his way out of it on his website," Lacey replies and frowns. "He must have gotten some better advisors. And now his face is everywhere because he finally got posters. Anyway, my lead against him is narrowing."

"But you can take her to the cocktail party, right Chase?" Amy asks. "I mean you're not involved with someone are you? I haven't a clue to be honest, but you've never brought a girl to a family function. Not since college and that was only once."

Amy's eyes narrow on me with speculation. Lacey just looks curious. I wish I hadn't stopped for flowers. "I'm single. But I'm not a great actor so pretending to be your boyfriend might not work out."

"You don't have to say you're a boyfriend. Just be my date. Once. For this stupid cocktail party the soon-to-be former mayor is holding for the candidates and the press," Lacey explains. "Look, some pictures in the newspaper with a handsome, successful man from a well-respected political family could go a long way."

"You could always ask Colin," I suggest. "He would drive down. And he needs a well-respected political ally like you and your family too. He's running for office next year."

Both women frown in unison. I have to laugh. "Your brother is a douchebag and you know it," Lacey says flatly.

"It's fine. Don't worry about it." Amy waves her paper coffee cup in the air between us. "I'm sure Hayden has some friends who are suitable. I mean if Chase here doesn't want to earn extra brownie points with his dad, the gate keeper of his pending inheritance, then we'll find someone else."

"I'll do it," I say without another thought, because Amy is right. My dad is good friends with Lacey's dad and he will love that I'm helping her out. It may even make him believe I'm entertaining political thoughts of my own. And more than anything, it will help him forget that I'm not as straight as he would like. "Text me the details."

Lacey hugs me and grins. "You are the best, Chase Ashton. I owe you."

"It's fine."

Amy also smiles, like she's Cupid and her arrow just hit a bullseye, which is not at all a look I want to see from her right now. Thankfully the flower vendor interrupts us. "Sir, are you still interested in flowers? I'm closing up."

"Text me Lacey," I repeat and give them both a wave. "Have a great day ladies."

I give Lily's hair another ruffle and she rewards me with another giggle. Then they go one way, and I buy my flowers and go the other way. I try not to overthink the whole thing with Lacey. I mean, after all, she's known me for years and she's never shown any romantic interest. I've never thought of her in that way either, even though she's very attractive and not exactly too old for me. She's closer in age to me than Bowen is.

And now I'm thinking about Bowen again. Shit. In an effort to squash those thoughts, I find myself walking down Church Street window shopping. Vino and Veritas isn't open yet, so I don't have to worry about being unable to control my urges to go into the place and look for him. But the bookstore is open — the veritas side of Vino & Veritas — and I find myself going in. I need a new notebook for song-writing. Well, need is a bit of an overstatement. I am unable to resist a good notebook though, and this bookstore carries some of the nicest, so I go in and decide to browse and possibly treat myself.

There's a guy behind the cash register who smiles at me as I enter. "Hi. I'm Briar. If you need anything or have any questions let me know."

"Thanks." I nod and even though I know where the journals and notebooks are kept, I wander down the aisles first. They have a great selection of books. I spend half an hour just plucking titles off the shelves. Everything from fiction to self-help to biographies. I'm reading the back cover of an unofficial biography of Joni Mitchell when I hear a woman's voice.

"Briar, have you read this one yet?" she says to the guy who greeted me when I walked in. "About a guy who has a crush on his best friend when they're teens. They drift apart but end up working together at a hockey camp when they're older. I started it last night and couldn't put it down. Finished it at three in the morning. Worth every sleepless second. So hot. Highly recommend."

My eyes slide over to the counter where the woman — a straw-berry haired college student — is holding up a book. Briar smiles. "Have I read it? Autumn, you have got to be kidding. I've read it like ten times. It's one of my all-time favorites."

Autumn.

Bowen's sister is named Autumn. How many Autumns can there be in Burlington? She turns and strides by me calling back to Briar, "I should have known I couldn't discover a great romance novel before you."

Now that I see her face, I have no doubt that even if there were five hundred girls named Autumn in Burlington, this particular

Autumn is Bowen's sister. Her hair isn't the same color as his, but her eyes are. And her nose is the exact same as his, only more petite and feminine. She smiles at me as she passes by. "Can I see that? Your description got me."

She stops and her smile broadens and her eyes light up. "Sure. On a scale of one to five I'd give it ten stars."

She hands me the book and I notice the hemp bracelets on her arms. Yep. She's a Whitlock. And at the very same moment she blinks and seems to recognize me. "Are you the singer from that band…. What was the name? Crap… I forgot. But you played at Vino and my brother helped you out when your drummer bailed."

"Imposter Syndrome," I say and she nods. "Yeah. Your brother is Bowen?"

I wasn't lying when I told Lacey and Amy I have zero acting skills. I don't. But Autumn doesn't catch on that I already figured out who she is. She just nods and her smile turns proud. "Yeah. Mr. Killer Drummer, Horrendous Bar Back is my flesh and blood. You're really good by the way."

"Thanks." I stare at the book she handed me for a second.

"Are you into romance novels?" Autumn asks. "Because Briar has a book club if you are. It's super fun and the novels are always good. Always. He's great at picking them."

I glance up at Briar and back at Autumn. Do they think I'm gay? Oh shit. Are they asking me to join a gay book club? Am I outing myself? The concern and panic in my eyes must be evident because Autumn starts to backtrack. "It's open to anyone. And the books aren't LGBTQ only."

"No. I mean sure. That's cool." Oh my God I couldn't be making a worse impression if I tried. "Anyway, I'm actually here looking for journals. Notebooks. For writing."

Autumn nods, taking my bumbling idiocy in stride. "Over here."

I walk with her to the wall by the check-out area where all blank notebooks and journals are. They've gotten some new ones since the last time I was here. And my eyes immediately land on a brown leather one with an A embossed on it. I flip through until I get to C and pluck it out, but I keep looking at the other ones. "So Bowen is going to keep playing with you, he said."

"Yeah. Which is great. He's amazing," I say and hope that sounds casual. "He picks up songs really easily."

"He and my dad used to jam all the time," Autumn tells me, her smile turning slightly wistful. "He stopped playing entirely, all instruments, when our parents died and he had to drop out of college, which is a shame. He was doing really well in the music program. He wanted to be a teacher. I am thrilled he's back at it, now, even just for fun. Gives me hope that one day he'll want to finish his degree after all."

I had no idea Bowen hadn't played since his parents died. Wow. And although I knew he'd been in college when the tragedy struck, I didn't know it was in the music program I have been coveting and hope to enroll in as soon as my inheritance comes in. I'm just staring at her kind of blankly, so she shakes her head and her cheeks turn pink. "I'm so sorry. That was a personal info dump and completely inappropriate."

"Please don't apologize." I smile at her. "I'm your brother's friend so consider me your friend too. I'm just a new friend so I didn't know he hadn't played in years. He was so brilliant at the gig, and at practice, and you'd never know he'd been on hiatus."

"That's because he's a natural." Autumn's beaming again. And then she tilts her head. "So, if we're going to be new friends, I need a name."

I laugh. "Right, I'm—"

"Chase?"

His voice floats across the room and seems to wrap itself around me like a hug. I turn to the door with Autumn and Briar. Bowen is standing there, in sweats and a tank top, his feet are in flip flops. His golden hair is unbrushed. He looks like he just woke up and it's sexy as fuck. "Hey."

"Hey," he repeats. "What are you doing here?"

"Buying stuff. What are you doing here?"

"My sister," he points to Autumn, "forgot her lunch."

He holds up a nylon lunch bag. I stare at it and then back up to his gorgeous face. Autumn walks over to him. Well, actually, she kind of bounces over. She's a very bubbly person and it comes out in her gait as well. "Thanks big bro. I was gonna have to go hungry if you didn't come through. No cash for extra meals these days with Woody's campaign sucking our bank account dry."

Bowen hands her the bag. His eyes are still on me but they slide from my face to the books in my hand. "You buying those?"

I look at the gay romance novel and the journal. "Yeah. I mean, the journal. Maybe the book."

Bowen walks over and takes it from me. I am acutely aware of two things — how my body reacts to his proximity and how his sister and Briar are watching us like we're animals on display at the zoo. The vibes we're giving off must be as awkward as they feel. He takes the novel from my hand and skims the back cover blurb. He grins that easy, laid-back smile that I find so damn appealing. "You aren't exactly the demographic for this."

"I guess not."

Ouch. Why does that hurt so much? Because he's forcing me to lie in front of them, to his beautiful face. He hands the novel back to his sister and then he looks at the journal. "Nice notebook though. For songs?"

I nod. He smiles again. "You should write something original for the wedding we're doing. That would be cool."

"Maybe," I shrug. I am so not ready for debuting my originals, but I'm flattered he would even suggest it.

"I'm heading back home. I still have half a field to prep. We're seeding in a couple weeks," he explains and turns away from me without hesitation, without a thought.

"Sorry I had to pull you away," Autumn tells him and bounces up to kiss her brother's cheek. "You're the bestest of the best for coming though."

"I know." Bowen smiles at her. He throws up his hand in a casual wave. "Later everyone. See you at practice tomorrow, Chase."

"Yeah. Cool."

But I feel anything but cool as I pay for my notebook and shove it in my bag with the produce from the farmer's market. I feel worse than I did earlier today. Because Bowen Whitlock is totally fine with just being my buddy. And that should fill me with relief and ease the anxiety I always get after a hook-up. But it doesn't. It hurts.

BOWEN

"Woody stop fussing," Autumn commands.

Woody sighs.

"And take off that stupid bow tie or I'm not going."

Woody looks at me with horror. "You're kidding right? Autumn, tell me he's kidding."

"He's kidding," Autumn replies, and now she's moved on from fixing the lapels of his suit jacket to trying to tame his shaggy blond hair.

"I'm not kidding," I argue, like an obstinate child. "He looks like a creepy weirdo with those bow ties."

Woody looks wounded, but then defiant as he adjusts his bow tie, only managing to make it more crooked. "It's my signature. Something for people to remember me by."

I roll my eyes but then Autumn glances over her shoulder and glares at me, so I make sure not to say anything else. I mean it when I say I think the bow ties are a bad idea, but Woody's ego has been kicked around a lot this week so I relent. Also, Autumn is not above punching me if I don't, so better to just back off.

"Why do you have a bee up your butt lately anyway?" Woody asks as Autumn finally stops fussing over him and we make it out of his bedroom. "Are you still struggling at your job?"

"Tanner told Harrison he's improving," Autumn tells Woody like

I'm not even here. "This week he managed to only drop one thing. It was a customer's dinner order. But at least it was before he left the kitchen and not in front of, or on, the actual customer."

"Thanks for looking at the bright side Autumn," I grumble. The fact is she's right, but the withering stare Joss gave me was almost worse than the customer's would have been. I hate disappointing him as much as I hate disappointing Tanner and Harrison. Joss, like everyone else at the bar, is great.

"Well, then he's improving. That's good," Woody smiles. "And the job has served us well. Mortgage payments are being handled just fine, and we even got free public relations help out of it from your friend."

"Chase isn't my friend," I blurt out and I don't know why. He is. I mean, we said that's what we would be, so I back track. "I mean he's a new friend. Bandmate is probably a better term right now."

One by one we descend the stairs. They creak and moan under our feet because they're old. This house was built in the late eighteen hundreds and our parents loved the noises it made, from the rattling eaves to the clack of the rain on the tin roof, to the creak of the wood floors and stairs. When we were teens, Dad used to joke it made it easier to hear us if we were sneaking in or out at night. And when we were all getting ready for an event, like a family dinner out or a vacation, Mom would call up the stairs to get a move on and we'd come lumbering down, like we are right now, and Dad would happily announce, "Here comes our herd, Cassie!"

Sometimes, like right now when we're rushing to something together, and we're on the stairs at the same time, it feels like I can almost hear him. It's always a jolt when we get to the bottom of the stairs and the house is empty. That feeling tonight does nothing to curb my already bad mood.

"Mildly homophobic bandmate," Autumn mutters.

"Chase? Hell, no. He's not homophobic," I reply sharply, my eyes wide. "Where the hell are you getting that from?"

"He was all weird about the gay romance book," Autumn explains as we grab our personal items off the table in the front hall. The table that still holds my dad's wallet and my mom's front door keys on her keychain that has little bells on it. We haven't moved them since the day we got them back from the hospital with their other personal effects. "He seemed all freaked out."

"Not because it was a gay book," I argue back. "We met him because he was performing at a gay bar, remember? And he's got me in his band. I'm out and he hasn't exactly minded."

Woody lifts an eyebrow at that, but my ever-protective, advocate of a little sister doesn't notice. "If you say so. I think something is off with him. Which is too bad, because he's hot. Like, smokin' hot."

"Can we just get going?" I bark a little too aggressively which raises Woody's other eyebrow. "We're going to be late."

Without another word, we lock up the farmhouse and pile into the car. Autumn gets behind the wheel while I climb into the passenger seat and Woody gets in the back. I clutch the door and grit my teeth to keep from lecturing her about her driving skills, or lack thereof, while Woody complains about the fact that we don't have an electric car yet. Even though he knows we can't afford one right now.

When we finally get to city hall, the parking lot is almost full. Autumn wedges the car into the last spot, with one hubcap grinding the curb as she does it. My tongue almost bleeds as I bite it to keep from bitching.

"I thought this was just the candidates and families," Autumn says, suddenly fussing with her floral dress as we walk towards the entrance.

"I thought so too," Woody replies but then we all notice the local television van and Autumn groans.

"I would have worn a nicer outfit if I thought there would be television people here," she complains. "Something dark and slimming."

"You look beautiful," I promise her and grab her hand before she can raise it to her hair, which is in loose waves.

"TV adds ten pounds," she whispers, and I pull her into my side.

"Who cares?" I reply. "You don't. You're my bad-ass, kick-ass, strong, body positive sister."

She looks up and gives me a smile, but it's not as confident as I wish it was. Autumn got teased a lot in middle school because of her weight. It took a lot of pep talks from our parents to keep her off the stupid diet trends that floated around in high school. And then Woody and I made a point of having her back after they died. She has grown into a really confident, happy woman and I refuse to let that slip away from her.

"He's right," Woody adds as we reach the door. "You look great, Autumn. And besides, I've already told them my family is off-limits. They can't interview you or bother you. They'll respect it because of the shit show they put us through with Mom and Dad."

That shit show was every news outlet and print publication in town trying to turn their deaths into fodder for the locals. Because they were beloved members of the community, because they left behind young-ish kids, because Woody and I had to get legal guardianship of Autumn, who was still a minor, because the road they had their accident on had been a problem for years and still no one had fixed the bend that was too tight, especially when it was icy, and lacked a guard rail. Sure, we wanted farming zoning changed but we also wanted to make sure things like that dangerous road that played a part in our parents' death didn't get ignored in the future.

"Okay. Good." Autumn sighs and reaches for the door handle to enter but pauses. "For the record, I would do interviews in florescent horizontal stripes if it gets you elected. All day, every day."

"And you'd still look great," I add as she opens the door, and we all step inside.

A security guard greets us, checks our identification, and leads us down the hall to the cocktail party, which is happening in a large conference room on the second floor. It's a lovely room, with ornate wood paneling and an impressive chandelier in the center. The wide, tall windows that line the exterior wall looks out over City Hall Park. I can barely see the view though, because the room is packed with people.

This is so not the intimate affair that Woody thought it was. That the current mayor pretended it would be. Ugh. I am not in the mood to be around this many people. "I need a drink," Autumn mutters.

"Me too," I agree and turn to Woody. "You go shake hands and kiss babies or whatever. We'll go get refreshments and blend into the background."

He nods, but I can tell he's disappointed and a stab of guilt pricks my heart. Woody is only doing this for the good of the farm and the city Mom and Dad raised us to love so much. I know he needs our support and I want to give it to him, I just… I've been a bitch since running into Chase at the bookstore. It felt so uncomfortable. And so did the band practice after that. I mean, the music went well, the other guys were in great moods and joking around. I smiled. I even laughed but… it felt off. And Chase was a little too quiet. So much so that Joe brought it up. But he just blew it off as having had a long day at work. We all stayed for beers afterward, but I barely finished mine before I made an excuse about needing to get back to the farm and left. Chase was holding the elevator open before I even got my jean jacket on.

And I haven't seen him since. He hasn't stopped by the bar, or emailed about anything, not even to see if the copy he helped us write for the website is working. I know we both said being friends would be easy, so why isn't it? I mean, hell, I've had hook-ups before that didn't amount to anything more and I'd been able to comfortably be around the guy afterward. I don't hold it against Chase that he's closeted, like I did to Trevor. Because Chase was honest about it from the get-go and has never asked me to be in the closet with him. So why do I feel like I'm holding a grudge? Why can't I act normal?

There're two bars set up in opposite corners of the room. Autumn and I both make our way to the one with the shortest line. I try to order three beers but Autumn talks over me and orders us three white wines instead. "It's classier. We need to look classy," she tells me. "Everyone here is classy. And beer makes Woody belch."

Oh. Right. Yeah, Woody loves to burp, loudly, with a beer. At least he does at home. I doubt he'd do it here, but she's right, we shouldn't take the chance. The bartender gives us three glasses of wine and Autumn leans in and whispers, "I didn't get red so if you spill it on yourself, or someone else, it won't be that obvious."

"Thanks." I frown at her, but she just smiles.

"I'll take Woody his glass," she volunteers. "Don't want to risk you dropping it, butter fingers."

"Whatever." I sigh and move my way through the crowd in the opposite direction. I feel more at ease sticking to the perimeter, so I wander toward the windows. Outside, the town looks peaceful and quiet. There's one couple in the darkened park with their French bulldog and that's it.

And then I hear his laugh. It's a sound that, in a short time, has imprinted itself in my brain. I'd recognize it anywhere. My eyes drift across the room and I see Chase standing by the other bar. He's talking to a tall, skinny guy in a suit that looks as expensive as his own. He is smiling, but I know Chase's smile — his genuine one — and this is not it. He's being polite. I watch him as he keeps talking to this dude and I realize how good he is at faking amusement and interest. I can't imagine having to fake so much of my life. Shit, why does he do it? I'm exhausted just watching him.

He leans in as a woman walks over and gives him a friendly kiss on the cheek. She's clearly the wife or date of the guy he's talking to, as she slips an arm through his after greeting Chase. Chase is telling them something and they're nodding. He moves his hands as he speaks, with his head up high and his shoulders back. He looks so poised and so at ease. He belongs here and he knows it. The woman starts laughing and motioning about something with her free hand and Chase smiles again, but his eyes lift a little, over her shoulder, and lock with mine.

That's when that smile suddenly reaches his eyes, but only for a second. And then it falls off his face completely. He blinks and looks anywhere but at me, his head moving right, then left. I feel like I'm a party crasher instead of an invited guest and he's looking for a security guard to escort me out. Well, you know what? Fuck him. Just like in the bookstore, I want to challenge him and his perfect demeanor. I start toward him, weaving my way through the crowd. His brilliant blue eyes widen just the slightest and the man, who is talking now, leans closer to Chase. I see Chase mouth the word *what* because he's no longer paying attention to the people he's with.

And then, as I'm within a few feet and can hear their conversation, someone else joins them. Lacey Baldwin. She links her arm through Chase's and tips her head up to him with a broad smile. "There you are! I've been looking for you."

"Well, you were busying dazzling everyone with your brilliant ideas for this fine city," Chase replies with a wink. "I didn't want to get in the way of that."

Holy shit. He's here with Lacey Baldwin. Like, *with* Lacey Baldwin. I abruptly turn around and smack straight into someone's back, my wine sloshing over the side of the glass and onto their corduroy jacket. Not just anyone's jacket, but Woody's. Fuck.

"Oops!" I say because I don't know what else to say.

Woody looks over his shoulder and smiles, but really, he's kind of glaring with his eyes. He's standing with the current mayor and his wife. They smile at me but look a little confused. Or maybe sympathetic. "Little brother, you have to watch where you're going."

"I know. Let me grab some napkins for you," I say. I turn and head toward the bar before anyone can stop me. I'm not in the right head space to make political small talk anyway.

I ask the bartender for some cocktail napkins and Autumn joins me. "Did you just pull a Vino and Veritas at an important political event? My God Bowen, what is going on with you?"

"I'm sorry," I mumble as the bartender hands me a small stack of napkins.

"Bowen, can I talk to you a second." Chase is suddenly standing behind Autumn, alone. She tips her head back to look up at him. He smiles at her. "Autumn, right? You look gorgeous tonight, Autumn. The green in that dress is your color."

"Thank you," she says but it's guarded. Her eyes start ping ponging between us.

I hand my sister the napkins. "Can you give these to Woody for me, please? I need to use the restroom."

I put my half empty wine glass down on the bar, pivot, and storm my way out of the room, luckily without smashing into anyone else. The restroom is down a long marble hallway far away from the party. I make it all the way there and am about to push open the door when I feel a hand grip my arm just above the elbow. He pulls me in the opposite direction, without a word, and I'm too shocked to stop him. Okay, well I guess I could stop him but the part of me that doesn't want to — the part that has longed for his touch and attention since the last time I had it — that part wins and I let him drag me into an office across the hall from the restroom. The name plate says Lacey Baldwin, Director Parks & Recreation.

That's when my feet stop moving. "I can't be in here! Do you know how bad it will look if I'm in Woody's opponent's office?"

"Shush," Chase commands, unbothered as he pulls me past her

desk to a small door at the back, which opens into a tiny private bathroom. He shoves me in and enters behind me closing the door.

"What the fuck are you doing?"

"I want to tell you something."

"What?" I demand and then his hands are in my hair, his lips are on mine, and his tongue is in my mouth. Everything about this kiss is hard, demanding, and fucking glorious. But I can't. I won't.

I reach up, put my palms on his shoulders, and push him away. "Chase, fuck. Stop!"

He looks embarrassed. "I'm sorry. I just... I... you look so hot. I've been thinking of you non-stop and you look so fucking hot. I'm sorry."

"You're here as Lacey Baldwin's date?"

"I am."

"Then I can't talk to you, let alone kiss you." I push him, trying to get by him so I can get the hell out of here. I'm so rushed and forceful he almost ends up toppling backward onto the toilet and has to grab the lapels of my crappy jacket to hold himself up.

I swivel so he's against the wall next to the sink, his body pressed between the tiles and my body. I pause out of pure, selfish need. I want to remember this feeling of him against me. I close my eyes for just a second and he whispers, "You've missed this too."

"Yeah." The word is gruff and thick on my tongue. "But so what? We aren't in the same place."

"I know," he sounds so sad. "I want to be. I will be. Soon."

"Well soon isn't now," I reply, finding my will power and stepping away from him. His lips are slightly pink and plump from that savage kiss and his eyes are so pale and so filled with longing it's almost tangible. It makes my chest feel tight. "And if you're supporting Lacey Baldwin, it doesn't matter anyway."

"I'm not supporting her."

"You're just dating her?" I question and he opens his mouth but no words come out. "Fuck, forget it. I have to go. I need a joint."

I fling open the door and step out into her office, storming out of it without a second glance. I need to get the hell away from him and this room, and this stupid party. I head toward the staircase, pushing open the door at the bottom, I gulp the fresh evening air. I text Autumn as I start down Church Street.

Bowen: *I'm sorry. I just can't. I'll wander around until you guys are good to go. Sorry.*

She texts me back immediately.

Autumn: *Are you okay? Do you need me?*

I sigh.

Bowen: *No. Stay and support W. I'll be at V&V.*

When I walk into the bar, it's bustling. Auden is working and sees me from across the room. He smiles and calls out. "Here to bust up the place on your days off too?"

"Ignore him," Molly says as she wanders by with a tray full of drinks and stops. "You look like you need a quiet place and a drink. Booth is open at the back over there."

She tips her head toward the last booth, and I give her a tight but appreciative smile. "Thanks."

Auden's face falls as he watches me go. I know he's just joking around, but I'm not in the right head space for it. I shrug out of my suit jacket and throw it and myself into the booth, with my back to the rest of the bar. I put my elbows on the table, rubbing my face with my hands. Suddenly there's a beer in front of me, but the hand putting it there is much wider and has hairier knuckles than Molly's hand. I look up and it's Auden. He gives me a sheepish smile. "This one's on me. For being a jackass."

"You're not," I reply. "I'm just having a shit night."

"Well, then it's definitely on me," Auden replies, his hands on his hips just above his kilt. "And seriously, I'm sorry."

"It's fine." My smile is less tight this time. "Also, thanks for the rush job on the posters."

"I had a brief chat with Woody when he came in to pick them up," Auden tells me. "I like his ideas for this city. He's got my vote."

I smile and it's less tight this time. "Thanks."

Auden nods and heads back to the bar. My phone buzzes in my pocket and I hope against hope it's my sister saying the party ended. But it's not.

Chase: *I still have things to say to you.*

I put my beer down and type.

Bowen: *Tell me at the next band practice, buddy.*

And then I turn off my phone.

CHASE

I know this is borderline insane behavior but that still doesn't stop me from pulling into the long driveway that leads up to the Whitlock farm. I glance at the clock on the dash of my car. It's a quarter to midnight. Yep, definitely not an appropriate hour for an unexpected visit. But that's not going to stop me.

I get out of the car and march toward the house. It's a modest white farmhouse with a peaked metal roof and an inviting wrap-around porch. There's a bench swing on one side of the front door and two wooden rocking chairs on the other. The matte black door is also flanked on either side by two big red pots with flowers and ferns in them.

The fact that I can see lights on inside helps me find the nerve to lift the brass knocker on the door. A few seconds later I hear footsteps and a small thud and then Autumn's eyes appear in the tiny glass window at the top of the door. She blinks, and then her pale strawberry blonde eyebrows pinch together and I know she's scowling. His sister doesn't like me much. I deserve that, a little... or maybe a lot depending on how much she knows. Either way, it still sucks.

The door opens. Autumn is standing there, next to a chair she must have brought over to reach the little window at the top of the door, in sweats and a T-shirt that says 'Book Boyfriends Do it Better'. "If this is some late night canvassing for Ms. Baldwin, we've already decided who we are voting for, thanks."

She starts to close the door, but I put my hand on it to stop her. "I am so sorry to bother you so late, but I have to speak with your brother."

"Which one?" she asks tersely, raising an eyebrow.

"Bowen."

Now both her eyebrows are up, like angry cats that see something they hate. I keep my hand on the smooth wood of the door, because I'm pretty sure she'll shut it in my face if I don't. After a few seconds caught in a stare down I don't think I'm winning, she takes a deep breath and exhales slowly. "Go around the back. He's out there fussing with Bert and Ernie."

"Okay..." I don't know who or what Bert and Ernie are, but I finally let her slam the door in my face. I'm picturing Bowen playing with puppets from the kids show as I make my way around the house and I almost smile.

There's a light glowing from a small shed situated to the left of the house. I assume that's where he is and make my way there. The ground is soggy and muddy in spots and probably ruining my pricey dress shoes, but I honestly don't care. I knock on the slightly open door, which is one of those sliding wooden ones. The shed looks like a newer addition to the farm, and handmade. The light inside is incredibly bright. I blink as Bowen yells. "Come in."

He looks over his shoulder and when he sees me, his shoulders tighten and his jaw flexes and his expression grows cool. "What are you doing here?"

"I told you I needed to tell you something."

"I told you to talk to me at band practice."

The walls of the small shed are lined with gardening tools. Not the professional farming kind, but the backyard, hobby gardener type. Plastic and terracotta pots, both empty and full with plants like tomatoes and strawberries and others I can't discern. Bags of potting soil, plant food, and watering cans are peppered about too. He's blocking the plants he's working on. I can't see them, but I can smell them. Marijuana.

"Are these the plants that produced the stuff we smoked together the night of the show?" I ask, stepping closer to him and tipping my head to peek around his shoulder. "That stuff gave me the best sleep of my life, by the way. I don't think I told you that."

"That was because it was Bert, not Ernie," Bowen mutters, like he's annoyed he has to explain it to me. Only he doesn't have to. He could tell me to get out, or just ignore me until I leave, but he doesn't. I take that teeny irrelevant fact as hope, because it's all I've got. "Bert is dried different than Ernie and with more CBD and less THC."

"Interesting."

"You shouldn't be coming to my farm in the middle of the night," Bowen warns me. "Not if you want to stay in the closet. Because my family knows I'm gay and the only boys that show up here this late aren't here to learn about cannabis."

I don't like to think about other boys showing up on his doorstep late at night. It makes my guts feel like I drank a gallon of ice water too fast. I swallow. "Tell them it was a band emergency. Please."

He sighs and turns to face me. Tugging off his gardening gloves and running a hand through his hair. He's changed out of his super cute suit from earlier and into a pair of very thin gray sweats and nothing else. I really want to admire his naked chest, but I have to focus. He didn't appreciate the impromptu mauling I gave him at the party. "Fine. I'll tell them that. Now can you tell me whatever you have to say that can't wait until practice? Because I want to be your friend, Chase. I do. But I can't have you blurring the lines. That's not fair."

"I agree." I shove my hands in my pants pockets. "But I wanted you to know the whole truth, about my reasoning for not being out, like you."

"It doesn't matter."

"Maybe it doesn't." I shrug. "But I want you to know, it's not by choice. I did tell my parents."

"That you were bisexual, even though you're gay. I remember."

I pace a little bit in the tiny space. I have never fully revealed the depths of my parents' reaction to my drunken announcement that I was bisexual to anyone before. "I mean, they said that's fine. Because they have to say that. But my dad also said he doesn't want that for his son. And, politically, which matters more, he didn't want that for his family. He decided it was a phase, and the general public doesn't need to know about my 'phases' so I am not to discuss it in public. Ever."

"That's fucked."

"Yep, but that's only the beginning." I keep pacing in the tiny space between the table that his plants are on and the shelves with piles of unused pots. "While my mother and father try to pretend they aren't bigots, my grandfather didn't care who knew it. And he put a morality clause in his will, which is governed by my father. So, I won't get my inheritance if I do anything that is deemed immoral or unbefitting the family name. My cousin Amy had a premature baby and he spent almost a year trying to block her inheritance."

"Are you kidding me?" Bowen looks appalled. It's hard to see him like that, knowing it's about my family. Yeah, they're horrible but I still hate seeing that reflected on someone else's face. Especially his.

"I wish I was. And she even married the guy. She'd always planned on marrying the guy," I explain, and my voice is as angry as his expression. "But it suddenly had to happen immediately, and no one admitted why. Anyway, the baby was born at seven months, but was over six pounds and healthy as a horse so… we all knew. And he would have denied her the money except my aunt got some doctor's note or something official that made him relent."

"Oh for fuck's sake, my parents had Woody before they got married. It's not exactly uncommon now." Bowen rolls his eyes and then sighs. He looks at me, studying me as I pace. "And he would do that to you for being gay?"

"Yeah. In a heartbeat," I reply with absolute certainty. I stop pacing and stare at him. He's so fucking gorgeous even in this harsh glaring light, and with a look of judgment twisting his rugged features. "And I want that money. I *deserve* that money. I'm a good person and I have good plans for that money. I want to go back to college and get the degree I wanted that he wouldn't let me have, which is music. I want to open up a music camp for LGBTQ youth when I graduate. I want to help people and this community and just be… happy. I deserve that and I'm not going to let him take it away because of my sexuality. It's not something I should be punished for."

"That's a lot of plans," Bowen says, his voice softer, less judgey. "How much is the inheritance?"

"Three and a half million."

"*Dollars*?" Bowen's amber eyes bulge out of his head.

"Yep." I nod and he blinks. "It's life changing. Not just my life either."

"Yeah. It definitely is." Bowen swallows. His eyes lock on mine. "And you get it when you're twenty-eight?"

I nod.

"And you're…?"

"Twenty-seven. With only six months and twenty-four days," I reply and pull my phone out of my pocket and punch a button and smile. "And nine hours until twenty-eight. I may have a countdown app set."

He smiles too. Finally. I step toward him again but make sure to shove my hands back in my pockets to avoid the temptation to touch him. "So anyway, that's why I'm not as out as you. It's not that I care, because I don't. Hell, if I had my way, I'd make out with you on stage in the middle of Burlington Town Square. In a rainbow flag shirt. Or in nothing at all. But I'm holding out for the money. And maybe that makes me a selfish jerk, or stupid, or whatever. But just so you know, I *do* want to be your friend. I don't expect you to wait around or anything but the day that check clears, I intend to hit on you relentlessly, in public, all the time. Unless, of course, you've moved on. I'll respect that. But if you haven't… I'll come knocking."

He's just staring at me, his face soft and relaxed. I think he's processing all of this, but I'm not sure what he's thinking at all. So I keep talking. "You know what's crazy? I named my firm Dauntless because it's my favorite word. It means fearless and determined, which I crave. How I want to feel, always, in every situation. But you… you make me feel the polar opposite. You're daunting. To me."

He quirks an eyebrow and tips his head a little to the left. "You're kidding, right? You're the smart, confident, fearless one. You always have a solution for shit and you can be calm and comfortable with anything, and I'm daunting? I'm an orphaned, college drop out with a pot habit."

"You're authentic," I reply. "The one thing I can't be. And I don't always have a solution. I don't have a way to be with you, which is all I want."

"Sure you do," Bowen says and leans back, his ass resting on the table behind him. He lets his hands rest just a smidge lower than his hips, next to the bulge under his shorts. My dick twitches involuntarily. "You could ask to date me anyway."

"I can't because—"

"Because I said I don't do closeted." I nod and Bowen seems to be thinking really hard for a minute. Then he looks me in the eye again. "Want to smoke?"

He reaches into the pocket of his sweats and pulls out a perfectly rolled joint. I eye it and then move my gaze to his face, which is staring back at me with the softest expression I've seen since our last hook-up. "I should probably be going."

"Oh. Okay." He walks to the door and holds it open for me. Then he follows me out into the yard after turning out the lights and telling his pot plants to "Sleep tight."

I smile in the moonlight at that. Bowen is delightful. We walk side-by-side through the backyard. He lights his joint by the side of the house, stopping to look at the fields just beyond. I watch the end of the joint glow as his perfect mouth sucks on the other end. Fuck, now I'm jealous of a joint. Jesus.

"When do you plant?" I ask, looking for something — anything — to get my mind off the sex we can't have.

"Soon. We'll till the soil again end of this month and we'll seed a couple weeks later," Bowen says and then he hands me the joint.

I shake my head. "I have to drive home."

"Do you?" he asks, still holding it out to me.

I sigh and shake my head with a heavy smile on my lips. "Look, I respect your boundaries. I even admire them. And I think this friendship will work, but I'm not ready to spend the night on your couch or whatever. And your sister kind of doesn't like me so I should go."

I start to walk away. His voice carries across the slightly over-grown grass. "So as soon as you hit twenty-eight, you're out?"

"I promise. Not you, but myself," I reply, turning slowly back to face him. He's blowing a cloud of smoke into the darkness and is moving toward me with a lazy, sexy gait. "And before you ask, if it costs me my family, I'm good with it. I've lived long enough by their rules, and it hasn't made me happy."

"What makes you happy?"

I watch the moonlight bounce across his high cheekbones. "Music. Gigs. Your blow jobs."

He chokes, but it quickly turns into a laugh. When he's recovered, he hands me the joint again. "You don't have to sleep on my couch. You can sleep in a bed. With me."

We stare at each other, my eyes scanning his face, trying to figure out what the trick is in that statement. There's got to be a 'but' or a catch of some sort. But there isn't. When I still don't take the joint he puts it to his lips, inhales deeply, and then holds it to the side as he very gently moves his mouth to mine. He's hesitant, waiting for me to pull away or resist, but when I part my lips it sure as hell isn't to say no. It's to let in the smoke and then, let him in. After I blow the smoke out my nose, our mouths tangle again in a searing kiss. Tongues searching, lips smashing, teeth nipping.

"Are you really okay with this?" I ask when we finally come up for air.

He steps away, untangling himself from me, and grinding out the flame on what's left of the joint against the wall of the house, as he nods. "Yeah. I am. You're not scared of who you are. This isn't a permanent place for you. And with the way I feel about this... I'd be an idiot to wait around for something to change."

He kisses the side of my mouth and then my neck, his hands wandering under my suit jacket. "So, you'll keep this a secret. Us? No one can know. Not even your family."

"Yeah. It's fine. For six months." He kisses his way to my ear. "And twenty-four days. And nine hours."

"Almost eight hours now."

"Look at that. Time flies." He palms my erection through my dress pants, and I swear my knees almost buckle. "Not a second more."

"Not a second more," I promise and shove my hand into the front of his sweats as our lips connect again. He's not wearing underwear and he might be harder than I am. Thank Christ. "But... your family."

"There's a studio above the garage my dad used for jam sessions. Separate entrance," he whispers against my mouth as I wrap a hand around him and glide my thumb over his leaking tip. "It's got a bed too for when his music buddies had a few too many beers. I can tell them we worked on a new song for the band and you crashed."

Is it slightly risky to spend the night with his brother and sister so nearby, regardless of the excuse? Yes. Am I going to do it anyway? Also, yes.

"Lead the way."

12

BOWEN

I don't feel one single second of trepidation as I agree to step into Chase's closet to be with him. The second he explained his story, I got it. He's not afraid of who he is or embarrassed by it. I would lie too for a chance at life changing money. I understand him and that's all it took to let this warm fuzzy feeling in my chest smother the deep scars of past heartbreak. Scars I didn't realize were still sore until I met Chase. And fuck, it's only six months. I don't want to miss half a year with him because of old wounds.

I kiss him one last time and take his hand and lead him around to the garage. I keep one eye on the downstairs windows, making sure the curtains don't move. Autumn is not known for giving me privacy. I don't want to lie to her about Chase, but I will, for him. We climb the wooden staircase and I push open the door and flip on the small lamp on the battered old table by the door. Chase looks around, taking it all in.

"My dad made guitars as a hobby. He sold some and gave some away to friends as gifts," I explain as his eyes sweep over the four we kept, all on stands in the corner of the room.

There's also a desk in the corner under the window where my mom used to do her crafting and bracelet making that Autumn has taken over. It's next to an old record player sitting on top of four stacked milk crates filled with vinyl albums. And then there's the bed. I gently push him toward it and walk over to stick a record on. I pick

Nirvana's *Nevermind*. It's not exactly soft and sexy music, but I keep the volume low. I like it because Chase thinks I have Kurt Cobain hair. He's smiling as soon as "Teen Spirit" starts.

Then I walk over to the one window and make sure the curtains are drawn tight, without gaps. I pull my lighter out of my sweats and light the small cluster of candles on the desk. I flip off the overhead light on my way back to him. He's shrugging out of his suit jacket as I start kissing him again. His mouth is warm and inviting and once his jacket falls, he starts undoing the cuffs of his dress shirt, and I have to pull back and watch because for some reason, it's an incredible turn-on. "I've never been with a guy as put together as you. All designer suits and cufflinks. It's sexy as fuck watching you… unravel."

"Your last boyfriend wasn't a suit guy?"

"He was a college kid like me," I explain, distractedly because my focus is on his fingers that are now making quick work of his shirt and with every button that opens, I'm treated to his glorious skin — taut and smooth. But then his words replay themselves in my brain, making it through the haze of lust. My fingers still. "Haven't had a boyfriend since my freshman year. Until now?"

It's a question because I didn't think he'd want to dive right into that label. But he used it first so I'm just seeking clarification. His shirt is completely undone now so he slips out of it, leaving it to fall to the floor at the foot of the bed on top of his suit jacket. "I've never had a boyfriend at all," Chase confesses. "Until now."

He steps into me and our lips connect. It's ten more glorious minutes of clothes coming off while our lips and tongues explore any inch of skin we can. When we're both naked, I push him back onto the bed and climb on top. Our dicks bump and rub together and the friction sends ripples of desire up my spine. "God, I have never wanted to fuck someone so badly in my life."

He tenses under me. Even his lips grow stiff against my neck and I realize that somehow, I fucked up. Before I can pull back enough to read his expression, he shoves his fingers through my hair and wraps one thick, muscular leg over the back of my calf, holding me to him. He kisses my neck softly and rolls his hips, our dicks rubbing again. "I've never done that. Yet."

That kind of throws me. I mean, it doesn't at all matter, I'm just surprised. He keeps talking in between featherlight kisses up my throat. "I've wanted to, more than once, but it's just… I didn't… I didn't want it to be a random hook-up and that's all I could offer."

"You're offering me more," I whisper and grind against him, my lips move to his ear, kissing the shell and nipping the lobe, which gets me a small, deep groan.

"Yeah. I am. But…"

"We've got time," I tell him before he can finish that sentence. "Lots of it. No rush."

As much as I want to fuck him, I want to do everything else with him too. God, this man is my catnip. Even the smallest taste is enough and not enough at the same time. "So, you haven't been fucked. Have you fucked a guy?"

I'm blunt, but we're naked here and I know he's as turned on as I am so no need to act shy. With one last push of my hips, I slip off him so we're lying side by side on the lumpy double bed with one of my grandma's quilts on it. Chase looks me square in the eye. "No."

I can tell it's hard for him to admit that. "But you've thought about it."

"Thought about it. Fantasized. Craved it. But it seemed like a bad idea with a one-night stand," Chase replies. "I mean, not for everyone. Just for me. Baggage and everything. I just didn't want my first to be with someone who… with a… well fuck, I sound like a romantic teenage girl."

We both laugh. "My sister would like you more if she knew. You sound like someone from one of those novels she reads all the damn time."

"Sorry." The light is dim, but I swear there's pink creeping into his cheeks.

"Don't be." I reach up, sliding my fingers over his chest, circling his left nipple and then his right. His eyelids flutter a little. And then I remind him of the most important thing. "I'm not a one-night stand."

"You aren't." His lips find mine again and we spend the next several minutes making out.

I roll away from him for just long enough to reach my arm down and under the bed, where I pull out the small wooden box I keep there. It's got guitar picks, extra strings, and some lube because sometimes I have urges and I'm usually up here at night when Autumn isn't. I grab the small bottle and turn back to Chase. "Hold out your hand."

When he does, I squirt some into his palm and then another squirt into my palm before tossing it off the bed and kissing him again. Each lick, each nip, getting more and more intense and passionate. Our lubed hands are wrapped around each other's cocks as we're side-by-side, making out relentlessly and giving each other hand jobs. We come almost in unison, my release exploding a millisecond before his.

After we clean up in the small powder room in the corner, we both throw on our boxer briefs and crawl back onto the bed. I pull what's left of the joint out of my sweats and re-light it. I'm sitting with my head against the wall at the top of the bed, Chase is lower, his head in the crook of my arm. We share the rest of the joint and talk – about my life, his life, our families. It's nothing but it's also everything. We couldn't have more different upbringings – his religious, political, rich, and full of expectations and boundaries. Mine simple, bohemian, working class, and with few rules or limits. Our life experiences, despite going to the same college, at different times, was also different. Chase was an athlete, lived in the dorms and then in a frat house, was an honor student, with a double major, and graduated top of both classes. I only did one year in my program, managed middle-of-the-pack grades, lived at home, and never went to a college sports event let alone participated.

When I mention how different our lives have been he smiles up at me. "But somehow the universe crossed our paths anyway. Kismet is a wonderous thing."

"How does your dad not see that you're way too deep to be a politician?"

He sucks hard on what's left of the joint and starts to laugh at the same time. Little puffs of smoke escape his lips, still pink and plump from our make-out session. I kiss him again. Eventually, with the joint gone, I slide down to lie beside him and we fall asleep.

When I wake up, sunlight is glowing behind the curtains. I feel like I haven't in a really long time – rested. I drifted off easily, with his warm, hard body against mine, and slept soundly. But now, as I stretch and open my eyes, Chase is gone. It's not really a shock, but there's still a pinch of sadness in my chest. I get off the bed and pull on my sweats, digging my phone out of my pocket and smiling at his name in my text alerts.

Chase: *Tough leaving you. Hope you slept well. You working tonight?*

I text back as I make my way out of the room and down the stairs. The morning air is warm and the sky is cloudless and there's a hum of machinery. Woody is out back on the riding mower.

Bowen: *Slept amazing. Hope you did too. Working 6-close. Stop by if you're bored.*

Autumn, as usual, is wrapped up in her housecoat, sitting on one of the rockers on the front porch. It's where she has coffee every morning, usually also reading a book. Although lately she's dug out our grandma's fancy tea set and started having tea instead, because she's on a historical romance kick and she says it's more fitting. Her eyes aren't on the book in her hand at the moment, though. They're on me as I climb the steps. Then they move up, back to the garage, and back at me. "Alone?"

"Yeah of course," I say casually and put my phone on my thigh. "Fell asleep after band stuff with Chase and a good joint."

"Huh." I don't like how unconvinced she sounds. "I didn't hear the drums or anything last night."

"We were listening to music, trying to figure out what songs we could add to our set list," I reply and then try changing the subject. "We're playing a wedding in Maine soon."

"Oh. Cool." Her hardened stare softens. "I'm so happy you're back into music."

"Yeah. Me too." I sit down in the free rocker, and she offers me some tea but I shake my head.

She frowns. "Even the Rakes in my romance novels drink tea, Bo."

"I don't think I fully understand that statement," I confess. "But I don't care what your fictional characters do, coffee is life."

She smiles while shaking her head, her strawberry blonde hair is a tangled mess since she hasn't bothered to brush it. She gets up and disappears into the house as I close my eyes and listen to the sound of the mower and breathe in the scent of freshly cut grass. Then another scent fills my nostrils. Coffee. I open my eyes just as the screen door slams and Autumn emerges with a cup of good old-fashioned Joe. "Here, you heathen."

I laugh. "Thank you, my lady."

She sits down again and opens her book, pausing to sip her milky looking tea with her pinkie finger high in the air. I bite my bottom lip to keep from laughing at her. "So you and our enemy's boyfriend are going to play a gig together in Maine?"

"Chase isn't Lacey Baldwin's boyfriend," I reply, sipping my coffee which she made exactly to my liking, black with a little bit of sugar. "They're old friends so he went with her."

"Friends, huh." Autumn looks like I just tried to tell her the earth was flat. "Sweetheart, no woman invites a guy that hot anywhere as just a friend."

The idea that Lacey may have had ulterior motives didn't cross my mind, because Chase seemed so confident in his explanation. And I definitely want to believe they're just good friends. "He's got no reason to lie to me."

"Because he's a spy for her," Autumn replies as the sound of the lawn mower somewhere behind us stops. "She sent him in here, to befriend you and infiltrate our campaign headquarters and get top secret information. Maybe that drummer you replaced went missing on purpose. Has anyone even seen him since that night he went M.I.A?"

I can't even try to stifle my laughter now. "Are you reading regency novels or *Bourne Identity*? Tom Clancy? Because Jesus, Autumn, your conspiracy theories are out of control this morning."

"Hey! You're up." Woody's voice interrupts our ridiculous conversation as he appears from around the side of the house. "I was just getting a jump on the chores before I head to the campaign office."

"You didn't have to do that," I reply. "I was planning on mowing the lawn before work."

He smiles and scratches his slightly unkempt pale brown beard that's peppered with red. "I know, but I've been slacking on the home duties and I've been feeling bad about it. But you can finish the last quarter of the lawn tomorrow or whenever the mower has recharged. It died."

I roll my eyes. Woody made us buy a very pricey electric mower which I was all for but we couldn't afford the top of the line, only the bottom of the line and the battery dies a lot. He walks right up onto the porch and plunks himself and the butt of his dirty work jeans on the railing across from our rocking chairs. "But for now, I want to run something by you guys. It's a bit of a wild idea."

"Shoot," I say and take another sip of coffee. "Nothing could be more wild than what Autumn's been saying this morning."

"I was thinking we should throw a fundraising event," Woody explains. "Here at the farm."

I tense and Woody noticed it immediately. He lifts both his hands like I'm holding a gun in his direction. "Hear me out. If we have people here, at the farm, it's personal. They can see us, what we do, who we are, and I think that would do a better job of showing people what I'm all about. You both know I suck at interviews and debates."

Autumn being Autumn goes right into planning mode. "What if we hire some people from V and V to bartend and what if we asked them to cater too? We could have a hemp theme. Joss makes those wicked delicious burgers with our hemp seed buns. We could create a signature mocktail and cocktail for the event, like the Woody Wallbanger or something. Do we have a budget for this? Let me look at the forecast and figure out the best day weather-wise for an outdoor event."

She snatches my phone off my lap to Google the weather as my eyes stay firmly fixed to the barn. Behind that barn is where I hid the last time we opened our house to people, which was our parents' memorial. I remember being out there, collapsed against the wall with its rough siding and chipped paint, sobbing like a baby. The reality of the whole nightmare had finally settled in, in the middle of their wake, and all I wanted was to be left alone. I didn't want to wear a brave face or listen to all these people with their consoling words that did not console me.

That barn is where I went to hide. Where I texted Trevor and begged him to come over and help me through this. Where I was when he texted me back with a firm. 'No. People will get the wrong idea.' And I had to go back inside and watch people poke around my sanctuary, pointing at our family photos and clutching their hearts like they cared.

"Look, Bo, I know you hate the idea," Woody says bluntly, and I blink and refocus on what's happening now instead of the past. "I know how much you hate people in our space, but it makes sense. Please."

"Yeah." I clear my throat because my voice is suddenly rough. "Yeah, I get it. We can do it. But I don't want them in the house or anything. Outdoor only and they can use the bathroom above the garage only. Not in the house."

"We'll negotiate that but yeah, I won't let them poke around the house," Woody agrees. "I know it'll give you flashbacks to the funeral."

I nod and stand up. "What day are you thinking?"

Autumn looks up from my phone, which I reach down and take back from her. "Week from Thursday is the best day weather-wise. Zero chance of rain and I also went on Lacey Baldwin's website and she has no events planned so we aren't going to compete for attendance."

"Cool. Do you want me to talk to Harrison and Joss or do you want to?"

Autumn smiles. "I'll talk to them. They like me better because I don't break things."

"Ha ha." I roll my eyes even though she's probably right. "Okay. I'm going to nap."

"You and your band buddy stay up late?" Woody says and I stutter step. My brain heard bed buddy and it takes me a minute to realize he said *band* buddy.

"You okay there big bro?" Autumn asks and her eyebrow is arched again. I fight the urge to reach out and try to physically push it down with my fingertip.

"I'm tired. I didn't sleep well last night, which is nothing new." I lie and head inside. Autumn and Woody go back to brainstorming this event.

I'm not thrilled with the idea, but it does make sense. I try to push it from my brain and concentrate on the fact that in a few short hours I'll be at work, and Chase is probably going to be there too. That's enough to make me smile and I haven't smiled about working a shift at Vino and Veritas since I got the job.

13

CHASE

I get to Vino and Veritas late. It's already pretty packed. Bowen is nowhere to be seen but I grab a bar stool as soon as two women get up to leave and smile at Murph. He gives me a little wave. "Hi gorgeous. Are you in a Pinot or a Cab mood today?"

"Cab, thanks."

He starts to pour me a glass as Bowen emerges from the back with a tray full of clean glasses. His face lights up when he sees me and he mouths the word *hey*. I give him a small, hopefully subtle wave, and bite the inside of my cheek to keep my smile from getting too big. Truth is, I want to grin like a lovesick teenager. He looks great, as always. He's given up trying to pull his chin length hair into a ponytail and it's loose. He's got on a simple black tee and a pair of black jeans that hug the curve of his ass. The shirt also lifts as he reaches up to slide the wine glasses into the holder above the bar and I see that perfect smooth ridge near his hip that I've had my lips on before.

My dick relives the moment in my pants and I shift on my bar stool and will my cock to simmer down. "Hey. Chase!"

I blink and turn to see Riley Meadows has slipped in between two occupied seats at the other side of the bar. We make eye contact, and he waves at me with a tattooed arm. Riley came back to town recently to take care of his grandfather and I helped him out with business applications through the Chamber of Commerce. "Riley. Good to see you. How's it going?"

"Good. Great, actually." Riley gives me a smile, which isn't something I'm used to seeing on his face so things really must be going well. I'm glad to hear it. He's a really nice guy.

"You wanna grab a drink?"

"I'm here with my… ah… Peter."

He tilts his head back toward the other corner of the bar and I see the lawyer from Sprysky and Gentry. Peter's eyes widen when he sees me and he waves. I nod in return with a friendly smile. It's weird seeing him in the wild and not across a conference table, trying not to grimace at the shit show that is my family.

"You've met before?" Riley asks.

"Yeah. My family does business with his firm." I lean closer to Riley. "If he ever comes home grumbly and annoyed, he's probably had a meeting with my family. Sorry."

Riley just smiles. "You here by yourself? Blowing off a rough work week or something?"

"Or something." I smile. "Just bored, really."

"You're welcome to come and sit with us," Riley offers as Murph slides him two Shipley ciders.

I shake my head. "No, thanks though. Enjoy yourselves without a third wheel."

Riley lifts a pint toward me in a 'cheers' motion before he takes the drinks and heads back to Peter. He's got to be Riley's boyfriend even though he didn't say it. I'm left with a bit of an ache in my chest. It looks so easy and effortless – date night. With a guy. I've always looked forward to the day I could openly do that too, but now it feels even more pressing. I want it more than I wanted to get into a college or make the swim team in high school, or open Christmas presents when I was really young and still thought Santa brought them. Because now I have an actual person I want to go on a date with.

My eyes find Bowen again. He's finished loading the clean glasses and is wiping the bar top where two customers just left. His eyes are on me though, until I look at him and then he looks away. His expression isn't readable. I walk over and drop back down on my bar stool and sip my wine.

An hour and a half later I'm standing at the end of the alley, waiting for him. The back door opens, and I hear him talking to someone. "Let's keep that streak going tomorrow night."

"I intend to," I hear Bowen say. "See you then, Tanner. Night."

"Night," Tanner calls back and then Bowen steps out of the shadows.

He smiles at me. "Hi."

"Hi." I walk over to him. I have my lips pressed tightly together to avoid the urge to kiss him. "My place for a nightcap?"

"Sure," he replies, and we start down the sidewalk. We walk half a block in silence and then he says. "You have a good night?"

"Mostly," I reply. "I was having a hard time keeping my eyes off you. I felt like Murph was maybe catching on."

"He knows you know I'm a klutz at work. Probably just thought you were keeping me in your sights so you could avoid any kind of disaster I might cause," Bowen jokes and tilts his head to shoot me this cheeky smile. It makes it hard to breathe for a second. I've never had breathing troubles with a guy unless he was giving me a hand job or a blow job. This is new. "Besides, even if Murph figured it out, he's not going to say anything to anyone. Not even me."

I nod. The wind is light and much warmer than it has been. Spring is definitely kicking into high gear and I'm loving it. Bowen isn't even wearing a jacket tonight and I probably don't need mine. The air smells faintly of flowers from the city planters and this musky, bergamot type scent I've inhaled while nuzzling his neck, so I know it's coming off Bowen. That scent warms me from the inside, and I've never been happier that my loft is smack dab in the middle of downtown as I am now, because it means it's not long until I can bury my face in his neck again.

When we reach the front door to my building, I punch the code into the pad and hold the door open for him. We walk to the elevator and I hit the button, a little shocked we have to wait for it. Usually it's sitting at the bottom, but maybe Grant has someone over and it's stopped on his floor.

"So," Bowen says, pulling my attention with his raspy voice. I watch him turn so his back is facing the wall to the right of the elevator and his body is facing me. "Is this private enough to touch you? Because it's all I've thought about all night and I'm fucking dying to get my mouth on you."

I glance at the front door to the building, which is basically all glass but I had the renovation team put an opaque film over it so with the lights off in the hall, like they are now, and the film, no one is likely to see us from the street. I contemplate explaining this to Bowen for about half a second but decide to just kiss him instead. I walk right up to him, place the flat palm of my hand on the top of his chest, at the base of his throat, and push him flush against the wall before I lean in. It's so similar to our first kiss, and I see the recognition in his eyes, only this time as I move in slowly, I don't hesitate one bit. "You looked so hot all night I could barely stand it," I confess, our lips brushing. "I contemplated going into the bathroom and jerking off."

"I hope you didn't," Bowen whispers back. "I have bigger plans for this."

He palms my erection through my pants, and I smash my mouth to his in a blinding, consuming kiss. It's equal parts satisfying and annoyingly inadequate. I want more. I want all of him. And then, through the noise of my thumping pulse and throbbing cock I somehow manage to hear the hum of the elevator stop and the swoosh of the doors opening. Light slices through our darkness and Bowen turns to stone under my touch. I *know* someone else is here. I jerk back and turn to see Bennie standing in the elevator staring at us through the open doors.

I'd like to think he didn't see anything but the expression of anger and pain on his face confirms the opposite. He saw everything. I step away from Bowen, who pulls himself off the wall, his backbone straight, shoulders back. "Hey," I clear my throat. "Bennie."

His wide brown eyes are moving between Bowen and me like a tennis fan watching a match. "Hey. Who's this?"

"Right. I forgot you two haven't met." I clear my throat again. I don't know why my voice sounds so off. "Bennie Johnson. This is Bowen Whitlock."

Bennie finally steps out of the elevator just before the doors slide shut. He turns his head to Bowen, jutting his chin out instead of taking the hand Bowen is casually offering. "You're the guy who took my job."

"Oh, you're that Bennie," Bowen replies. "I didn't steal your job. I just happened to be there when you weren't."

"Is that how you see it?" Bennie asks, but I'm not sure who the question is directed at because he's turned to glare at me again.

"I guess you were hanging out with Grant?" I say, changing the topic. Sort of. Jesus tonight has taken a turn.

"Yeah," Bennie's voice is hard and colder than Vermont in January. He takes a couple steps, pausing only when he's face-to-face with me. "He told me you'd found someone to replace me. He clearly wasn't just talking about the band."

Bennie turns and walks straight for the door, shoving it open and disappearing into the darkness beyond. I stare after him for a second. I hear Bowen let out a long breath. "So, that's the drummer who flaked?"

"Yeah."

"Looks like he's not thrilled about me taking over."

"Yeah." I turn from the door and punch the elevator button again. "It's been weeks since that gig and he's just now contacting one of us, so I don't give a fuck how he feels about it."

I step into the elevator and watch Bowen hesitate before stepping inside with me. He stands directly beside me, facing forward as we both watch the doors close in front of us. "Sounds like he was more than a drummer."

"He wasn't," I reply, clenching my jaw as I figure out how to address this. Fucking Bennie, always making a bad situation worse. "I mean he was. For one night. And I was very clear about the one night thing. He said he got it. He was cool with it."

"He ain't cool with it," Bowen replies.

"Yeah. I guess he's not." I inhale and then can't seem to exhale as I say, "Do you care?"

There's a heartbeat of silence and then Bowen speaks but doesn't answer the question. "That guy in the bar who you were talking to, he also one of your one night stands?"

It takes my brain a second to figure out who he's talking about. "Riley? No. Not at all. I helped him out with a Chamber of Commerce thing."

The elevator opens on my floor, my dark loft coming into view but when I step toward it, Bowen doesn't follow, so I turn to face him instead. "You're jealous?"

"No," he replies quickly. His eyes, with those flecks of golden amber, can't seem to find my own. He's looking over my shoulder, at the elevator wall, the floor. And then, in a rough whisper he says, "Maybe. And I don't do jealous, so I don't like how this feels."

I reach out and cup the back of his head, leaning forward to brush our lips together. He leans closer but I pull back. "I've always been honest with you. Just like I was honest with Bennie. He was a one-time thing. You're more."

I step right up into his space. He doesn't move or flinch, not even when my hands slip under the hem of his dark T-shirt and my fingertips ghost across the waistband of his jeans. My fingers grasp the bottom of his shirt and in one fluid motion I slide it up as he lifts his arms to allow me to pull it right off him. I throw it in the general direction of the loft behind me. I move to kiss him. His mouth is already slightly parted, his tongue slipping out onto his bottom lip, eager to meet with mine. I feel the need to taste him – his mouth, his tongue, his everything – so deeply it makes my balls ache. His hands grab my face and I bury my fingers in his hair and press my hips to his, our cocks glancing off each other.

He pushes me backwards, into the loft just as the elevator doors try to shut. They bounce back open and we go tumbling into the hall, tripping over each other's feet. I end up on my back on the smooth concrete, Bowen on top of me. Neither of us broke the kiss, and we keep kissing until we've got my jacket and shirt off and both our pants and underwear are at our ankles. Only then, do our lips find other places to explore.

BOWEN

I wake up the next morning to an empty bed. Once again, I slept like the dead. It was amazing. I woke only once to use the bathroom in the wee hours of the morning. I considered leaving. I should have left, but when I walked back into the bedroom, Chase's lips were parted in a sleepy smile and he had the sexiest bed head and he murmured, "Stay." He held back the duvet for me to climb back in and I lost any and all willpower right then. I've never been able to cuddle. Trevor was so worried someone would know we were more than friends, he never let me stay in his dorm room, even though he had a single room. And since my parents died, until Chase, I've always had trouble sleeping. So even on the odd occasion my hook-up and I drifted off to sleep together, it never lasted more than a couple hours and then I was wide awake with no chance of drifting off again, so I'd leave.

But after crawling back into Chase's bed and curling into his naked form, I fell asleep again without issue. What wakes me up now is my phone ringing. The ring tone is a Stevie Nicks tune — "Edge of Seventeen" — which is specifically for Autumn. I grab my phone off the bedside table, where I had the sense to put it last night after round one, before round two. It hits me as soon as I see her number on the screen I forgot to update her on my whereabouts. So I answer the call with a blunt, "I'm alive."

"Bowen, why didn't you text? Call? Anything?" Autumn's voice is filled with relief but also sharp with anger. "We have rules! You *know* why."

"I know. I'm sorry. I just fell dead asleep," I say and immediately regret my choice of words. "I'm fine. I'm sorry. It won't happen again."

I turn and realize I'm not alone. Chase is standing in the doorway to the bathroom, in shorts and a T-shirt with a toothbrush in his mouth, and damn, he looks good. "We never break this rule Bo! Never. You're the first! It's not okay!" Autumn has a way of getting really upset about shit she cannot change. I hate that. I always accept things for what they are. "You can't just break that rule. It exists for a reason."

"I did it. I'm sorry. I won't do it again," I promise firmly.

"When I woke up and Woody said you weren't home..." Her voice wobbles deeply on the last word and my heart thumps heavily with guilt.

"I stayed with a… friend," I say and Chase raises both eyebrows but turns and heads back into his bathroom. "I'm good."

"Since when do you sleep well? Let alone well somewhere that isn't your bed?" Autumn wants to know. I can visualize her brows pinched together like they get when she's totally confused.

"Since now," I reply, hoping the annoyed tone in my voice cuts this interrogation short. "I'll be home later, in time to help with whatever you need to make this event happen."

"Okay fine. I'll grill you then," Autumn says, and I roll my eyes. "And do not do this again. I don't care how good the sex is."

The line goes dead and I almost smile. Chase appears in the doorway again, still looking casually gorgeous. I must look like a troll that's been woken up from his sleep under a bridge. Self-consciously I run a hand through my hair and it promptly gets stuck in tangles. "She's a real gate keeper about where you are, huh?"

I nod. "We all have to check in if we're not coming home or we're going to be late."

He seems puzzled by that and so I guess we're starting this morning on a sad note. "My parents lay in that car for hours because we didn't think to worry."

"What?"

"They called home when they left the Christmas market they'd attended in New Hampshire. Told us they'd be home in a little over an hour, in time for dinner," I explain, and I hate talking about this. I haven't, with anyone really, except my siblings. We spent months after they first died blaming each other and ourselves. "When they didn't show up for dinner, we just assumed they stopped somewhere. We didn't call the cops or highway patrol. We ordered pizza and then Autumn convinced me to watch a movie instead of studying and Woody went out to meet up with friends. It wasn't until like midnight that we thought, maybe we should try their cell phones. And when they didn't answer those, we called Woody who called the police. So, we promised each other to always check in. Always. And I fucked up last night and didn't."

He looks stricken, which is to be expected but it still makes me uncomfortable. It was the worst night of my entire life, and I don't like thinking about it let alone talking about it. Or seeing his handsome face washed in sympathy. I turn away from him and start grabbing my clothes. "Relax. You don't have to run out of here now that she knows you're okay, right?"

"I guess not. But you look like you're going somewhere," I mutter pulling on my shirt and then reaching for my pants. "I should get out of your hair."

I tug my underwear over my ass and as I straighten, his hand lands on my shoulder. He gives it a gentle squeeze. "Bowen, I'm sorry."

"About what?"

"About making you talk about that," Chase replies softly. "I should have figured out why you guys are so anal about checking in. I know what happened. But you guys have to realize that you didn't do anything wrong. It's normal not to freak out about your parents being late."

I nod. Our family therapist told us the same thing but none of us cared and still don't. Woody, Autumn, and I will hold that mistake deep in our heart until they stop beating. He, thankfully, changes the subject. "What event are you working on?"

"Woody is having a cocktail thing at the farm. A campaign fundraiser," I explain. "You'll get the invite because you're on the city thingy."

"Chamber of Commerce?" he asks, and I nod.

"Yeah, the chamber thingy." I smile, he shoots one right back at me and it's beyond stunning. Fuck, he's the best looking guy I've ever known in real life. And he's my boyfriend. That revelation calms my agitation a little. "But I get it if you can't go since you're friends with Lacey."

"Lacey isn't my boyfriend," Chase replies and steps into my space, the fabric of his loose shorts brushing against my thighs and he wraps his arms around my neck. "I may not be able to say that in public but I can still support you. It'll look like I'm just fulfilling my duty as a Chamber of Commerce member but really, I'm there for you. And also your brother has my vote, even if I also can't say that out loud."

"I want to kiss you, but I haven't brushed my teeth," I confess and he brushes my lips across his lightly anyway.

"I left a new toothbrush on the counter." He breaks our embrace. "I have to go teach aquafit at the community center so brush them quick so I can kiss you good-bye."

I head into the bathroom, he leans on the door frame and watches me. "You know you can stay as long as you want. Use the hot tub or just take a shower. Play around with my guitars if you want."

I meet his eye in the mirror as I spit out the toothpaste and grin. "I'd love to play with something but it's not your guitars."

He grins. I rinse the toothbrush, and he walks up behind me, takes it, and puts it in the holder next to his. I keep my eyes on him in the mirror and bend a little at the waist, pushing my ass into his groin ever so slightly. He doesn't startle or move away. "Tell me more about this aquafit thing?"

"I used to be a lifeguard as a teenager," he explains and picks up a comb from the counter next to my right hip. Chase starts gently brushing my hair. And he also starts gently pushing his erection against my ass. I'm not sure which action is getting me hot. Maybe it's both. "Then in college I took an online certification for this, on a lark, and started teaching. Wanted extra spending money I didn't have to ask my parents for. I kept teaching for free to help the community."

"I feel like I'm dating a Saint," I reply and tilt my hips to rock into him a little harder as he rubs his cock against me again. "Which is weird because you fuck like a demon."

"We haven't fucked," he reminds me. He stops combing my hair and grips my hip.

Our eyes meet in the mirror again and he holds my hip tighter and rocks into me, his cock pressing against my crack.

"Close enough," I whisper, arching my back a little, showing him how easy it could be. How perfect. He leans forward, kissing the back of my neck and pumping himself against me. Oh, how I wish we were naked, but I know he needs it slow. So if he wants to hump like teenagers in front of the bathroom mirror for now, I am not about to stop him.

"One day," he murmurs, his hips growing still but his hard length still pressed to my ass. I straighten a little and twist my head and kiss him so long, hard, and deep that we're both sporting wood by the time it ends. He steps back and palms his cock through his sweats. "How the fuck am I supposed to face the aqua ladies with this?"

"Do I have time to fix the problem for you?" I ask, and he pulls his phone from his pocket.

"Probably not. I have to leave in five minutes," he replies, and I grin and slip down to my knees.

"You underestimate me," I say, pulling down the waistband of his shorts.

Four and a half minutes later, Chase is groaning so loudly the walls are probably rattling as he comes into my mouth. His hands are splayed on the counter above me and his knees are bent, on the verge of buckling as he gasps for air. I slowly slide my mouth off him and look up, grinning in victory. "Better?"

He laughs. "But I have no time to return the favor."

"Lucky for you I take rain checks." I stand up as he pulls his hands off the counter and yanks up his sweats. "Hope the ladies enjoy the class as much as I enjoyed that."

"You should come," Chase suggests. "Find out for yourself."

I laugh but he doesn't. "Seriously?"

"I've got an extra suit," Chase offers. "It's a decent workout."

"How would we explain me at an aquafit class full of seniors?"

He shrugs. "I don't know but at least it would give them something to fawn over besides me. It's like having forty grandmothers. They're constantly asking me if I'm eating enough vegetables and if a lady has caught my eye yet."

I laugh. "I should go just to watch that. But I have to get back to the farm. Autumn is annoyed enough as it is, if I don't help with this event, she'll be unbearable."

"Okay." He kisses me and then I finish getting dressed and we head downstairs.

As we wait for the elevator my mind goes back to Bennie finding us in the hallway. "You going to do anything about the Bennie thing?"

Chase frowns slightly. "I guess I should. But how do I handle someone who has feelings I explicitly told him I couldn't, and didn't, have?"

"Well, having been the Bennie in a relationship," I say carefully, because for Trevor that's exactly what I was. I didn't see it at the time, but I had feelings he did not. "I don't think you can fix this. He probably thought that after you two hooked up you'd see things differently."

"I didn't."

"I know. And that sucks for him. There's no way to make that unsuck unless your feelings change," I reply as we step into the elevator.

"That's never going to happen." Chase scrubs his face with his hand. "I guess that friendship is gone forever."

"Maybe. Or at least just for now," I reply and then add a thought I'm not sure I should be sharing. "Are you worried he'll say something? Out you?"

Chase shakes his head quickly and without a second of hesitation. "No. Bennie isn't out either. That's what convinced me we could have a quick, discrete moment."

"Oh."

The elevator opens on the ground floor and we walk down the short, narrow hall to the front door. Outside the air is slightly crisp and the sky is overcast. He looks at the time on his phone screen. "I have to go. Sure you don't want to come to class?"

"I can't, but the thought of you all buff in a bathing suit is tempting," I keep my voice low, almost a whisper, even though the closest person is a stranger walking on the other side of the street.

He shifts his weight and then makes a bit of a face. I tip my head quizzically and he grins. "I had to catch myself there. Wanted to kiss you good-bye."

I smile. "One day, right?"

"Six months, twelve days," Chase replies quickly and winks before turning and making his way down the sidewalk.

It takes everything in me not to stare at his ass until it disappears from sight. Instead, I force myself to walk the other way, back to my own car near the bar. Time to go face my ornery sister.

15

CHASE

I have to admit, they've done a great job. Bowen says the whole thing was planned by Autumn — everything from the color of the candles to the menu to the way the tables are arranged in little clusters around the side yard, overlooking the hemp fields. It's not that I expected this to be a horrible event, it's just that I know their budget is limited and they've struggled compared to Lacey, who has unlimited funds from her wealthy family and their friends who have all contributed to her campaign, including my own parents. They told me flatly when I spoke to them over the phone yesterday that I was expected to donate as well.

I mumbled something about putting it at the top of my To Do list and got off the phone as soon as possible. I have been to two of Lacey's events, including a fundraiser she had last night. It was a fancy dinner with entertainment by members of the string section of the Vermont Symphony and boring as hell. The town's political columnist said as much too, which I'm sure Lacey is fuming about. I haven't called on her to check though. I had assumed I was going as a member of the Chamber of Commerce, just like I'm here as one, but when I got to the event, I found out she'd seated me at her table, as her date. I spent the night listening to her try and woo people with her arm curled around my bicep. Then I texted Bowen, drove to his house, and explained the whole unwanted experience to him. I didn't want him to read about it in the paper or hear about it and think I was keeping it from him. We smoked a joint, fiddled around with his dad's guitars, and got naked. I left the farm as the sun rose and now I'm back here as it sets.

But instead of being upstairs above the garage, sucking on Bowen's perfect dick, I am glancing at one of the many silent auction items set out on long tables that line their front porch. None of the items are all that great. A bunch of gift certificates for free meals and discounts at local restaurants, some movie passes, a couple ski passes for next season, and a weekend getaway to a bed and breakfast in Maine. I bid on that because it says it can be redeemed anytime in the next twelve months. I intend to use it in slightly less than seven months — with my boyfriend, because I'll be able to call him that out loud by then.

"Having a good time?"

Speak of the devil. "Not as good as I had last night."

"At Lacey's event?"

"Oh hell no," I whisper vehemently and he smiles. "Afterward. Up in our sex attic."

He laughs but it's cut short by the appearance of his sister. She's wearing the same lovely sundress she wore to the outgoing mayor's cocktail party. "Autumn, hey. You look beautiful."

"Thanks. You said that last time," she mutters with a polite and fleeting smile. She grabs her brother's arm. "I need your help with something."

"No, you don't," Bowen replies, refusing to move when she tugs him.

"Yes, I do."

"With what?"

She tugs again and when he still doesn't move, she sighs. "Okay, *you* need *my* help to get you to stop conversing with the enemy."

Bowen and I exchange glances. Autumn gives me another smile that is anything but friendly. "I know you're dating Lacey Baldwin so, although you're going to tell me you're here as just a Chamber of Commerce representative, I can't believe you. And neither can my brother. Even if you do make beautiful music together."

Both my eyebrows and Bowen's shoot up at the exact same time.

She means the band, it takes me a minute to realize. She uses that moment of shock to finally get Bowen to move and she drags him off toward the group of people surrounding Woody as he discusses the farm and how they would expand to marijuana production if they could.

I know exactly how zoning marijuana farms in Burlington would work under Woody's mayoral plan, because Bowen told me in detail after band practice the other night. In fact, he told all of us as we drank beers on my roof top, so he's got both Joe and Grant's votes too. So instead of listening to it repeated, I wander over to admire the tulips sprouting on the side of the house. There's also a lilac bush just at the back corner of the house, which I remember smelling that night I came over to talk to Bowen. It's in the last stages of bloom but I walk over to enjoy what's left of the scent and I hear someone laughing. It's a sharp, cruel laugh. One I grew up with. I turn and see Colin walking toward me. "What on earth are you doing here?"

"It's the United States of America, Chase," Colin says acerbically. His blue eyes, a muddier blue than my own, roll. "It means I can travel from one state to another easily. And without telling you about it."

I fight a frown because any sign of annoyance with Colin has always been like waving a red cape in front of a bull. He will keep saying and doing things that upset me if I give him any inkling that he's started to piss me off. So instead, I say nothing. I raise my half empty red wine glass in his general direction. "Well, have fun."

"Were you just sniffing the flowers?" he asks.

I was about to turn away, but I stop and answer him. He'll just follow me if I don't. "Yes. I like lilacs. They remind me of Grandma Bette."

Bette McDaniels was the only member of my family I think about with fondness. She was married to Ned and all the inheritance money actually came from her, not my grandfather. Bette was the only child of a very wealthy real estate developer from New York. She never wanted for anything and despite being able to marry anyone – because she was beautiful and smart and kind – she somehow ended up with Ned. I like to think that Ned changed over time, once he got more and more into politics, and that they had this loving, wonderful marriage, but I don't know for sure. All I do know is that Bette was sweet to me. When we'd stay with her every summer, she let me help her in the kitchen with every meal and when Colin told me to 'be a man' and come outside and play football with him and Granddad, she chastised him and told him I could do whatever I wanted. In fact, doing what I wanted made me more of a man than doing what was expected. She died of ovarian cancer when I was ten, but those words have stuck with me my whole life, even if I haven't exactly followed them. Yet.

"She wore lilac scented perfume, Colin," I add when he's just standing there blinking at me. "Don't you remember. It engulfed you when she gave hugs and stayed on your clothes."

"That's what that smell was?" He walks over and leans a little to sniff the flowers and then promptly wrinkles his nose. "I used to hate that. Smelling like flowers. I guess you like it because of your... other side."

He makes it sound like being bisexual means you're Two-Face from the *Batman* comics. Like my left side likes men and my right side likes women. "Why are you such a Grade A asshole?"

He actually looks upset by that. "Jesus, Chase, why so sensitive? I'm just making light of your mistakes."

"Sexuality isn't a mistake," I hiss out through a clenched jaw and then my eyes fly around the yard to make sure no one was close enough to hear what I said. Thankfully almost everyone is starting to sit at tables and get ready for the dinner part of this night.

"Telling Mom and Dad about it before getting your hands on the cash was," Colin replies and sips his drink. "Also, for the record dude, we all went a little *loco* in college with the sex stuff. But the three-ways are supposed to be boy-girl-girl not boy-boy-girl, *hermano*."

"You spent one semester in Barcelona years ago, stop trying to throw Spanish words into everything you say," I bark. "And fuck off."

I turn to leave but then someone behind the shoulder of Colin's designer suit jacket catches my eye. Bennie Johnson is walking toward us from behind the house. Well, shit. Could this night get any worse? I step around my brother. "Hey Bennie. What are you doing here?"

I know my face, which is blocked from my brother, must reflect the panic I feel at the sight of my ex-drummer-slash-ex-hook-up and the dude who caught me with another dude. Bennie sees it too and he smiles, but it's even less friendly than the one Autumn gave me earlier. "My father thinks this guy might be a good candidate and he donated an auction prize, so he got a ticket to this thing. But then he caught the damn flu and so here I am instead. I'd rather be eating glass."

Colin chuckles at that. I just nod because I am too uncomfortable with this whole situation to do anything else. It feels a little bit like I'm in one of those rooms in horror movies or whatever where all the walls start closing in at the same time, and there's no door to escape. "And you?" Bennie asks casually. "You here to support your new... Musical partner?"

"What?" Colin asks.

"Bowen Whitlock has taken over for Bennie in the band," I explain. I know that Bennie's choice of words and pregnant pause were meant to up my anxiety and I hate that it worked.

"Oh." Colin chuckles and smiles at Bennie. "You finally gave up that stupid hobby, huh? Good for you. It was fine when you guys were in college but now it's kind of weird, or maybe it's sad, I don't know. But grown men with real careers don't need to spend weekends pretending to be Queen."

"We don't cover Queen songs," I tell him through gritted teeth, like it matters. I turn back to Bennie. "What were you doing back there?"

He shrugs. "Looking for the bathroom."

"Isn't it in the house?"

"The chubby Whitlock said something about using the one by the barn or something."

I'm horrified he just said that. "Watch your mouth."

Bennie levels me with a hard, icy cold stare. "You don't think I'm watching what I say? Because if you think this isn't being careful..."

"Don't comment on a woman, or anyone, like that ever again. It only shows the world how truly lacking you are of character," I snap, and Bennie looks shocked, and then furious. I step right up into his face, so close I know he can feel my breath when I exhale sharply. "And you can say whatever the fuck you want, Bennie. I'm not so scared of the truth that I'm going to keep my mouth shut when you're a cruel asshole to someone who doesn't deserve it."

"Oh shit, do you have the hots for Whitlock's sister?" Colin asks, completely missing the subtext of this. It's like a jumbo jet, but somehow it soars right over his head unnoticed.

"Hey gentleman," I hear Woody's voice and immediately turn to face him. "We're about to sit down to some awesome food, courtesy of Vino and Veritas, if you'd like to join us. Simple but good stuff, all with local ingredients."

"Sounds great," I say and turn away from both Colin and Bennie.

The faintest look of relief passes over Woody's face. I'm fairly certain he doesn't know exactly what was going on, but he's clued in that it wasn't good. "Unfortunately, there aren't any seats left at the same table, so I hope you all don't mind sitting at different ones."

"There is nothing unfortunate about different tables," I say with a smile I hope looks more relaxed than I feel. Bennie marches past me and sits down in the closest empty seat. I notice there isn't an available seat at Bowen's table, which makes me relieved. I shouldn't sit with him, it would only annoy Bennie even further, and I definitely don't want my brother sitting with him.

I claim a seat at a table as far from Bowen's as possible, but still facing his table so I can steal glances. He looks as comfortable as a trout in a tuxedo and I love that about him. He's not all about this stuffy, formal, political bullshit and neither am I. I just pretend better than he does.

The rest of the night is uneventful, thankfully Bennie left right after the food and Colin right after the auction winners were announced. He won the ski passes. I won the weekend at the bed and breakfast. As I'm driving home, I realize I never did get a straight answer as to why Colin was there, so I call him. He picks up but there's a shit ton of noise in the background. He must be at a bar.

"Hey. What?"

"You never told me why you were at a political fundraiser in Vermont when you live in Rhode Island," I find myself shouting in my car.

His laugh comes out of the hands-free speaker. "Chase Ashton, you're a nosey little fuck. I'm in town for a meeting with Iris regarding my investments. Gotta free up some cash for my election run."

"Oh. Okay," I say lamely. "Well, still doesn't explain why you were at a political fundraiser."

"A mutual friend asked me to check it out," Colin says vaguely but obviously he's talking about Lacey. "The bigger question is why were you there when you're dating the opponent?"

"I'm not dating Lacey."

"That's not what people think," Colin counters. "And that's not what Dad thinks. He told me that you were spending a lot of time with her lately."

"I was. Friends spend time together, Colin. Do you not have any, so you don't know that?" I'm being exceptionally bitchy but I don't care. "And I was helping her. Sort of. But I'm an undecided voter and a member of the Chamber of Commerce so I attend all political events."

"Whatever. I don't care. Want to join me for a night cap? I'm at the Biscuit in the Basket," he explains. "The college hockey team just won and the place is packed with happy, horny college girls."

"You're thirty."

"And rich and good looking," Colin adds with a chuckle. "And I don't look a day over twenty-six, according to History major Brittany and her friend Environmental Biology major Chelsea. Night, little bro."

He ends the call and I growl in annoyance. I don't expect to hear from him again, so when my text message pings four consecutive times as I'm getting ready for bed, and all the messages are from him, I'm surprised. The more I read the further my heart sinks.

Colin: *Reported back to Lacey about the Whitlock fundraiser.*
Colin: *She said her own event was a bust. No one liked the music.*
Colin: *I volunteered your band for her next one.*
Colin: *See? I support your lame ass hobbies. Aren't I a good bro?*

What the fuck? Imposter Syndrome can't perform at Lacey's fundraiser. At least not with Bowen on drums. I'm so pissed, but there's nothing I can do about it at this hour. And now I'm too worked up to sleep. So, I head back down to the living room, grab a guitar and my song journal, and play.

I don't want to play at Lacey's next fundraiser. I'm sure the pay will be stellar but I know it would hurt Bowen. That idea more than anything feels unbearable. I think of him and how well he seems to handle everything, except maybe working at Vino and Veritas. I know if I tell him, he'll encourage us to do it, and he'll easily step aside but I don't want to perform without him. I don't want to do anything without him. That realization is both scary and exciting.

BOWEN

I'm the last to show up at Chase's place. I'm not late but nearly. And I have to be dropped off by my sister, like a toddler going on a field trip, because we share a car and I can't just abscond with it for over twenty-four hours. I jump out of the passenger seat almost before she's come to a stop at the curb. Grant, Joe and Chase all turn to greet me. "Sorry. Had to help with some farm stuff before I left. Hard to ask for a weekend off when we're gearing up to seed soon."

"It's not a whole weekend," Grant argues. "We'll be back by noon tomorrow."

"It just made more sense to spend the night," Chase adds.

I nod. I know. It does make sense. The drive to Old Orchard Beach, Maine, is almost four hours. The wedding will likely go late into the night and driving home after midnight and a long gig is stupid. Besides, secretly, I'm excited to spend a night away with Chase, even if it's not technically for romantic reasons. As I'm reaching back in to grab my overnight bag off the back seat, Autumn lowers the passenger window and cranes herself toward it. "Hi boys! You all have fun!"

They all wave and nod. "Bye Autumn."

"Bye Bowen. Love you. Hope you packed your toothbrush. Stay safe and make good choices!" she bellows like a helicopter parent and it gets the effect she wanted, the guys all snicker.

"Love you too but bite me. And drive safe!"

She laughs as she pulls away from the curb. Grant grins. "I have a sister too, Bo. I get it."

"I wish I got it," Chase adds. "My family dynamic is not nearly so amusing."

"We should hit the road," Joe interjects, checking the time on his phone. "We've already loaded the equipment into the van I borrowed from my cousin. Grant will ride with me and we'll follow Chase who will take Bowen."

"Sounds good," Chase replies casually.

"Wait. Why does Bowen get to ride with Chase?" Grant wants to know.

"Because he's the new guy and I'm not ready to subject him to Joe's shitty road trip music," Chase replies. "We can't lose another drummer."

I smirk but Grant's eyes narrow on Chase. "What car are you taking?"

I didn't realize Chase had options when it came to transportation but clearly, he does. Chase doesn't respond to his friend with words, he just smiles very slowly. Grant swears. "Ah come on! I want to ride home with you!"

Chase doesn't bother to respond again and instead clamps a friendly hand on my shoulder and pushes me toward the alley that leads to the back of his building. "Come on, quick. Before Grant tries bribing you for your spot."

"I'll give you half my gig money!" Grant calls out.

But I'm too stunned to answer. My eyes have landed on the car they're arguing over. I'm not exactly sure what it is, because I'm not a car guy but it's old, in mint condition, and gorgeous.

"1969 Ferrari Dino 246 GT," Chase tells me.

"I have no idea what that is, but I'm impressed anyway," I reply as my eyes slide over the low, sleek lines of the low, glossy cherry red car.

"It's a classic car, ridiculously expensive, and totally impractical for New England," Chase explains. "My grandfather gave it to me for college graduation. My brother got a 1964 Maserati Gihbli which is equally as pompous and ridiculous."

I look up and smile at him. "But you love it."

"My Ferrari? Yeah. I fucking do." He grins, his eyes somehow lightening in color and his cheeks blushing sheepishly. "But not Colin's car. That thing just looks like an older version of a Mazda Miata. A bathtub with wheels. This… My Patrizia, she's a beauty."

"You name your cars?" I ask as he opens the trunk for me to put my bag in, next to his which is already there. Then he walks around to unlock my door as he nods.

"Yeah. Always have."

"Me too," I reply and get into the car. It's a bit of a tight squeeze lowering myself into it but it's spacious enough once I'm seated. And way more comfortable than it appears. I reach over and unlock his door and he climbs in too. "My parents used to do it, so I guess I do it because it feels like tradition."

"What's the name of the car you and Autumn share?"

"Clark," I reply and open my mouth to explain but Chase's face lights up.

"Because it's the same car they have in *National Lampoon's Vacation!*"

I nod and he laughs as he puts the key in the ignition and the engine roars to life with a purr. "You hold onto that thing long enough and it'll be a classic too."

"Good to know, because we don't have the money to get rid of it." I want to smile but can't quite make my mouth do it. "Anyway, let's hit the road."

Chase nods and reverses. The first little bit of the drive is mostly silent. He tells me to find a radio station I like, so I do. He passes the van with Grant and Joe and leads us onto the freeway heading toward Maine. We talk about the scenery, and I tell him about my latest disaster at work. I tripped carrying two glasses of red wine and spilled them. Luckily it was just all over me and not a customer.

"My shirt was black so I tried to just suck it up and keep wearing it, because you couldn't really see the stains, but do you know how sticky wine is?" I ask as the pine trees and rocky hills blur by outside. "And the only person who had an extra shirt was Murph."

Chase laughs loudly. "Oh my God, he's half your size."

"Yep," I tip my head back and squeeze my eyes shut at the memory of the one glance I dared to take in the bathroom mirror. "It was so tight I could barely breathe. And short. My bellybutton was exposed for the world to see. And it was pale pink with a unicorn on the front."

"Tanner must have been thrilled with your look," Chase says through his belly laugh.

"Harrison was more horrified than Tanner," I mutter but I'm chuckling a little too. "Tanner joked we should make it the new uniform."

"I'd have bought an extra couple of glasses of wine with that as my entertainment," Chase says as he shifts gears. The interstate is busy and there's a lot of slowing down and speeding up as he maneuvers through traffic. My eyes slide to him at the same time his slide to mine. "Put your hand on the gear shift."

I cock an eyebrow and quirk my lip. He grins. "I said *the* gear shift not *my* gear shift."

I lift my hand from my lap and drop it on the gearshift.

He drops his hand on top of mine. It's warm and solid, and comforting. "It's as close as I can get to holding your hand in a manual car."

A Pearl Jam song comes on the radio so we both spend the next few minutes harmonizing with Eddie Vedder. Then we go back to talking — about everything. Unimportant stuff like his favorite food, Italian, to my favorite TV show, anything on Discovery Plus but especially the scary shows about paranormal activity which for some reason floors Chase. And then we talk about not-so-unimportant stuff like his family and how he feels so unattached to every single one of them, and my family and how my siblings are as vital as limbs to me. When I see the sign saying we've entered Maine, I'm shocked.

"I'm not a huge fan of car trips. Never have been, even when we were kids and the trip would end at Disney World or a beach or whatever, I still hated them," I tell Chase, studying his rugged profile as he drives. He's got shades on now because the sun is shining brightly, so I can't admire his baby blues, but I drink in the sexy stubble on his strong jaw and the way his perfect mouth is curled ever so slightly upward in a content smile. Because he's as happy to be with me as I am with him. "But this road trip is going to end sooner that I want it to."

"I could pretend to get lost," Chase suggests and his eyebrows wiggle. "Find a secluded back road somewhere and…"

He doesn't have to finish the sentence. I know what he's insinuating. My dick is growing in my pants at the thought. I readjust it with the hand not still on the gearshift. "In this tiny car it might cause one of us permanent injuries. I think getting to the motel as fast as possible, so we can make sure we get rooms as close to each other as possible, is a better idea. Because I'm totally sneaking into your room tonight Ashton and I don't want a long walk."

He grins and moves his hand off mine, reaching for his phone which is wedged under the parking brake between us. "Then you better map the exact location of the motel so we can get there already. Password is 1,2,3,4."

"Original." I chuckle and unlock his phone. I'm about to pull up Google Maps when it starts ringing and his brother's name appears on the screen. "Umm…"

I turn it for him to see. He curses under his breath. "Hit ignore. No. Wait. If I do that, he'll just keep calling. Colin is a bit of a bitch that way. Hit answer and speaker."

I do both and his brother's voice fills the car. "Why haven't you called Lacey?"

"Afternoon, bro. How are you?" Chase snarks.

"Hey. Hi. Yeah, I'd be peachy if you would call Lacey and confirm."

"I can't do that right now. I'm driving." Chase's voice right now is nothing like I've heard before. It's clipped and hard and as cold as a Nor'easter. "And I can't talk to you either. I'm in the Ferrari. No hands-free. I'll call you back when I stop."

"Don't," Colin says, his voice very similar in tone to Chase's voice. "Just call Lacey and tell her your stupid band will do her event. I told Dad you were doing this for her and he was actually pleased with you for once."

Chase doesn't respond. He also doesn't look at me. I'm biting my bottom lip to keep from blurting out "oh hell no!" His brother knowing I'm in the car with Chase won't make this conversation go any smoother. Finally, Chase sighs. "I haven't asked the band if they're available. You know Grant and Joe have lives and jobs too.

And also, obviously, there's no way I would ask Bowen to do this. You should have thought of that."

"I did," Chase replies. "I just didn't care. Get Bennie to do it instead. He's voting for her. He won't mind."

"Colin, I am not just going to —"

"He hung up," I finally speak when I see his screen go dark. Chase shoves his sunglasses up into his hair and glances over at me. His expression is a mask of guilt. "I was going to tell you. I just was trying to figure out when. And I haven't told the other guys yet. I wouldn't do that without asking you first."

"Asking me what?"

"Do you mind if we do it? I know Colin made it sound like I can't say no, but I can," Chase says and pulls his sunglasses from his hair and hooks them into the neck of his shirt, and then he glances at me again still looking contrite. "My dad isn't going to deny me three and a half million dollars over this. Hell, he hates that I'm in a band and would probably be happier if none of his political friends find out."

"I'm sure she'll pay you well," I reply after a couple seconds of looking out the window trying to figure out how I feel about this. I don't like how I found out but he's genuinely upset about that. And I definitely can't play with them, but as the newbie in the group I also don't feel comfortable telling them they can't.

"I don't need the money."

"But Joe might," I remind him. "And I doubt Grant would turn down extra cash."

"But I don't want to play with Bennie again," Chase confesses. "I don't even want to see him again. He's not exactly being mature about this."

"I noticed," I reply. "At my brother's event he was more than a little unpleasant. When my brother thanked him for coming, he said he wouldn't have if his father didn't make him and stormed off. He also glared at me so much during the dinner part that Autumn asked me if I dropped something on him at V and V."

Chase tries not to smile at that but fails. It's fleeting though as he starts frowning a couple seconds later. "Sorry about that."

"You didn't make me kiss you and grope you in that hallway," I reply and put my hand over his on the gearshift, giving it a gentle squeeze. "I wanted to do it and I don't regret it. And I'll do it again."

"I hope so," Chase says quickly. "But still, I won't do this gig if you don't want me to."

"I don't care if you take it. Honestly," I tell him and push my hair back. "Seriously she can have your band and be your date to shit. I just don't want her to get your vote."

"She doesn't have my vote. Your brother does, I swear." He reaches over and grabs my hand and pulls it to his lap, pressing my palm into his hardening cock. "And she definitely does not have this. This is all yours."

I am grinning like a lunatic. "Good. Now as much as it pains me to say this, give me my hand back so I can get us to the motel."

He lets go and I regretfully lift my hand from his crotch. Half an hour later we're parked in front of a short, squat ocean front motel that looks like it hasn't had a lick of work done to it since it was constructed in the mid-seventies. We get out of the Ferrari and Grant turns to us. "Seriously? This place looks…. Like it isn't a five star."

"We're a cover band, not The Rolling Stones," Joe tells him squinting his dark eyes to look up at the building. "It got great reviews on the booking site and it's literally two buildings over from the hotel the reception is in."

He points to the wood and brick high-rise that looks infinitely newer and fancier than the place we're about to check into. "And before you say anything this place is eighty a night and the other one is two-twenty and only had two available rooms. We're not bunking up like this is sleep away camp. You snore, Grant."

Grant is about to argue when Chase adds, "And you fart in your sleep. Loudly. You used to wake me from a dead sleep in boarding school with those freaking fog horn sounds."

"Only when they had Taco Tuesdays in the cafeteria, shithead," Grant mutters and I think he says something else, but Joe and I are laughing so hard I don't hear it.

We check in and they give us two rooms side-by-side on the third floor and two side-by-side on the second. Chase grabs all the key cards and hands them out casually, like he isn't making sure I'm the one next to him, but that's exactly what he does. We both have the top floor rooms. Joe and Grant are beside each other one floor down on the other end of the building. This couldn't be more perfect.

"So, we've got about an hour before we should head to the venue and set up," Grants says. "Let's get comfy and meet back here in forty-five?"

We all nod and head to our rooms. I unlock mine and start to step inside, but Chase passes me to get to his room, grabs me by the arm and drags me with him. "Shouldn't I at least put my stuff in my room. To make it look like I'm staying there?"

"Nah." He taps his keycard on the lock panel and the green light flashes, so he pushes the door open. "They both know I've been with dudes before and although they probably don't want me to hook up with you because of the band dynamic, they aren't exactly going to do a room check or anything."

"They know?"

"Joe was my college roommate," he reminds me. "That's when I started messing around with guys and so sometimes, while he waited in the study lounge for the sock to come off the door handle, he'd see who left. And Grant, well I told him because he lives below me and we work together and he's my oldest friend. I trust both of them with my life. They're not going to tell anyone."

"But you don't think they'd be cool with us?" I ask as I follow him into the room.

"No," Chase answers flatly as he pauses to pull back the curtains on the large window at the front of the tiny, but clean room. There's nothing but beach and ocean stretched out before us. It's honestly pretty fucking great. I walk up behind him to admire the view. "Not because they don't like you, but because they know me. I've refused to do anything more than a one-night stand before. And, well, Grant knows that fooling around with Bennie is what had him bail on the band."

"Ah. I get it," I say as Chase turns away from the view to look at me. "But if they knew this wasn't just a one-time deal, and that I'm not going to throw a tantrum and leave the band, would they be cool with it?"

"Yeah. I think they would," Chase replies. "We'll find out in six months, two days and…. Roughly five hours."

He leans close and drops a slow, easy kiss on me. I snake my arms around his waist. I can't wait for Chase's birthday. I push my hips against his but he moves back. "Sadly, we don't have time for any really fun stuff. I wanted to run the set list with you again."

"Argh," I let out a garbled groan of sexual frustration. "I hate being responsible."

He laughs and pushes me back until I've dropped into a small shockingly cozy chair by the window and then he pulls a crumpled piece of paper from his back pocket. He starts reciting our songs. We are doing a lot of stuff we haven't done live together, but they've done with Bennie. I'm confident I can pull it off, and did well with all of them in our rehearsals, but I think they're all still a little nervous.

"I feel like we need another slow tune," Chase scratches his chin and his eyebrows pinch as he thinks about it. I look out the window and something pops into my brain.

"That notebook of yours had lyrics in it about an ocean." I turn to look at him. "Something about the audacity of oceans or something. I remember it sounded cool."

"It's called Dauntless," Chase replies.

"Like your business?"

"Told you it was my favorite word. The song came first. When I was in college." Chase looks wildly uncomfortable suddenly. He's bouncing his weight from one foot to the other. He starts pacing. Five steps toward the door, five back, and repeat.

"It's about the man I want to be. That I intend to be. One day," Chase says in a voice that's a pained, whispered confession. He clears his throat and stops pacing. "I feel like the ocean is dauntless. Like it's scared of nothing and if it's determined to claim something — a ship, a beach, a person, whatever — it does it. Boldly and without regret. So I use it as a metaphor in the song. Anyway, why are we talking about this?"

He is so agitated discussing his music that when he starts pacing again, I almost think he's going to go more than five steps and open the door and head right out without another word. But he doesn't, he pivots back toward me after that fifth step. I pull myself out of the chair. "It's a slow song, right? I could tell by the chords you jotted down next to the lyrics."

"You're a nosey fucker with a photographic memory, huh?" Chase laments but he seems more awed than mad.

"Yeah. Kinda." I give him a gentle smile and reach out and grab his hand not currently death-gripping the set list. "You could always perform that. Acoustically. I'm sure you've done it a hundred times if it's the first song you ever wrote."

"Yeah. Alone. Never in front of an audience." Okay now his agitation seems to have exploded into full-blown anxiety judging by how wide his eyes are.

"Just an idea," I comment casually and squeeze his hand reassuringly. "I mean eventually when you go back to school, you'll have to perform your own stuff so I just thought, this might be a good opportunity to test it out. The bride and groom probably won't even notice. And if they do notice it'll be because they love it."

"I don't know."

"Okay. No biggie. You don't have to do it. I honestly think we're good with the songs we have," I tell him and it's not a lie. We've got a lot of material.

"You really think I could pull it off? In front of people."

"I know it."

And then I kiss him, hoping I can quell his fears that way. We make-out standing there in the middle of the room for so long that there isn't time for any more conversation. We have to rush downstairs and meet Joe and Grant.

The gig goes without a hitch. We play three sets, which are interspersed with DJ sets. Halfway through the last set when we're supposed to do "Heaven" by Bryan Adams, Chase turns his back to the dance floor and his eyes lock with mine and I know. I stand up from the drum kit. "Guys, he's gonna do an acoustic number. Let's take a minute."

Joe and Grant look slightly confused but put down their instruments and follow me to the back corner of the stage as Chase says. "Let's try something new here. Since we've got this amazing ocean front location, I thought you might enjoy a song I wrote inspired by the ocean. So grab someone you love and hit the dance floor for this one."

The song, in its entirety, is simply amazing. Chase's voice is strong, the lyrics are beautiful, and the melody brings almost every single guest onto the dance floor. The people without partners are swaying in their seats or on the side of the dance floor and I swear they clap louder for his original tune than they have for any of our covers.

He doesn't react though when it's over. He just motions for us to come back. As I sit down and pull my sticks out of my back pocket, I'm more than ready for this night to be over so I can get back into that motel room and show him exactly how incredible I think he is.

17

CHASE

I'm nothing but adrenaline and lust when we get back to the motel. All I want to do is grab Bowen and lock us away in my room, but of course I can't. Joe and Grant want some celebratory beers so we all gather in Grant's room, on his balcony facing the ocean, and sit and toast a great night.

"I've never heard the whole song you sung tonight," Joe says. "I've only heard bits of it over the years. I wasn't even sure you had a whole song."

"I've never played it in its entirety for anyone until tonight," I admit. "Bowen thought it was time and he was right."

"He was," Grant adds and smiles at Bowen, clinking the tops of their beer bottles together. "You've got a magic touch, Bo. He's been refusing to play his originals in public for almost a decade."

Bowen shrugs and his eyes meet mine as he lifts his beer bottle to his lips and takes a slow pull from the bottle. I grin because I've never felt like this before and I'm pretty sure it isn't just because I bared my soul on that stage when I performed that song for the first time. It's because I'd already bared my soul to him. "He does have a magic touch. You should give up bartending and become a therapist."

Bowen laughs. Joe puts down his empty beer. "Speaking of therapy, you know what would really help me sleep right now?"

Bowen's grin deepens and he pulls his cigarette pack that doesn't contain cigarettes from his pocket and tosses it at Joe. "Be my guest."

143

"Thanks man." Joe promptly lights up one of the joints, tosses the box back to Bowen and after a long drag, passes the joint to Grant.

After a good long inhale, Grant passes the joint to me but I shake my head. "I'm actually not ready for sleep. I want to enjoy the moment a little more."

I also don't want to be too buzzed when I'm alone with Bowen tonight. I want to feel everything and forget nothing. I blink, because I know my gaze is getting heated, and stand up, finishing what's left of my beer in one big gulp. "I'm gonna head to my room, and maybe fuck around on the guitar a little. I'm wired."

Joe smiles, shaking his head. "Creative bug stronger than ever, huh? Good for you, Chase. I can't wait until you're a zillionaire and can do this full-time."

"Yeah, me too," I reply and leave my bottle on the small table. "See you all in the morning for the trip home."

"Hold up," Bowen says casually. "I'll walk upstairs with ya. I am dying to take a long shower and catch some Zs. Unlike the rest of you I have to work when we get home tomorrow afternoon. My brother and I have to install a new watering system for the fields."

"Party-poopers!" Grant calls behind us as Bowen follows me out the door.

We don't speak or touch until we're on our floor. He leans on his door next to mine as I swipe my keycard and push it open. And then I leave it open for him to walk through behind me. I don't turn on the lights, I just open the curtains so the moonlight bouncing off the roaring ocean can fill the room. I hear the door click shut and then feel his hands snaking their way around my waist. And when his lips ghost over my neck, I shudder in relief. "Fuck I have been thinking of this all night."

I turn in his arms and he kisses me. It's aggressive and dominating and I am fucking here for it. Our tongues slide across each other and I fist his hair and he grabs the hem of my T-shirt and yanks it up. Our kiss breaks. "Too many fucking clothes."

He growls those words and I feel it in my balls. I don't think I've ever been this turned on. But I think that every time Bowen and I are together. I'm going to have a really hard time not telling the world how I feel about him for another six stupid months. My shirt is suddenly up over my head, and he reaches behind his back and yanks his own up and over his head while my hands make quick work of his battered old brown leather belt. I get it undone as he toes out of his brown boots, which I've noticed he hardly ever ties up properly. I unzip his pants and he runs a hand over my hair and then down my back. "You really were amazing tonight. That song is fucking gorgeous. Like you."

"I'm glad you like it so much," I whisper as my lips graze across his and then I press them to his ear. "It's about the man I want to be… that I will be one day."

"I hate to break it to you, but it's kinda who you already are," Bowen murmurs, his head tipped back as I suck on his neck like a starving vampire. "At least it's how I see you."

"I…" *love you.*

His head tilts back as he searches out my face, because I've stopped sucking, and stopped kissing, and stopping breathing. I was honestly about to say that out loud. And that's fucking terrifying. Because I can't say that to a guy I can't even hold hands with in public. At least I don't want to. Not like this. Not now. "You… what?"

"I want to be naked." I make my thoughts do a complete one-eighty from the emotional to the primal. It's actually not that hard. "On that bed. With you."

The lazy, easy smile that tugs up the corners of his mouth is hot as fuck. "You don't have to ask me twice."

He pops the button on his pants and then it's only another couple of seconds until I get exactly what I want. We're both on the bed, naked. We're kissing and Bowen reaches down and hooks my leg behind the knee and pulls it up over his hip. We grind together like that with my hand on our cocks between us, rubbing them together, creating a blissful friction.

"I want you to fuck me. If you want it."

Bowen's words are soft and tangled up in our kisses, so it takes a minute for their meaning to hit me. When it does, my eyes slowly open, and I pull my mouth away from his. His eyes flutter open, the moonlight making the amber flecks glimmer a little. "I know you said that you don't want to be fucked yet, but this is different. You'd be doing the fucking. I mean, I haven't bottomed in a while, actually in years but… I'm babbling and killing the mood, aren't I?"

"No. You're not," I promise him and plant a quick, soft kiss on his lips. "I'm just processing."

"Forget I asked. I'm not trying to pressure you." He leans in and kisses me again, and I let it happen for a second, but before he can slip his tongue back into my mouth, I pull away again.

"I want you."

"I know, I got the memo." He reaches down and wraps his hand around my hand that's holding our dicks. I smile. He smiles. "But do you want to fuck me?"

"More than anything," I reply, and my voice is calmer and steadier than I thought it would be given that my heart is pounding so hard against my rib cage I'm sure he can feel it.

He kisses me again, fiercely, before letting go of me and moving off the bed. He grabs his overnight bag and unzips it and digs around. He walks back over to the bed and puts a small bottle of lube and a roll of three condoms on the night table. Then he climbs back onto the bed and on top of me. His weight presses into me as his lips capture mine and his tongue sweeps into my mouth. We make out and grind against each other a little longer, and then he stretches out one of his arms and grabs the lube. His lips kiss a trail over my jaw to my lips. "Use your fingers on me. Fuck me with them like I did to you," he whispers. "Use this too."

He uses his thumb to pop the top as I hold out my hand and he squeezes some lube onto it. I rub it around my index and middle finger as I move my hand between his ass cheeks. I kiss him hard and deep as I push the tip of my index into him, breaking that first ring of muscle. I've only ever done this to myself, so I set a pace I know I like and go with that. After stroking in and out of him with one finger, up to the second knuckle, I add another, starting slow again and then going deeper until I'm moving both of them in and out of him at a hearty pace. I must be doing a good job of brushing his prostate because he's writhing and groaning into my mouth. Pushing back against my hand he orders, "Grab a condom." He rolls off me as I grab the condom and slide it over my dick. I am so excited even the feel of my own hands and the latex makes my cock tremble. Bowen is on his back beside me, watching me. "Remember, this was just a suggestion. If you don't —"

"I want to fuck you."

He smiles and I kiss him. I'm not lying, I want this, but that doesn't mean I'm not a little bit nervous. I've never done this before. Penetration. With a man. I just don't want to suck at it. I know I don't suck with women. I've never gotten a bad review, but I mean… this is Bowen, so it matters more than it ever has before, with anyone.

He pulls his legs apart and my hips slip between them. "It might be easier if I turn around."

"I want to kiss you and see you," I reply, almost sheepishly.

He cups the back of my head and brings our mouths together again. "I was hoping you'd say that."

He's still holding the lube so when I lean back on my knees between his legs, he sits up and coats the condom with it. After he takes a minute to suck on my right nipple and then my left, he falls back onto the bed, taking me with him. His lips brush my chin, and he moves his legs, wide, bending the knees and lifting them up. I grip my cock and slide it across his balls and lower, between his cheeks. My heart is running some kind of Olympic sprint. It feels like one beat doesn't have time to end before another starts.

I rub the lube covered condom over his hole and then, just as he impatiently whispers, "Chase" I push into him, just a little. Just half of the tip.

He inhales sharply and pulls his knees closer to his chest. "Remember, it's been a while. Slow and steady."

I nod and push a little more. This is…. Not at all what I expected. It's tighter, warmer, and much more intense. I feel a rush of heat pulse though me and push some more. Bowen groans and I freeze. "Good groan. So, fucking good."

I push. And push. And holy fuck, my dick is buried from tip to balls inside Bowen and my entire body trembles with pleasure. "Don't stop, Chase. Fuck me. Come on."

"This is going to be embarrassingly short," I whisper through gritted teeth as I pull back a little and move forward again.

His dick jerks between us and he wraps one of his big hands around it and tugs. "You're telling me," he lets out on a pant.

His mouth is open and his head is tipped back and I hook one of his knees and pull his leg up to my shoulder while the other one stays bent at my side and I pump in and out of him at an erratic, unsteady pace, fighting the urge to come with every movement. "Are you good? Is it good?"

"So fucking good," he moans and reaches up and cups the side of my face. I turn my head to kiss his palm and he groans as my hips swivel and slam into him. "Oh. God. Yes."

He strokes himself harder and then, just when I realize I'm definitely about to lose this fight and come like I've never come before, his hand is behind my neck pulling me down until I'm flat on top of him. Our lips meet and the kiss turns into a series of expletives as I pull out and snap back in. "Oh God this is better. How did it get better? Again. I'm gonna…"

I don't answer him because damned if I know. Then I feel his release hit my stomach and chest as he comes. I pull back until I'm almost completely free of his hole and then push back into him hard and fast. He swears and his whole body shakes and after another two pumps, I explode. I yell out something even I can't understand and my head snaps back and he cranes his head up and nips my chin then kisses and sucks on my neck.

I swear I've never come like that — so long and so hard — and when I'm done, I can't think straight or hold myself up and I collapse onto him. Now we're both covered in his release and I couldn't care less. This is perfection. He is perfection. I feel like I am still lost in post-orgasmic bliss, but I manage to gingerly grab the base of the condom and slide out of him. Then I roll out of the bed and make my way to the bathroom. I clean up and bring a fresh damp wash cloth to the bedroom and wipe him down.

"Thank you. Now get back here and enjoy the aftermath," Bowen says, grabbing my wrist and refusing to let go. I drop the washcloth on the floor beside the bed and lie down beside him. I bury my face in the side of his neck as he slowly reaches out and grabs my hand, pulling it up and bringing it to rest, palm down, on the center of his chest. I can feel his heart thumping as wildly as my own and that makes me feel euphoric.

"I bet you wish you hadn't waited so long," Bowen mumbles, sleep already grabbing hold of him.

"Nope. I'm glad I waited." I feel his breath hitch and I know he just opened his eyes even though I can't see it. I'm still buried in the side of his neck. "Doubt it would have been this good with someone else."

He doesn't respond. He just drops his hand over mine on his chest.

CHASE

I was hoping to be awoken by the feel of Bowen's lips on some part of my body, preferably in the lower region, but that's not what happens. I'm woken up by someone knocking on my motel door. Loudly.

"Chase! We said nine!" Grant's voice filters into the room.

I jump up and hunt, blurry-eyed, for my underwear. Bowen sits up slowly, running a hand through his hair and yawning. I find my underwear and yank it on. Bowen stretches like a fucking cat coming out of a coma. Not a care in the world. And then he's about to speak, so I leap closer to the bed and clamp a hand over his mouth. Now he's awake, judging by the size of his eyeballs as he stares at me, blinking.

"Shh!" I whisper, swiveling my head toward the door. "I'm awake. Be down in five!"

"Do you know where Bowen is?" Grant calls out. "Joe said he wasn't answering his door."

"No," I bark back. "Maybe coffee run or something."

"Okay…" Grant says, barely audibly.

Bowen points. We left the curtains to the massive window open last night. It faces the ocean but also the front door and the open hallway Grant is standing in. I let go of Bowen's mouth and bolt across the room, hurdling over his bag and my guitar and I see Grant's hair and a flash of forehead. The nosey asshole was going to peer in the window. I manage to yank the curtain closed before he gets the chance to see anything important — namely Bowen naked in my bed.

"I said I'll be down in five," I bellow, annoyed. "Stop trying to peep on me, perve."

I hear muffled laughter and then Grant yells, "Fine! Meet you downstairs."

I exhale loudly and turn back to Bowen. He's gotten out of bed and is hunting down his own clothing. He looks fucking gorgeous doing it. His blond hair is messy, his sculpted frame and perfect ass are on full display. The ass that felt so incredible around my cock.

"Sorry. I kind of forgot for a minute that we can't... that this is secret," Bowen mutters and pulls on his underwear.

"No worries. I don't think he saw anything," I reply.

"I thought you said Grant and Joe know," Bowen replies and pulls on his T-shirt. Then he grabs his overnight bag and walks into the bathroom, so I follow.

"They know." I nod and watch him pull a toothbrush out of his bag and pull off the little plastic travel holder around the bristles. "I mean, that I'm bi. Yeah. But they don't know that you and I have been involved. And they can't."

He grabs my toothpaste and puts a dollop on his brush. I figure maybe I should do the same, so I grab my toothbrush and take the toothpaste from him. We brush in silence, shoulder-to-shoulder, our eyes locked on each other in the mirror. Bowen spits first.

"You don't trust them with your secrets?"

I spit and rinse my brush. "If you were a one-nighter, they could know."

"If I was a one-nighter, they wouldn't need to know."

He seems... annoyed. Bowen has never shown any real big emotions around me, so maybe I'm reading this wrong, but he definitely isn't as easy going and chill as he usually is. So my brain scrambles to find the right words through my sex hangover. "I trust them, but I promised myself I wouldn't have anything serious before the whole inheritance thing was done for a reason. Because I didn't want to put other people in the position to cover for me. Obviously, that's changed a little. I mean you'll have to cover for me. But I don't want them to have to lie or watch their words around my family or anything. I know Joe and Grant would feel horrible if they said something to someone by mistake and it got back to my brother or some-thing. They're both friendly with my brother and Joe's wife is in some play date kid's group with Amy, my cousin."

I'm rambling, I think, and judging by the unchanged look on Bowen's face, it's not helping. He just nods and then takes his tooth-brush, shoves it back in his bag, and starts peeling back out of the clothes he put on. "Okay well, I'm going to take a quick shower. You can head down and tell them you couldn't find me. I'll come down a couple minutes later and tell them I was in the shower, which is why I didn't hear anyone knocking on my door."

"Good plan." I walk back out into the main room and start grab-bing clean clothes out of my bag to pull on. I hear the shower turn on.

I glance up and through the open bathroom door just in time to see Bowen slip behind the shower curtain. His dick is at half-mast. I feel like there's something wrong. An unpleasantness hanging between us, and this is not at all how I wanted the morning after to go. I curse to myself and grab my phone off the night stand and text Grant.

Chase: *Gonna be longer than 5. Need a shower. Sorry.*

He texts me back immediately.

Grant: *Figured. We're already at the diner across the street. Show up in time to pay ok? Because this is on you.*

I shake my head, smiling, toss my phone on the bed and walk back into the bathroom where I strip naked and pull back the curtain just enough to poke my head in. Bowen looks at me over his broad shoulder. There're water droplets peppering his skin. "This sucks. I suck. I'm sorry and I want to make it up to you."

"Sorry for what?" He turns right around so the spray is at his back, and I can't stop my eyes from taking a long slow look at all of him.

"Sorry I couldn't tell Grant you were in here with me," I reply, my voice getting huskier with every word. "Sorry I can't tell him or Joe or the dude at the front desk when we check out that you let me fuck your brains out last night and it was the best experience of my life."

That gets me a smile. A real, lazy but authentic Bowen Whitlock grin. "I'm not sure the front desk dude would be all that impressed."

"He should be," I say and then ask. "Can I join you?"

"What about the plan?"

"I have a new one. Sent Joe and Grant for breakfast across the street," I explain, and my eyes drop to his hand which is covered in soap and tugging slowly on his now fully erect cock. "Said I needed a shower."

"Then you should get in here and shower," Bowen replies.

"Can I suck your dick first?" I ask as soon as my feet land on the slick porcelain bottom of the tub.

Bowen laughs and reaches for me, pulling me into a kiss, which I take as a yes and when it breaks, I lower myself to my knees.

It costs me twenty-two bucks to pay for Grant and Joe's breakfast plus an extra twenty to bribe Grant into riding with Joe again, instead of switching with Bowen as he wanted. I would have paid triple. It was worth it. The car ride home with Bowen was supreme. I dropped him off right at his farm because Autumn has their car and is working a shift at the bookstore.

"You have to take the gig with Lacey," Bowen says to me as I pull to a stop in front of his house. "I can't do it with you, but it's great money for the others and great exposure for future gigs that I can do with you."

"Are you sure?" I ask, reaching across the small distance to lay my hand over his in his lap. "Because I, personally, have no problem steering clear of anything and everything political. I hate it all. No offense."

"Hell, no offense taken. Woody has been campaigning for just two months and I'm already over it." Bowen sighs and tips his head back against the seat. "I've refused to get too involved, but Autumn has gone with him to interviews. Everyone wants personal details on our parents' death. Why didn't they have snow tires? When did we realize they were missing? One reporter even asked him if he had regrets. Who the fuck doesn't have regrets about their parents dying?"

I squeeze his hand. He looks positively anguished and I hate it. "I hope he told the reporter to go fuck himself."

"Of course he didn't," Bowen sighed. "But I would have, which is why I'm not the one running for mayor. I don't have the temperament. Woody might stutter and look a bit like a hillbilly, redneck, or whatever it is the polished business types call him behind his back, but the truth is, he's levelheaded, and practical and smarter than his school records would indicate."

"I really don't want to do this gig," I tell him.

"Yeah, but Joe has another baby on the way. On a teacher's salary. So you have to at least give him the option, don't you think?" Bowen opens his eyes and stares at me.

"I wish I could kiss you right now," I reply.

His eyes dart toward the front porch of his farmhouse and back to me. "Woody wouldn't tell even if he's home and happens to be looking out the window."

"You sure?" I feel fear start to beat in my chest alongside my heart.

"Of course I'm sure. My brother would never hurt me," Bowen replies.

So I lean in, without even glancing around, which I desperately want to do. I kiss him like I'm not hiding anything. Like it's six months from now. Like I'm free. And Bowen is the one who has to break it off because I swear, I could keep this up for hours. He pulls back slightly, panting but with a smile pulling at the corners of his mouth. "That was worth the risk."

"Hell yeah it was," I murmur and rub my thumb across his bottom lip. "Now get out of my car before I do it again."

He chuckles and gives me the smallest, quickest whisper of a kiss before opening the door and getting out. I turn off the engine and walk around to open the trunk for him to get his bag. The thing about cars built decades ago is there's no automation whatsoever and I can't open the trunk from the inside. He grabs his bag and I slam down the trunk again and impulsively reach out and grab his face and kiss him again. It's just as needy and just as perfect.

"Fuck me." Bowen steps away and his eyes dart up to his house and then around to the fields and the road at the bottom of the long drive. There're no prying eyes. I don't look but I can tell by the way his flushed face remains impassive.

"I've already done that, but I'll gladly do it again," I reply, and he laughs.

"I've created a monster." Bowen walks backwards towards the stairs that lead to his porch.

"You really did." I walk around and get into the car. "I'll text you later."

"Okay." Bowen turns and climbs the porch steps before turning back. "Ask the guys. I swear I'm okay with it."

"Okay." I nod.

He turns and pushes open his front door and disappears inside. I am grinning like a lunatic the whole way down his driveway, and most of the ride home until I find Joe dropping Grant off outside our building and I ask them their thoughts on the event.

"I know this sucks for you, Chase, but if I'm being honest," Joe says with sympathy shining in his dark eyes. "I need all the extra cash I can get."

"I wouldn't turn it down either, not because I need the cash but because I love playing," Grant replies. "And I know Joe needs that cash and Baldwin has deep pockets backing her so we could give her a stupid fee and she'd likely pay it."

"Yeah," I nod, resigned.

"But only if Bowen is cool with it," Joe adds, and I give him a smile. I love that he thought of him. "I'm not voting for the chick, but I'll take her cash."

"He's cool with us doing it, but obviously he won't play with us." They stare at me and wait for me to state the obvious. I look over at Grant. "So maybe you can ask Bennie to play for us."

"He's not going to want me to beg him. He's gonna want you to do it," Grant replies. "I'm not the one he's pissed at."

"Yeah. Yeah," I grumble and yank my phone out. Then I pause and shove it back in my pocket. "I should probably do this in person."

"I'm sure the puppy dog eyes would help sway him," Joe replies with a snarky grin.

I flip him the bird but he just laughs and drives off. Grant and I are left standing there. He raises an eyebrow. "This is going to be awkward as fuck for you."

"You think, Captain Obvious?" I quip and Grant laughs.

He puts his overnight bag over his shoulder and digs his keys out of his pocket and lowers his voice. "Maybe you should stop banging our drummers."

Our eyes meet and I know in that instant he is fully aware of where Bowen was this morning. "This is different."

"How can it be? You giving up that inheritance?"

I shake my head. "No. But Bowen knows about it and he's cool with keeping us on the down-low until I get it."

"So, he's what? Your secret boyfriend."

"Yes. And then one day he'll be my not-so-secret boyfriend," I reply. "But not for another six months so can you just pretend you know nothing."

"Yeah of course. So, you're… gay now?"

I blink. "When was the last time you saw me with a woman?"

"I don't see you with anyone."

"I like Bowen. Only Bowen. He's a dude."

Grant still looks slightly confused, but not in a homophobic way. "Wow. Well, cool. You know I am there for you no matter what and I won't breathe a word to anyone."

He starts to walk toward the front of the building. "But if you cost us another drummer, I will kick your ass."

"I won't. I promise," I reply and pull my phone out and text Bennie and ask him where he's at and if we can talk. He responds that he's at home and I can swing by anytime. So I sigh and tell him I'm on my way.

Bennie lives in a residential area of Burlington where the streets are canopied with mature trees and the houses should probably all be on the Historic registry. It's not his house. It's his parents'. He still lives at home. Our reasons for not being out are different though kind of the same which is what bonded us. Bennie is trying to stay in the closet long enough for his homophobic parents to die and-or hand over the reins to the family business. Not an inheritance but close enough.

He opens the bright red door before I even knock. He's wearing a pair of joggers and a Moo U Track shirt that barely fits because Bennie didn't keep up with his track star workouts after he graduated. "Hey. Come in. My parents are at some church mixer or some such shit."

I step inside. The house is full of dark polished wood and spacious rooms with high ceilings. The whole place smells vaguely like cookies and coffee, the way I imagine it's smelled for decades whether or not someone bakes. I half expect his mom to emerge from the kitchen wearing an apron and calling him Beaver. "What do you want, Chase?"

"To apologize," I say as we stand face-to-face in the foyer. "I thought I was really clear about the rules, and I thought we were on the same page, but obviously you got hurt so I must have been wrong."

Bennie frowns, tilting his head to look in my eyes. He's shorter and thinner than I am, but with a bit of a soft belly that developed after he stopped running track and started working in the front office of the family construction company instead of as part of the construction crew on school breaks. I used to find his dad bod attractive but now, well I'm only into one body, and it's Bowen's. "So, you're sorry I feel bad but not sorry you used me?"

"I didn't use you," I argue and sigh, rubbing my eyes with my thumb and forefinger as I take a breath. "What I mean is I honestly believed that we were using each other. That it was one night of mutual fun but nothing else."

"It was one night of fun, but I don't understand why it can't be more than one night," Bennie replies and the frown slips from his dark features and there's a pain in his eyes I've never seen before. "I mean we get along. We both have our reasons for not wanting to date publicly so I just thought maybe we could date privately, you know?"

"Yeah. I know." I nod and sigh. "I mean I get why you might want to go in that direction but I just don't. I'm sorry."

He cocks an eyebrow. "You don't want a relationship?"

He's thinking about catching me with Bowen. I have to choose my next words very deliberately. "I told you before, I'm not trying to find anything serious until I get through this inheritance shit."

"Yeah. And then you'll stop working, go back to school, and be out and proud," Bennie frowns again. "It's a fucking gay fairytale."

"I'm hoping it is," I reply frankly. "And you're not on the same timeline. There's no set date when your dad will finally, legally give you the company."

He shakes his head. "And you won't wait for me."

"I love you Bennie. As a friend," I say, and he actually physically flinches at the words no one with a crush ever wants to hear. "But even if it was more, I'd have to say no. I'm not waiting for anyone. I've spent way too many years not fully honest about who I am, and I don't want to do it for a second longer than I have to."

"And the drummer guy? Ben?"

"Bowen." My tone is clipped and harsh which is not at all how I should sound right now. I'm supposed to be making amends not making things worse. I clear my throat. "He can't do a gig we have booked and so I was hoping that you could."

"Guess he couldn't handle your one and done rule either, huh?" Bennie seems to be taking a lot of satisfaction from that assumption and as much as I don't want to burst his bitter little bubble, I have to be honest. Well, honest-ish.

"It's not that he doesn't want to play with us, it's that he can't. Because the gig is a Lacey Baldwin campaign event and with his brother being the opposing candidate, it's not exactly a good idea."

"Oh." Bennie looks disappointed that I didn't break Bowen's heart, which makes him a bigger dick than I realized. If I had more time before the gig I would walk out of here and find another damn drummer, but unfortunately the event is in less than two weeks and finding a guy who can fill the spot and knows all the songs might be impossible. I can't risk it.

"Come on. For old time's sake," I beg. "And the pay will be great. Grant and Joe would love to have you back."

"And you."

Ugh. Fuck. I suck all the air I can into my lungs. "I never hated playing with you Bennie. Or hanging out with you. I still consider you a friend."

That isn't exactly what he was hoping to hear, I can tell. But as he runs a hand through his dark hair and scratches his head, I realize it's close enough. "Fine. I'll do it. I've missed playing anyway."

"Awesome." I give him what's supposed to be a quick hug but he holds onto me longer than I expect.

I'm about to panic about what, exactly, he's going to do next when I hear a high-pitched female voice. "Chase Ashton? Well, we haven't seen you in ages."

Mrs. Johnson appears at the end of the hall in the doorway to the kitchen. They came in the back door. Thankfully, judging by the friendly smile on her face, she didn't overhear much of our conversation. Bennie jumps away from me like her voice is a cattle prod suddenly jabbing him in the back.

"Hello, Mrs. Johnson, it has been a while," I say and brush by Bennie to give her a hug. She loves hugging. She extends her arms as I approach and I notice Mr. Johnson staring behind her with a pained smile on his face.

"You hug too much Karen," he chastised his wife. "That's why Bennie is hugging dudes like it's normal. Nothing normal about coming home and finding my son with his arms around another dude."

I hug Mrs. Johnson extra hard after that comment and give him a smile as bright as the sun. "Hey Mr. Johnson. So you don't want a hug? I can challenge you to a duel or something if that's more manly?"

Mrs. Johnson giggles. Bennie smirks at me when I turn back to him. Mr. Johnson mutters something under his breath but I don't catch it because I'm already on my way to the front door. "I was just on my way out."

"But we have leftover cake from the church mixer!" she calls out. "And fruit salad!"

"I've really got to go, but thank you," I reply, and my eyes meet Bennie's. "Can you practice with us, say, Friday?"

He nods and I give him another hug good-bye, just to piss off his dad, and leave.

BOWEN

I can't believe I'm doing this, but I'm doing it. I pull open the door to the community center. The cavernous entry smells faintly of chlorine that gets stronger as I head towards the aquatic area. I see the changing rooms side by side on the left and I poke my head into the men's one, making sure he's not in there. There's one guy in front of a locker and I can hear a shower running but I doubt Chase showers before he teaches. I enter and find one of the empty lockers and quickly change into my bathing suit and grab my towel out of my bag before walking down the hall to the indoor, Olympic sized pool.

I don't know why I'm nervous. I shouldn't be, but I totally am. I have barely seen Chase this week and it's been killing me. Tanner scheduled me a lot because Molly was sick, and Chase had a busy work week. The band practice they had last night was with Bennie because he agreed to sub in for the Baldwin gig. Even though I gave my blessing, I hate that he's drumming with them again. Chase hates it too, I know. And he even offered for me to come over and have drinks with them after practice, but I thought it might annoy Bennie. I can tell he still likes Chase as more than a friend and if I showed up it would be salt in a wound. Because I wouldn't be leaving that loft with the rest of them. I'd stay and spend the night. So instead, I spent my night at home sulking so badly Autumn asked me if I was PMSing. Then I went to my room and jerked off to the memory of the sex we had in Maine.

So now, unable to go another minute without seeing him, I walk into the pool area, which has about twenty gray and white haired ladies milling about in swimsuits. One of them glances up as I walk in. She's in a one piece black and red floral bathing suit with a red scrunchie keeping her long white hair up in a high bun. "Hello gorgeous. Are you lost?"

That gets the attention of a few more of them, and the chatter starts to die off, which gets the rest of them to look up. Now, all twenty senior ladies are staring at me, some of them lewdly. I have an overwhelming urge to blush. "No, ma'am," I say quietly. "I'm here for the ten-thirty aqua aerobics."

"You are?" another says, her jaw just about on the tile floor. She's wearing a tangerine, high-waisted two piece that I'm pretty sure Autumn owns. She cocks a hip and puts her hand on it as she picks her jaw up. "Well, I'm Leslie. What's your name?'

"Bowen."

"Well, Bowen, you can stand in front of me in the pool. I want a good view."

A bunch of them giggle. And then there's a whistle. "Hello ladies welcome to…" Chase's voice stops completely when he sees me standing amongst his usual clientele. He is trying not to smile, and failing desperately, so I grin right back. "Make that ladies and gentleman. Thanks for coming today. If you'll make your way into the pool, we'll get started. There's free swim immediately after the class so don't feel like you have to rush off."

I hang my towel on one of the hooks on the wall by the door and follow the gaggle of ladies down the wide steps and into the pool. Chase's eyes never leave mine. Neither do Leslie's or any of the other ladies. One of them has her head turned almost all the way around to keep her gaze on me. It's flattering, to be honest. I wink at her and she blushes.

"Don't give Jane too much attention," a lady to my left says. "She's been widowed for ten years. Might just ask you on a date."

"Give the man some breathing room, Rachel," Chase calls out with a chuckle to the woman who just warned me about Jane. "You know there's a lot of arm movements in class, we don't want to be hitting each other."

"Hitting *on* each other is a different thing altogether," Leslie chimes in.

"I'm going to start the sound system. Leigh, I'm counting on you to keep these ladies in line," Chase points to a woman with short gray hair closest to the edge of the pool.

"Honey, I make no guarantees," Leigh replies. "I might just leave my dear Eddie for this one."

More laughter.

Chase walks over and leans over the edge of the pool, right in front of me. "I can't believe you're here."

"You said it was open to anyone."

"It is, but…" Chase grins. "There seems to be some serious sexual harassment. I promise Johanna, Leslie, Leigh, Rachel, Jane and Lori are all harmless. Myrtle, I make no guarantees about. She might goose you."

"I'm cool. Are you cool?"

"Getting to see you? All wet and half naked? Yeah. Cool." He stands back up and walks over to the sound system tucked into the wall.

Music starts to flood the cavernous room from speakers near the ceiling and Chase unzips his hoodie and hangs it on one of the wall hooks. He's in gray and red swim trunks with a dark gray tank with the community center logo on it. He looks smokin' hot and one of the women who hasn't yet spoken to me leans in. "There's a reason why we girls never miss a weekend class and it's not because we enjoy the scent or chlorine or need the exercise. We have a walking group and chair yoga twice a week."

I lift an eyebrow and she laughs. "Oh, come on, you're here for the same eye candy we are."

"Myrtle!" Chase calls her name sternly but with a smile. "Eyes up front."

"Not a hardship," Myrtle calls back with a grin.

The class is forty-five minutes and actually more of a workout than I anticipated. Chase is a great instructor, giving out options for each exercise at varying degrees of difficulty. I always pick the hardest but so do a lot of the ladies. My only objection is that he's instructing from the pool deck. I was hoping he'd be in the pool with us.

When class is over they all clap and some of them even whistle. It's cute. A few stick around for the free swim but most head out. Jane and Leslie invite me to grab smoothies with them at the juice bar around the corner, but I politely decline and promise them next time.

As I grab my towel off the hook and wrap it around my waist, Chase walks over. "I'm beginning to think you don't do this for their benefit but to boost your own ego."

He laughs and flashes me a sheepish grin. "It's a perk. So was having you show up."

"I wasn't sure if you'd be cool with it, but I just really wanted to see you," I confess, and he leans his shoulder against the tile wall beside me.

"I really wish our lives weren't so busy this week," Chase whispers. "I've wanted nothing more than to see you every single night this week."

"Yeah, me too."

"Wanna do something now?" Chase asks. "I usually swim a few laps, but I'll skip it if you want to hang out. I'm sure I can find a way to get my cardio another way."

My dick hears that and twitches in my trunks. I groan. "I had a hard time slipping away at all this morning. We have a whole crap ton of farm work to do today. We're starting the seeding for the crops."

"Argh," Chase let's out a strangled sound. "When can I see you again?"

"Tomorrow night? I'll be tired and sore but you could swing by and we could chill in the room over the garage. Play with the guitars." I wiggle my eyebrows. "Make a little music up there."

Chase lowers his voice. "That sounds like such a fabulous idea I can forgive the ridiculous pun."

"Aren't you two adorable."

The light drops out of Chase's face like a fuse has blown behind his eyes. His smile disappears. He turns to see Johanna standing there, wrapped in a towel with her floral bathing cap. Myrtle is beside her smiling brightly. Chase blinks. "What?"

He's panicking. Never mind that his tone is suddenly curt and his voice abnormally deep, I can feel the panic radiating off him. "You two. You're so cute the way you smile at each other. You remind me of my grandson and his boyfriend."

"We're just friends, Johanna," Chase says, his voice firm like he's reprimanding her. "He's in my band."

Myrtle swats at her friend. "Of course, Jo, don't you remember? We saw Chase in the paper with that Miss Baldwin who is running for mayor."

Johanna pinches her eyebrows as she thinks about it. "Oh dear. Right. I remember now."

I wait for Chase to correct them. I know he won't say I'm his boyfriend, but he could explain to them he's not dating Lacey. But he doesn't explain anything. He just keeps blinking and frowning. Now Johanna's cheeks get red. "I didn't mean to offend. I just… I made a mistake."

"I'm not offended," I pipe up and give her a gentle smile. "I'm gay."

"I'm not," Chase says before I can even close my mouth after speaking.

Myrtle and Johanna both nod and then Myrtle leans towards me. "Well, if you're single, my nephew is gay, and probably near your age."

"I'll keep that in mind, ma'am."

She smiles and walks out of the pool area pulling Johanna with her. Neither look at Chase again. He frowns. "Is she mad at me?"

"Yeah. Maybe," I admit, and he looks crushed. "You get so adamant it sounds kind of homophobic."

He looks wounded now, like I've just hurt his feelings. I feel guilty, but I have to speak the truth. I didn't with Trevor. I swallowed too much down and it made things worse. He runs a hand through his hair. "I'm sorry. I don't want to sound like my brother or any other asshole like that. I just… I panic."

"I know." I pause and try not to say anything more, but I can't help myself. "And you let them say you were dating Lacey."

"They didn't say I was dating her," Chase replies, his voice firm but flat. I stare at him. He blinks again. "They just said they saw me with her. Don't you think it would have been worse if I corrected an assumption they didn't actually say out loud?"

"What a very political answer," I snap and he looks even more wounded than before. Maybe I'm being harsh but this is all too familiar in the worst way. Trevor used to use these tactics too, avoiding responsibility by splitting hairs and confusing the issue.

"I'm sorry."

"You said that."

Our vibe has definitely evaporated. "I should go. I promised Autumn I'd also bring home maple donuts."

"From the Maple Factory?" Chase asks and I nod and give his shoulder a small squeeze as I pass. "Still want me? To come over tomorrow night?"

I glance back over my shoulder. He looks remorseful and a little bit guilty and a whole lot lost. All of that swirling on his face makes him look younger too and it hits me that, when it comes to being comfortable in your own skin, I'm the veteran. He's the rookie. This suave, smooth, confident, intelligent, and capable guy is like me at Vino and Veritas — a bumbling klutz.

"Bowen, I really am sorry," he whispers.

That whole thing sucked, yes, but I can't help but believe him now. But, he's allowed to screw up. And he has a lot at stake and I knew what I was signing on for. "Yeah. I do want you to come over tomorrow."

His shoulders sag a little in relief. "See you then."

I wink at him and leave the pool. I head to the changing room and tug off my bathing suit and throw on dry clothes. I skip the shower because I'm just going to get sweaty and dirty on the farm anyway. I can shower after a long day of seeding. But even though I have four messages on my phone from Autumn and Woody both reminding me about the maple donuts and how fast they run out, I take a minute before I leave the community center to peek back into the pool and watch Chase swim laps.

He's doing butterfly in the far lane, his body cresting the water and diving back under rhythmically. Every muscle is taut and bulging at the same time. When he gets to the end he pops up and shoves his soaking hair back with his hand as water slips down his broad chest. I smile. He looks like that capable, confident guy I was in awe of when we met.

This too shall pass, I think as I make my way out of the community center. He'll find his way and conquer this coming out thing the same way he's conquered everything else in life, with ease. I'll be there right beside him, making sure of it.

When I get to the Maple Factory I don't see any maple donuts in the case but I ask if there's any in the back. The guy behind the counter actually chuckles. "It's almost noon. We run out of these things by ten on a bad day."

Shit.

But the guy speaks again as I turn to leave. "Unless… are you Bowen Whitlock?"

I nod.

"Oh yeah. Then we've got your six in the back for you," he says, and I am beyond confused. "Some guy called and paid for them and told us to hold them for you."

"Was his name Chase?"

"Yep," the guys says, emerging from the back with a small box and a slip of paper. "Sorry he wanted us to give you a dozen but we only have six left."

"Six is plenty. Thank you," I say, taking the box, the sugary maple scent wafting out of it even though it's closed.

"Don't thank me," the guy calls after me. "Thank him."

"Oh I will," I say to myself, not him, as the door closes behind me and I make my way back to my car with a smile from ear to ear.

I carefully put the box on the passenger seat and am just buckling up my seatbelt when my phone rings. It's Autumn. I hit answer. "I got the donuts. Relax. I'm on my way now."

"The police are here," she says, her voice shaking so badly everything inside me turns to ice. "And they're looking for you."

BOWEN

The sight of the police cruisers in front of my house as I pull up the drive has me gripping the steering wheel with white knuckles. My heart is beating erratically, and I feel cold and yet I'm sweating. I get out of the car and my legs feel shaky as I approach the porch where an officer stands talking with Woody.

Woody sees me over the officer's shoulder. "You okay?"

I swallow but my throat feels like it's coated in dust. "What's going on?"

My voice is distorted, even to my own ears. Woody steps around the police officer, his blond brow pinched. He's wearing pajama bottoms and a white T-shirt and that somehow increases the panic collapsing down on my chest, making it hard to breath.

"Bowen Whitlock?"

It's Matt Lockheed. I went to school with him. He was in Autumn's class. Why is he acting like he doesn't know me? Is that some kind of bullshit police protocol? "You know it's me."

"I think you need to sit down," Woody tells me, his voice soft and low, the way Mom used to talk to me when I got the flu and was laid up at home.

"Where is Autumn? I need to see Autumn," I say and my voice still doesn't sound right. I know this is a PTSD type thing. The last time police cars were at my house was when they came to tell us our parents were dead. I'm reacting to the sight with the trauma of the past. Woody was wearing pajamas then too.

"She's in the shed with the other cops."

"What? Why?" I blink as Woody takes me by my shoulders and pushes me gently until I'm sitting on the bottom step. It's easier than it should have been considering I don't want to sit down, but my legs are made of Jell-O and toothpicks suddenly. "I need to see her. I know it's stupid, but I need to see she's here. Okay?"

"Yeah. Okay." Woody stops crouching in front of me and stands up. He stakes several steps but stops. I don't think he wants to leave me so instead he just yells, "Autumn! Come! Now!"

"No screaming," Matt barks at my brother and then he turns to me. He's wearing reflective aviator sunglasses even though the sun is behind the clouds and has been since I left the house this morning. I see my face in them and Woody is right, my skin is the same color as the white washed pine porch. "Bowen, we came here today with a warrant to search your premises."

"Why?"

"This is why. This slander piece." Woody shoves his phone in front of me. I didn't even realize he was holding it earlier. It's open to the online version of the local newspaper.

I have to really study it to understand what the hell I'm seeing. The headline says "Mayoral Candidate's Brother is Suspected Drug Dealer."

I read it four times but it still won't compute. There's a picture of Bert and Ernie in my back shed. As I scroll further down there's another picture with both the pot plants and the rows of our tomato plants behind them. With the dark lighting of the shot it looks like rows and rows of pot plants.

"We need to take you down to the station for questioning," Matt says gruffly.

"No, you don't," Autumn's voice fills the air, high and somehow menacing at the same time. "Your buddies have only found the two plants, which is all they're going to find. Which, legally, is allowed under the current recreational marijuana laws for the state of Vermont."

"Autumn, don't tell me how to do my job," Matt grumbles at my sister.

"Well, someone's got to," Autumn retorts and storms right up to him. She's furious. Her strawberry blonde hair is wild, unbrushed, and she's in a pair of jean shorts and an oversized Beauty and the Beast T-shirt, which she always wears when we have farm work. "Isn't it your job to know the penal code? Because here's a part you seem to have forgotten. As of July first, 2018, adult cultivation in private of up to six marijuana plants – two mature and up to four immature – is no longer punishable by criminal or civil penalty. Those who cultivate marijuana for their own personal use may possess at home the total quantity of the harvest."

"Didn't know you were pre-law at Moo U, Autumn," Matt says with sarcasm dripping off his words. He turns to me. "The question is whether you consume it recreationally, at home, or whether you sell if for profit, Bowen. We need to question you about that."

"So do it here," Woody interjects. He points to me. "In case you didn't notice he's not exactly doing well right now."

"I'm fine."

"Is that because he's about to get caught?"

"No, you fuck wit," Autumn barks. "It's because the last time police cars ambushed us, we became orphans."

"Autumn!" Woody snaps.

Matt turns slowly towards my sister, and I finally find my legs and stand. "I'll go with you. Whatever you want. Just cut her some slack."

Matt ignores me and faces off with my sister who would spit nails right now if she could. "You can't talk to me like that Autumn."

"Freedom of speech."

I can see his jaw clenched so tight the vein in his neck bulges. "I'm going to cut you the slack your brother asked for because I get that this might be traumatic."

Autumn opens her mouth to speak but I cut her off. "Say thank you Autumn and absolutely nothing else."

Her eyes find mine. "Please."

"Thank you," she spits out.

Matt turns to me. "Can we just talk? I don't think you're a drug dealer but I gotta do my job which is due diligence."

Three more officers come around from the back of the house. I know them all by face but not by name. None of them, thankfully, look happy to be here. "Just the two plants. And we've looked everywhere."

"Okay good," Matt says. The guy loves being an authority figure, clearly, but right now he's not leaping off into the asshole abyss and I appreciate it. "We can talk here, I guess. Somewhere private because I don't need the peanut gallery chiming in."

Autumn opens her mouth but I glare at her so she closes it promptly. I nod at Matt and am about to suggest he come inside and we chat in the kitchen, when Woody starts yelling. "This is private property! Leave!"

"Holy shit. Are those reporters?" Autumn gasps.

I squint down at the end of the driveway, near the fence and sure enough there are five people and two cars and a god damn news truck. Two guys with cameras are snapping away. "Matt! Can you make them stop?" Autumn asks.

"I'm just a fuck wit," Matt shoots back with a shrug.

"Let's go inside before you have to arrest her," I say, lifting a hand toward Autumn in a stop motion as I lead Matt up the porch stairs and pull open the screen door for him and his partner.

"I'll handle this," I hear Woody say just before the door closes behind us.

Inside Matt and his partner ask me a half hours' worth of questions about my weed and what I do with it and if anyone has ever paid me for it. I answer it all honestly, because I've never accepted payment for it. I share it with friends, in the privacy of our own homes. I don't distribute it. I even offer him the number of my therapist who treated me after my parents' death, who was the person to recommend weed for my anxiety and insomnia. Finally, he closes his little notebook and sighs. "I don't have enough evidence to arrest you. Today."

"You sound disappointed by that, Matt," I reply, trying not to sound as offended as I am.

He folds his arms across his chest. His partner sighs and speaks for him. "They're pretty riled up about this at city hall."

"The article is a slander piece, pure and simple," I reply.

"Yeah. Looks that way," Matt adds. "And I don't want to arrest you, Bowen. I just want to do my job and not get my ass handed to me by my bosses because I don't arrest you."

"I'm not a drug dealer."

"I think whoever fed the paper the info knows that," the partner says. His name is Martinez and he's older and oddly way more friendly and relaxed than Matt. For some reason I expected the opposite. "And they aren't actually expecting you to get arrested. This isn't about you. It's about ruining your brother's chances in this election."

"And they've succeeded, haven't they?" I feel that elephant of panic sitting on my chest again. We've invested everything into the election run. Everything. Woody can't lose because of me.

"They've made a dent," Martinez admits and stands up from where he's been leaning against our kitchen countertop. "Look, kid, I'm not a political genius or anything but if I were you, I'd look for the source. Start with the names in the article and figure out who could have been on your farm and got the shots in the paper."

"You've been stabbed in the back," Matt adds. "Anyway, I also have to say don't leave town. This investigation isn't closed."

Martinez rolls his eyes behind his partner's back and leans in. "We might have to follow up with you is what Matt is trying to say in the most Bad Cop Movie way possible."

I just nod. The humor is lost on me. There's nothing funny about this. I follow them back through the house and out the front door. I'm relieved to see that the media appear to be gone, along with the other squad car and officers. Matt and Officer Martinez get into their car and leave without another word to any of us.

As soon as the car has left the driveway, Autumn breaks down in tears. She's full-on sobbing and I walk over and hug her. "It's okay. I've done nothing wrong."

"I know that but the damage is done," Autumn sniffles into my shirt. "Woody will never win now. We may lose the farm. People will still point and whisper at you for ages. We could even have the paper print a retraction and it won't matter."

"I don't give a shit about whispers and stares, Autumn," I reply. "And Woody won't necessarily lose."

"Can your PR friend Chase help us figure out how to minimize damage?" Woody wants to know. "I need all the help I can get."

"Chase…" I let go of Autumn who is crying less and wiping at the tears that have fallen on her cheeks. "I never got to read the whole article. Can I see it again?"

Woody illuminates the screen on his phone and hands it to me. I read the whole thing. It says a concerned and legitimate source found what they believe to be a grow-op on our farm. The name of my plants is mentioned and the picture... well, the only person who I told the names to was Chase. He's also mentioned in the article, as it goes on to mention my brother is running for mayor against Lacey Baldwin who has traditional ideas about marijuana distribution and comes from an upstanding political family and "is dating Chase Ashton son of staunch conservative congressman Charles Ashton."

"I told you he was bad news," Autumn's uneven voice pulls my eyes from the screen. I realize I whispered that dating line out loud. "He is dating Lacey."

"This article is full of lies," I say, but my voice is weak. "It's lying about me why would it be telling the truth about him?"

"If he is dating Baldwin, then he seems like the logical suspect in this, Bo." Woody says. His eyes are filled with sympathy but his voice is hard with frustration. "You've been hanging out with him a lot."

"I sent him to the shed to find you that night," Autumn reminds me of the little fact that has been making me feel sick this entire time.

"Shit. Bowen..." Woody buries his hands in his messy blond hair. "I don't think we should ask him for help on this. I don't think we should ask him anything anymore."

I swallow and the dust seems to have settled in my throat again. Along with a very large lump. I get up and dig my keys out of my pocket. The donuts are still sitting on the passenger seat so I open the door and hand them to Autumn. "I need to swing by work and make sure I'm still employed because the article mentions them. If I were Harrison, I would fire me."

"He wouldn't do that," Autumn argues. "He's smart enough to know slander when he sees it."

"I've got to make sure," I reply and open the driver's side door.

"What do we do?" Woody wants to know,

"Farm work," I reply. "We've still got Mom and Dad's legacy to keep up. For now. Let's not let them take that without a fight."

I leave them in the driveway staring after me.

It's too early for the bar to be open but I knock on the delivery door in the alley. Tanner and Harrison often come in around noon to work on schedules and pay roll and stuff. As soon as Harrison opens the door, I know he's read the article. "I had no idea small-town politics could get as dirty as the big city politics."

I nod. "Yeah. Me either."

"Come inside," Harrison holds the door wider so I can pass.

He leads me through the bookstore to his tiny office at the back, which is a windowless, claustrophobic room if you ask me. He picks a stack of papers off the extra chair and moves them to his desk, motioning for me to sit down. I do, but then I stand up again. "Relax, Bowen. You don't have to plead your case. I'm not even thinking about firing you."

I drop back down into the empty chair, my whole body sagging with relief. "And you won't fire Autumn either? I have to ask because she's also freaking out."

"Of course not," Harrison gives me a warm but sympathetic smile and pulls off his glasses, tossing them on the desk, ruffling paperwork as they land. He rubs the bridge of his nose. "I think you should talk to a lawyer though. You probably have grounds for a libel suit and even defamation. Especially if you could find out the source."

"I think I know the source," I swallow but that lump makes it nearly impossible. Harrison studies my face. "We don't have money for a lawyer and it likely wouldn't go down in time to save my brother's campaign."

"Sadly, that's probably true," Harrison sighs. "But it could get you some money to balance your books if you brother doesn't win. I know you guys put all you had into this."

I tent my arms on my knees and drop my face into my hands. "I can't even think about all that right now."

"Because you know the person that planted this garbage?"

"Yeah."

"And you trusted them."

"Worse. I was falling in love with them," I confess and that's when my vision blurs and my face feels hot. I'm about to cry. I fight it with every ounce of my soul. I don't want to give in to it in front of my boss. I'm embarrassed enough. And even more so, I don't want to give in to it over Chase. I cried over Trevor and that got me nowhere. No one cares if they hurt me. I blink away the tears and stand up. "Anyway, I'll deal with it. Thanks for the advice and for not firing me or my sister. I've got to get back to the farm."

I stand abruptly and Harrison does too, grabbing his glasses and putting them back on. "Hey, one other thing Bowen. If your brother wants to use the bookstore or the bar for anything like an event or even just to hang posters, tell him to give me a call. I think it's time my businesses show their political alliance."

"Thanks. That means a lot."

He smiles and I can't return it. I head out onto Church Street but when I reach my car around the corner I don't drive out of town toward the farm. I head to Chase's loft. It's a very short drive but with every foot my junky old car travels, the anxiety and anger inside me grows tenfold. I'm spiraling. I don't want it to be Chase. I'm furious I have to even consider it, but how can I not?

I pull into one of the visitor spots behind his building as he's about to get into the Ferrari. As soon as he recognizes the car he runs over and is pulling open my door. "I was just coming to the farm to see you."

"Not a good idea." I snap as I get out of the car and stand there with the open door between us. I grip it like it's a shield that can somehow protect me even though I feel like I'm already wounded. He steps closer but only one step.

"Woody and Autumn must be so upset. I'm sorry."

"Sorry you did it?"

"Did what?" Chase blinks those big, blue eyes I loved looking into. "Wait. You think *I* told that paper?"

I stare at him. He's confused and I wonder if, like everything else in his life, this is just an act. I hate that I doubt him, but I do. I'm just a tangled mess of re-opened wounds right now. Between the sight of the cops at our farmhouse giving me flashbacks and all the garbage I went through with Trevor feeling like it's repeating itself... "I shouldn't be here."

"Where should you be?" Chase asks, his tone is heavy.

"Not with you," I snap back and I don't even know if I mean in this moment or in every moment. He doesn't know either, I can tell by the way his handsome face crumbles.

"Bowen, I can help you with this. I can help Woody spin this."

"Before or after you help Lacey out with her fundraiser or go to an event as her fake boyfriend?" My voice is loud. Too loud.

"Shh!" He snaps his mouth shut as soon as the sound escapes his mouth. "Sorry. I just…"

"Will do anything to keep your secret."

We stare at each other, the distance between us feels like a hell of a lot more than a few feet now. It's the grand fucking canyon. And it's filled with emotional baggage. The hurt of his face is morphing into something harder. "Not anything."

"They knew the names of the plants. I don't tell everyone that."

"You told me."

"Exactly."

"Well, I didn't do it, Bowen. Fuck. You really think I would?" His mouth snaps shut into a hard line when I don't answer him instantly.

"I haven't told anyone else the names of my plants except my siblings," I reply. "Not one person."

"Why would I do that to you?"

"Because your family wanted you to." It's a guess. A horrible burning suspicion, which as soon as I say it out loud, I realize how hurtful it is. "Chase, you've spent your life lying about yourself. Why not lie about me too? You're so close."

Saying it out loud hurts. I can't seem to take a deep breath and those tears I fought at V and V are trying to escape again. I clench my jaw and blink them back.

"Yeah." He gives me a smile I've never seen on his perfect mouth before. It's snide. "I thought I was close too. I thought *we* were. But you know what? That was a lie too. You were never okay with us."

He walks away from me. I knew this was where we would end up as soon as I read the article but somehow it still feels like the rug is being pulled out from under me. And the part that really upsets me, is that I knew better.

"And I'm going to make sure that person pays for what they've done," I tell him, thinking of Harrison's idea of suing the liar, and maybe even the paper.

He stops walking so suddenly that the parking lot gravel skitters around his feet. He turns to face me. "Are you going to… you're threatening to out me?"

His handsome face warps into a look that can only be described as disgust and horror. I feel what's left of my heart drop into my boots.

"No. That's not what I'm saying. I wouldn't do that to you, for any reason. Who the hell do you think I am?"

"Who the hell do you think I am?" he counters angrily. "Because I get that you were burned by someone in my... sort of predicament. But that doesn't give you the right to —"

"No one else knew the names of the plants!" I yell. "Explain that to me."

"I honestly have no idea," Chase snaps back. "The only thing I do know is that we're done."

I open my mouth to argue but it hits me like a bowling ball to my chest that there isn't anything left to say. So I stand there and stare at his back as he storms away.

21

CHASE

We finish the last song and I can't wait to take my guitar off. I've never struggled with band practice. It's never felt like a chore or a nuisance but every second of the last two hours has felt like pouring vinegar on a paper cut. But that's been how everything feels lately. Since the afternoon I left Bowen standing behind my building.

"Chase?"

I suddenly realize I'm staring at the guitar I just hung back on the wall at the foot of the stairs. Motionless, ignoring my bandmates, and Bennie. I turn around when Joe says my name and realize he must have asked me something. "Yeah. Sure."

Now Grant, Joe, and Bennie are looking at me funny. Grant cocks an eyebrow and crosses his arms. "Yeah? Sure?"

I shake my head. "Sorry. What did you say?"

"I asked if you knew if Bowen was doing okay after that bullshit article in the paper," Joe repeats.

"And you answered yeah sure like he asked if you wanted a beer," Grant notes.

"A beer sounds great," I say, ignoring the original topic and walking over to the kitchen.

"So, you haven't talked to him?" Grant asks as I pull some cans of IPA out of the fridge. I gently lob them to everyone. I can't help but notice Bennie is staring at me intently, waiting for my answer just as much as everyone else.

"I talked to him only long enough to find out he thinks I might have planted the story," I reply.

Grant chokes on his first gulp of beer. Joe slaps him on the back, but his eyes are wide and glued to me. "You? Why would he think that?"

"Because I'm mentioned in the article," I explain, taking a sip of my beer but it doesn't taste enjoyable so I put the can on the counter. "Because the article gives his nicknames for his pot plants and he told them to me once."

"Oh. Shit," Grant whispers, shaking his head.

"You would never do that. Would you?" Joe asks.

"Of course not!" I bark out. Then I notice Bennie tucked into the sofa at the other end of the loft. He's sipping his beer with his feet up on my coffee table, watching us like we're the half-time show at the Super Bowl.

He notices me noticing him and decides to speak. "Well, it looks like you might be needing me for more than this one gig, then?"

"I guess so," Joe answers for me, not bothering to look back at Bennie. We exchange a glance that says neither of us are happy about it and when I look at Grant's face he doesn't looked thrilled with the idea either.

I hate the idea of Bowen not playing with us again so much that I swear bile rises in my throat. The idea that Bowen and I are over, before I can even tell anyone we happened, that also makes bile rise in my throat, while my chest aches like it's been used as a punching bag. And the best part is I have no one to blame but myself. I'm the one holding onto the lies for money. Lying, hiding, pretending to please a bunch of bigots I share a bloodline with. For cash. I hate me.

Bennie has brought up the Stanley Cup playoffs and since Grant's favorite team is a first-round match-up against Joe's favorite team the conversation is easily swayed. I listen, kind of, but in reality, I'm just holding a beer I don't want to drink, surrounded by people I don't want to be with. I just want to be alone to sulk and stew and hate myself in private.

Finally, Joe mumbles something about having to get home to his wife and they all decide to leave. Bennie is the last one out the door. He pauses before joining Grant and Joe in the elevator. "You want me to stay? You look like you need company."

I shake my head. "What I need is a good night's sleep."

That's not a lie. I haven't managed more than four and a half hours since the fight. Or break-up I guess you can officially call it since Bowen hasn't reached out once.

"Well, send me any other upcoming dates," Bennie says and gets in the elevator with the others. He doesn't seem pissed off at the rejection tonight, which is good. We need him for the gig. I mean, personally, I would be fine if he bailed again and we couldn't perform. But I don't want to screw over Lacey or take cash away from the guys.

Fuck. I am so sick of doing shit for everyone else.

I'm pacing my apartment deciding whether I should go to bed and stare at the ceiling or continue pacing when the elevator pings. Lacey Baldwin steps off. She's in a pencil skirt and white, short sleeved blouse. Her blonde hair is smooth and tucked back behind her ears and the make-up looks fresh. She looks like she's starting her day, not ending it.

"Sorry to show up unannounced," Lacey says with a sheepish smile. "I was going to text you, but Grant walked Bennie out and saw me outside. He punched in the elevator code for your floor and told me it would be fine if I just came on up."

"I was just on my way to bed," I tell her.

"You look like you haven't slept in a while."

"I haven't."

"Is it because your friend is in trouble?" she asks, still standing just a couple feet away from the elevator, like she might change her mind and leave any second.

"Yeah," I sigh. "And he isn't my friend."

"Your bandmate."

"He isn't just that either," I reply. "Look, I know I'm locked into this thing for you, because of our families and because I can't let the guys down, so I'm not going to fuck you over. I just want the truth. Did you plant that story?"

"No. I swear, Chase," she replies without hesitation, her eyes staring straight into mine. She takes a couple steps forward. "I know this seems like something either one of our parents would pull from their bag of tricks in order to win, but I didn't, and I grilled my staff to make sure none of them did it either."

"I want to believe you," I reply.

"Good. Because it's the truth." Lacey digs in her shiny black over-sized leather bag and pulls out a single piece of paper. "In other news the reason I'm here is I've got a list of songs to avoid for the gig. Stuff my dad's publicist thinks might be too controversial for my supporter base."

"Barf," I say and roll my eyes. "You sound just like them."

"I guess sometimes I am," she says with a twinge of remorse in her voice. "I actually want to do good if I get in, Chase. I fully intend on being more moderate on a lot of stuff than our parents are. That's why I wrote an editorial to the same paper that screwed over Woody, in defense of his hobby plants."

"You did?"

She nods. "I may not be for adding marijuana farms within the city limits but I'm not going to try and undo a bill that's long passed when it comes to the recreational usage."

"Your dad voted against legalized marijuana of any kind," I remind her and she smiles.

"I'm different. I told you."

"And gay marriage?" I can't help but ask, since we're talking her politics here.

"Like I said, I'm not about trying to change what's already decided," Lacey replies and just as I'm starting to feel like she might not be a bad consolation prize if Woody Whitlock loses, she adds, "Although I do think we can put in some bylaws to tone down the rainbow flags and the rainbow crosswalks and all that. It's a bit too in-your-face and Church Street still has a lot of young kids who hang around there."

"There's a lot of young kids who are gay," I counter back.

Lacey freezes. "I don't want to argue with you about my platform. I just wanted to say I'm sorry about your friend."

"He's not a friend."

Her mouth puckers out of agitation and she cocks a hip. "You said that. He's not your friend. Not just a bandmate. Then what is he?"

And once again, I'm faced with the opportunity to come clean... and I don't take it. I don't drop all this stupid, heavy self-made baggage. "He's nothing anymore because he thinks I had something to do with the piece. We don't speak."

"Chase, I'm sorry. Of course, you wouldn't do that to someone you care about." Lacey finally walks into my apartment, dropping the list on the kitchen island and walking over to give me a hug. I let her, but I don't return it. She pulls away. "You are one of the kindest, most reliable friends I've ever had. You're also the guy who stands up for everyone, not the guy who tears everyone down."

"Thanks, but he doesn't see it that way," I say.

"You know who I think did it? Someone at that fundraiser Woody hosted at his house," Lacey says to me. "I mean, I have no proof, I wasn't there. But the plants were, right? So it makes sense that would be the time someone could have found them."

"But everyone there was supporters of Woody. That was the whole reason they were..." I pause. "Except my brother. He was there because you asked him to be."

"Your brother isn't bright enough to think out this level of sabotage," Lacey replies with a wry grin. "And also, the work it would take to execute it would interfere with all the time he spends hanging out in bars trying to pick up college girls or admiring himself in the mirror at home."

I actually laugh. She joins in. "You're not wrong about Colin. And also, he would know he'd be the prime suspect."

Lacey lets out a sigh. "Well, maybe I'm wrong about the event. It's just an idea."

She walks back over to the elevator, steps inside but doesn't hit the down button. Instead, she pokes her head back out and says, "You should tell Bowen to review the guest list."

"Yeah. I guess." Just before the elevator doors shut, I call out. "And you shouldn't touch the rainbows, Lace!"

I head up to bed. Lying there staring at the ceiling I muster up the courage to message Bowen.

Chase: *Hey. I think you should review the guest list at the event you guys did. Everyone there had access to the shed/plants.*

I hit send. Stare at my ceiling again for a millisecond and then send him another text.

Chase: *I hope you're okay.*

I watch until I see he's looked at the messages, which takes about fifteen minutes. Then I give myself another fifteen minutes to stare at the screen before I come to terms with the fact he's not going to message me back. So, I put the phone down and go back to staring at the ceiling.

22

BOWEN

Half an hour into my shift, everyone in the place decides to place food orders and Joss gets slammed, and Tanner asks me if I want to go help in the kitchen. I jump at the chance, even though I hate the idea of wearing a hair net. Luckily Joss lends me one of his bandanas to cover my hair instead so that's one problem down. But he has this incredibly chaotic and intense working style that has me kind of stressed, on top of the stress I already feel because I'm terrified of disappointing him. Still, it beats working up front with customers. Since the article came out, I get a lot of stares during my shifts. From staff it's always sympathetic, from patrons it's a bit more of a mixed bag. Some stare at me with curiosity, some with sympathy, and some like I'm the devil incarnate. One dude even asked me if I could hook him up with cocaine. Tanner swiftly asked him to leave when he overheard.

Still, any chance to hide from all of it, I'll take. So here I am, carefully dipping and dredging haddock filets in the batter so Joss can cook them up and make the fish and chips dish that is beyond excellent. Raw fish filets are more slippery than they look, and two almost land on the floor. Joss misses the first one but catches me fumbling the second one and his stare borders on a glare.

"Careful," he warns gently. "Don't want to have to toss a filet in the bin because of your butter fingers."

"I won't drop one. I promise," I vow. "How are you?"

I'm just trying to make small talk, because we've been in this kitchen together for about twenty minutes and he hasn't said much other than to give orders. I have never felt like he likes me much and I want to change that. But all I get is a grunt and a nod as he concentrates on plating a burger order. It's just a burger and fries but he makes it look, and taste, incredible. I'm actually really proud that our hemp buns are part of it, so I mention it, and add, "I hope you won't let the bullshit in the paper affect our business relationship."

That gets him to lift his eyes off the plate. "I didn't believe a word of that rubbish, Bowen."

"Good. Thanks."

He smiles. "Besides, I have to keep buying from you. It annoys my fella when I tell him I get my buns from a hot farmer."

I laugh. "You tell him that?"

"I did, yeah. And he hasn't forgotten," Joss chuckles with me. I shake my head and almost drop another filet. I curse under my breath and manage to get it on the plate and hand them all to Joss to cook. "I'm glad I could be used to rile up your boyfriend. See? I'm good for something."

Joss grins and takes the plate from me and starts cooking the four fish and chips platters that are next up. He's everywhere. The fryer, the prep station, the fridge. He moves erratically at warp speed but somehow it looks like a choreographed dance. "Can you run the finished burger plate out to Molly? It's for table twelve."

"Sure thing." I take off my apron and bandana, and grab the dish, walking it carefully to the front.

Molly is by the bar, putting a drink order on her tray and she smiles at me. "Trade ya a burger plate for a lawyer."

"What?"

Her high pigtails, which look like two poufy curl balls, jiggle as she flicks her head toward the back of the bar. "There's a guy in the back booth who wants to talk to you. He's a lawyer."

She grabs the burger plate out of my hands as I ask, "A lawyer for who?"

"I didn't ask him that." She spins and grabs the tray full of drinks too. Auden, Tanner, and I all hold our breath as we watch her carry both at the same time.

Once she's done and hasn't dropped a thing, I can hear Tanner sigh in relief. Then he turns to me. "Why don't you take your break and find out what he wants."

"Okay," I reply numbly. I don't know how these past few days can get worse, but maybe I'm about to find out. All the worst-case scenarios take turns dancing through my head. It's a lawyer for the city, they're suing me for something. It's Officer Matt's lawyer, he's suing Autumn for calling him a fuck wit. It's Lacey Baldwin's lawyer because when Woody gave that interview in his pajamas to the reporters who had gathered while the police searched our property, he more than subtly insinuated that he thought her camp might be behind the lies.

Never once do I think it's going to be lawyer here to help me. But when I get to the booth, it's someone I know. Aaron Morin. He's Autumn's friend. She knows him through his brother Jamie. I know them all, sort of. I mean we've hung out before when Autumn has dragged me out one of the many events that fill her calendar.

"Hey, Aaron" I say, feeling very confused. I thought he went to school out of state. I hardly ever see him around. "You're here to see *me*?"

"Yeah. Hey." He gives me his hand to shake. "You got a minute?"

"Sure." He motions for me to sit down across from him. He's dressed in a pair of jeans and a polo but somehow still looks very much the buttoned-down lawyer. He puts his arms on the table between us and folds his fingers together. "I was asked to talk to you by a friend. About the article about you in the paper."

"Is someone suing me?" I don't know why my brain goes straight there, but it does.

"No. No." Aaron smiles lightly. "But you can sue. The paper. And I was asked to give you a little bit more information about that."

He turns and reaches down into a messenger bag I didn't realize was on the booth seat next to him. He pulls out a small stack of papers held together with a paperclip. "I'm not a defamation lawyer. I'm not actually a lawyer at all yet, but it's something I have covered in school and so this is just advice. Not exactly accredited legal advice but more like an informed legal opinion."

He slides the stack of papers at me, and I pull it closer and thumb through them. It's a bunch of examples of court rulings on defamation cases similar to what happened to me. I think. I mean that's what

I get from scanning the first two pages. I'm trying to figure out what to say to him when suddenly there's another person slipping into the booth next to Aaron. His boyfriend Jeremy.

"Oh! You started without me. What did I miss?" he asks and wraps one arm around Aaron's broad shoulders while placing his other hand under the table on Aaron's knee I assume by the way Aaron's eyes widen for a second. I remember that these two are the definition of opposites attracting. "And thanks for sitting down so I have an excuse to squeeze into this side and press myself against my man in public. He's not a huge PDA boy and I like pushing his boundaries a little."

"A little?" Aaron repeats and lifts an eyebrow at the same time his mouth lifts in a smile. They're cute and then some. And it makes my heart long for what I never got to have with Chase.

"So, you totally have to sue the pants off the reporter, the newspaper, and whoever the hell their bogus source is," Jeremy announces. "You'll be rich."

"I don't want to be rich," I reply but then I think about how we might lose the farm if Woody doesn't win because of this. And how, although Autumn refuses to admit it's the cause, her online hemp jewelry sales have taken a total nosedive since the article. "I just want to repair the damage they've done."

"Money can fix a lot of things," Jeremy tells me. "Not everything by all means, but some."

"Even just filing the lawsuit and making it public will help change public opinion. The world loves when someone stands up for themselves and fights back. Staying silent makes them think you're guilty," Aaron explains.

"Woody has spoken out."

"Yeah, in his pajamas. I saw it," Jeremy cringes. "Oh, and he needs new PJs. Something silk maybe?"

Aaron rolls his eyes good naturedly at his other half. "Legal efforts always hold more weight than just words to a reporter. But think about it."

"I will. Thanks." I grab the stack of papers and stand up.

"I can't represent you, but I already have feelers out. We're looking for a local lawyer who would handle something like this," Aaron explains. "Just in case you go down this road."

I nod and try to give them a confident smile. Truth is I wouldn't have the money to hire a lawyer anyway. "I'm going to go put this away and thank Harrison for asking you guys to help."

"Harrison?" Aaron looks completely confused.

"He isn't who asked you to help?" They both shake their heads in unison. "Autumn?"

"No, my friend Peter asked me to help," Aaron tells me.

"I work with Peter over at Sprysky and Gentry," Jeremy explains. "You've met him once or twice before. With the gang at game nights."

Right. Peter Landry. He's a great guy. I'm trying to figure out why Peter has decided to help when I haven't talked to him about this, when Jeremy drops the real bomb and almost knocks me over. "It was actually his client Chase Ashton who asked him to find someone who might be able to help you."

Chase did this? Even after that blow-out fight? Is it because he feels guilty that he blew up my life and he's trying to make up for it? Or is it because he still cares despite the fact that I accused him of something he didn't do? I didn't even bother to return his text message a couple days ago and now I'm getting free legal advice because of him. Am I the asshole or is he? Fuck, I wish I could know for certain. My heart tells me one thing, but my heart is the biggest masochist I've ever met so my brain won't let me listen to it anymore. After all, my heart duped me into believing Trevor had real feelings for me for far too long.

"Bowen?" Jeremy has lifted his hand off his boyfriend's knee and is waving it in front of me. "You just totally zoned out."

I give my head a small shake and smile. "Sorry. A lot to process and I'm kind of not good with a lot of processing all at once. Anyway. Thanks. Truly. I appreciate it."

"When I get the name of a lawyer, I'll let you or Autumn know," Aaron promises.

"Cool. Thank you again." I head back toward the bar, slipping behind it.

Auden looks over. "All good?"

I nod. Tanner walks by as I'm rolling up the paperwork and trying to shove it into my back pocket. It sticks up but it shouldn't fall out. "The food rush has calmed down. Now I need you bussing some tables."

"Sure thing," I say and grab a tray.

My mind revisits all my suspicions that led me to accuse Chase in the first place as I clear dirty dishes and empty wine glasses. Everything seems tenuous now. I spent a good chunk of last night going over the guest list for that party too, like Chase said I should, and it just made me angry. Because I don't know what I'm looking for. I have no reason to think that the out-going mayor or a member of City Council would sabotage us like that. And all the citizen donors were there because they support Woody as the future mayor. Every single business owner or person had donated before and also come to other events. Heck some of them even canvass their neighborhoods with him and have his posters in the windows of their homes.

I'm debating calling Chase and asking to meet him, but then it dawns on me what day it is. Lacey Baldwin's fundraiser. The one he's playing with Imposter Syndrome. Without me. And with that Bennie guy who is probably ready and willing to console Chase if he's feeling sad about me.

"Whoa there!" Auden says. I realize I slammed the tray down a little too hard on the bar.

"Sorry."

"Are you mad at the empty cheddar dip bowl or something else?" He lifts an eyebrow and gives me a smirk.

"Something else."

"Don't let the cockwaffle behind the smear piece win, Bowen," Auden says.

"No. I won't. That's not what I'm riled up over." *It's thinking about my ex moving on without me.* "I got some legal advice for that, actually. That's what the lawyer thing was about."

"Well, if there's a lawyer giving free advice in the house tonight, send him my way," Auden replies, which shocks me.

"Everything okay?"

He chuckles. "Yeah I'm joking. Probably."

"That jerk is not going to sue you, or me, or Harrison," Tanner replies as he slips past me holding a couple bottles of wine to restock Auden's wine fridge which is getting low.

"What happened?"

"The other night, you weren't working, but we had a real piece of work in here," Auden explains. "He'd been drinking before he got here, I think, because I only served him two and he was slurring his words."

"And what words they were." Tanner frowns. "He was hitting on a guy at the bar, which would have been fine but the dude needs to take classes in how to pick up or something because he was saying all the wrong things."

"Bragging about his dad's construction business. How he's gonna be rich when he takes it over and how his ex was too stupid to see it," Auden explains and rolls his eyes.

"Just what every man wants, right?" Tanner lets out a soundless laugh. "A dude with daddy issues who still wants his ex back. Thank God I'm married."

"Anyway, the guy he was trying, and failing, to pick up finally told him to fuck off. Like exact words." Auden is grinning but then it slips into a frown. "And he gets stupid belligerent. Yelling obscenities and disturbing everyone so I told him he was done. I wasn't serving him anymore and he would have to leave."

"What happened?"

"He didn't want to leave," Auden replies. "So I called Tanner, who came and backed me up but he still didn't want to leave."

My eyes are bouncing between Tanner and Auden and I almost laugh as I picture this. Tanner is all tattoos and muscle and has got the dark broody look down. I can't imagine being drunk enough to lip off to him. He looks like he would end you. And Auden is built like a brick wall so this guy must be a moron on top of drunk.

"He changed his bitchy little tune when I told him I was going to call the police," Tanner adds as he crosses his arms over his wide chest. "And you'd think that would shut him up. But it didn't. He started telling me that I was going to pay. That the whole bar would pay. He was all about the payback. Just ask the last guy who screwed with him. He stole his drums and this guy made sure he got what was coming to him."

"Wait… what?"

Auden is laughing as he uncorks a bottle of Prosecco. "Aye. Mr. Wanker McWankerson compared Tanner kicking him out of here to a dude stealing his drums. Like Tanner is a criminal who stole his toys."

The hair on my arms starts to stand on end, and the goosebumps keep crawling up my arms and up my spine until the hair on the back of my neck is also on end. "What was his name?"

Tanner shrugs. "Well Auden calls him Wanker McWankerson apparently. But I never got his full name because he left before I had to call the cops."

"I wrote his name down along with a description for the other bartenders in case he dared to come back." Auden points to a scrap of paper taped to the back bar where the staff sometimes leaves notes and To Do lists for each other. "Got his name off his credit card."

I walk over and read it. Benjamin Johnson. Dark hair, dark eyes. Around five foot eight. Medium skin tone. Wanker.

"Bennie."

"Yeah!" Auden's eyes widen. "That's how he introduced himself to the guy he was hitting on. Please don't tell me your friends with the wanker?"

"Hell no." And then it hits me.

I went over the fundraiser guest list looking at the names that RSVP'd, not the people who actually showed up. A Chris Johnson from Green Mountain Construction was a donor and was supposed to attend. But Bennie Johnson was the person who showed up. I remember him talking to Chase and his brother that night.

On the side of our house.

Near the shed.

"Fucking Bennie."

"Bowen?" Tanner looks stunned and unimpressed, and I realize I said that a little loud for a crowded work night.

"Sorry. I'm so sorry," I reply.

"Did you drop something again?" Molly asks, bouncing up to the server station, her round eyes even rounder with excitement. "If you break one more dish or glass, you've beat my record."

Auden laughs. I want to laugh because that is funny but I'm reeling. "I think that Bennie kid is the one who planted the fake story with the news. He was at Woody's fundraiser at our house."

"Holy..." Tanner has the common sense not to finish that in front of the customers.

"Yeah. Holy..." I pull my phone out of my pocket. "Can I make one very quick text?"

"I'll consider this an emergency if you're going to nail this guy's you-know-whats to the wall," Tanner replies. "Go ahead."

"Thanks."

I walk into the storage area and punch out a quick message to Chase.

Bowen: *When you're done your gig can we talk. Alone. Please. I know who slandered me. And you should know too.*

I'm about to shove my phone back in my pocket when I decide to tell Chase one more thing.

Bowen: *I don't expect you to forgive me but I am going to beg for it anyway.*

I head back into the bar where Auden asks me to grab him white wine glasses. I hand him red wine glasses. He frowns and explains my error. I put them back and reach for the less bulbous white wine glasses, I have no idea how I'm going to make it through the rest of my shift without losing my mind. All I want to do is be with Chase, tell him everything and find a way to get him to give me a second chance.

And that's when I drop one of the glasses.

"Woo hoo!" Molly calls out in victory. "Ladies and gentleman, we have a new record holder."

Fuck. My. Life.

CHASE

Another thing I hate about politicians; they don't dance. And when they do dance, it's not well. And it's not to cover songs from the nineties. They do like the eighties songs we've got. Unfortunately, a couple of our better ones are on that banned list Lacey slapped me with the other night. We finish the cover of "Jack and Diane", which despite being about two teenagers deflowering each other, it wasn't on the banned song list. Neither was "867-5309 Jenny" even though it's literally about stalking a woman whose number is scrawled on a bathroom wall.

"And now everyone, a word from your host tonight. Lacey Baldwin!" I announce, stepping back from the mic. I remove my guitar and put it at the back of the stage near the drums with Grant and Joe's and follow them off stage. Lacey gives me a tense smile as she passes and a curt nod. She looks pissed. Or stressed. Maybe both.

"Well now I know what it feels like when a comic is up there not getting any laughs," Joe mutters quietly as we gather just left of the stage.

"Yeah."

"Well, the money is good." Bennie remarks. "So who cares?"

I grit my teeth and force myself to not respond. This really is just a way to get out of his house. He doesn't care about the band or the quality of what we do, but I do. I know this isn't going to be a career or anything, but I still want it to go well.

Lacey is on stage thanking everyone for coming and going through her plans for the city again. She doesn't look upset but I know she is. I know this isn't the event she was hoping for. She invited us and held it outside at a park, with food trucks because she's hoping to lure the younger voters. But the average age of the people who showed up is more like fifty. And a lot of them are career politicians and friends of her dad. Including my Aunt Hilda. She's frowned through almost every song we've done. Amy, God bless her, and her husband are here too and they danced a little.

Lacey's campaign manager, a short, wide guy with a mustache that looks so seventies porn star I've never seen one like it in real life, stomps over to me. "You didn't follow the script."

Oh right. They told me to say something specific. "Sorry. I totally blanked."

"You were supposed to sing her praises, call her the future mayor, and thank her for having you," he reminds me.

"I'm sorry."

"Hrmpf."

He pivots and stomps away again.

"So we only have a song to get through after this?" Grant says hopefully.

"Two. But yeah, then it's done."

"Thank God," he whispers. "Should we stick to our set list. Because something tells me they're not going to get their groove on to Nirvana."

"Umm," I think about it. "They haven't gotten their groove on all night anyway."

I'm giving up. And I never do that, but fuck. What's the point? I can't win.

"What about doing a Bon Jovi song? We all know most of them?" Joe suggests.

Grant and Joe debate Bon Jovi songs, while Bennie consults the list of banned songs and I pull my phone out of my pocket and ignore them all because I don't think changing the songs will help anything. I check my text messages and all the chatter around me fades into the background when I see an alert with Bowen's name on it.

I read his messages and then reread the last one three times and then I just stare. He wants *me* to forgive *him*? He thinks he has to beg for that? Like I haven't been lying awake thinking of nothing but him every night. Missing him. His laugh. His easy-going smile that somehow made these lies I've been living so much more bearable.

"You're smiling. Why?" Grant asks suddenly and nudges me with his shoulder.

"Because Bowen is talking to me again."

"What?" Bennie says at the same time Grant says, "That's great!"

"What changed?" Joe wants to know.

"He knows I'm not the one who lied to the paper," I say and my smile grows.

"How could he figure that out?" Bennie snaps and he sounds both angry and… something else. Incredulous? "That kid and his brother are dumber than a bag of hammers."

"Whoa." Joe frowns.

"He's incredibly smart and a way better drummer than you," I reply and Bennie flinches. I don't feel the least bit bad because as I look at him with his wide eyes and skittish expression, Lacey's suggestion rumbles through my head.

"You know who I think did it? Someone at that fundraiser Woody hosted at his house."

My eyes narrow on him. "You did it."

"Me?" His indignation is so over the top it's almost ridiculous.

"Sounds like you definitely did it," Joe remarks. "Fuck Bennie. Why?"

"Exactly! Why?" Bennie says, his voice getting so loud that Grant shushes him. Lacey is still giving her speech. "Why would I do that, Chase?"

"You know why," I growl.

"Thank you again, for a wonderful evening," Lacey's voice cuts through our argument as it booms from the speakers. "And now let's finish off the night with a couple more songs from my dear Chase and his band Imposter Syndrome."

"Her dear Chase?" Grant repeats and lifts an eyebrow.

"I don't know what the fuck that is about," I grumble and follow Joe as he heads towards the stage.

"She's being a good beard," Bennie adds, falling in step with me. "You should be thrilled."

"Shut up," I snap but his words stick to me as I climb the stairs to the stage and make me feel dirty. "If I could kick you off stage right now, I would."

"Your accusations are unfounded," he whispers back. "I'm right about her and you know it."

He *is* right. If I hadn't met Bowen, pretending to be Lacey's boyfriend would be no big deal at all. It would actually probably be a welcome lie. One last extra thing to placate my dad and guarantee my inheritance. What more could I want?

Bowen I think as I pick up my guitar and slowly walk over to the microphone. Bowen is the more I could want. And I do want him. So much. More than I want that stupid money.

Joe talks to the audience and announces the song, which will be "Living on a Prayer" apparently. I should have probably paid more attention. But I can do this one without even thinking about it. As I strum out the melody and sing the lyrics, my brain wanders. I think about what the next few months will be like if Bowen takes me back and we continue our secret relationship. And then I think about what the rest of my life will be like if Bowen takes me back and I say fuck it and just live my life out loud, in public, the way I've yearned to for years. And it's only then that I smile.

Sure I might have to go into debt to go back to school. And I might have to sell the Ferrari and maybe even give back the loft and the business space, but I'll still go after everything I've dreamed of. And I can be proud of myself while I'm doing it. And I won't be living a second more of my one and only life for anyone else but me. And the world will know how much I adore Bowen Whitlock. How special he is. How lucky I am.

The song ends and Grant stares over at me from his position on stage. That song did get the crowd going at least a little bit, so we're greeted with almost exuberant applause.

"Before we do our last number, I want to thank Lacey for having us here tonight," I say into the microphone. "She's an old family friend, as many of you probably know. My grandfather was a local politician as well. Ned McDaniels."

I see my aunt just to the left of the stage perk up at the mention of her late father. A wave of fear washes over me but it's gone just as quickly as it came. I know this is right.

"I never saw eye-to-eye on politics with my grandfather," I say calmly. "Or on a lot of other things. And the same might be said of Lacey and myself, but I appreciate that we've remained friends anyway."

Her annoying campaign manager is freaking out at the corner of the stage. I can see his arms flailing from here. Luckily, he's still whispering whatever irate words he's saying. I smile. The enraged look on his face only serving to calm my nerves. Lacey, on the other hand, doesn't look angry, just confused. My eyes move to someone standing just behind them.

Bowen. He's wearing black jeans and a black T-shirt and if it wasn't for his golden hair glinting in the park lights, he'd be basically invisible. Our eyes meet and his mouth lifts in that perfect, effortless smile of his. And I smile back and I feel twenty pounds lighter. It must be the fact that the emotional cinder block that has been parked on my heart for years is finally gone.

My eyes move to Grant and then Joe. "You guys and the drummer can go. I've got this."

I turn back to the crowd who all look either confused or annoyed. I clear my throat. "Let's be honest, this band wasn't really your cup of tea tonight. So instead of leaving you with another loud cover tune, I thought maybe I would play you an original. It's softer, slower. Feel free to grab someone and dance to it."

I put down my electric guitar and walk to the edge of the stage where Grant hands me my acoustic. I get to the mic and clear my throat and move my eyes back to Bowen. They don't waver or blink as I continue. "I wrote this song about who I want to be one day. I didn't have an actual person in mind when I wrote it, just someone who lives fearlessly and with determination. I've met someone who, in spite of all the horrible things life throws at him, lives that way. And I love him for it. So, this goes out to my boyfriend Bowen Whitlock."

And then, my eyes still on him, I strum the first few chords of Dauntless. I'm not so sure anyone hears them, or the words I'm singing, over the murmurs and gasps in the crowd when they realize I just dedicated a song to the opponent's brother and alleged drug dealer. But I really don't give shit. I'm singing this for me and Bowen who is listening and smiling and being my everything.

When I'm done there's a smattering of polite applause and a

bunch of loud clapping from Joe and Grant. Bowen is wolf whistling. I put down the guitar, leave the stage, and head right for him. I stop abruptly, suddenly afraid to touch him. Does he forgive me? Is he going to take me back?

That lazy smile is no longer lazy. He's beaming. "Did you just come out? On stage? By calling me your boyfriend and telling a bunch of conservatives you admire me?"

"Yup." It's as much of a sentence as I can make right now.

He blinks and I watch his Adam's apple bob as he swallows. "Wow."

"Yup." I take a step closer to him. "And I think the word I used was love, not admire."

"Right. It was." Bowen shoves his hands into his hair and does the most unexpected thing. He laughs. "Dear God, Chase. And you think I'm the fearless one? You're… you may be giving up millions."

"I definitely just gave up three and a half million dollars," I confirm and it sinks in. It sobers me a little, but I have zero regrets. "Also I think Bennie is the asshole who lied to the paper. He went in your shed at that fundraiser and the names of the plants are written on the backside of the pots."

"I was coming here to tell you the same thing."

"I'm sorry. He did that because of me," I reply.

"I don't blame you." Bowen puts a hand on my shoulder and squeezes. "I can't believe I was stupid enough to believe you'd ever do that to me. I'm sorry."

"Forgiven." We're standing almost on top of each other so I reach out and cup the back of his neck, tipping my head toward his until our foreheads are touching. "So can we kiss and make-up now?"

"Right now?" I nod and Bowen smiles, moving his lips against mine ever so slightly. "Why the hell not?"

And so I kiss him like we're re-enacting the final scene in a romantic comedy, minus the comedy part because behind me I can hear Lacey's campaign manager yelling about contract violations and who I'm sure is my aunt Hilda gasping, and my cousin Amy is the voice declaring "Oh my God!" loudly.

But I block them all out and just kiss Bowen, my boyfriend, for the whole damn world to see.

24

BOWEN

"I'm glad you talked me into going back to your place," Chase says as I pull off Route 116 and inch up the long driveway to the house. "I know my parents will show up at my loft at the crack of dawn. My aunt has definitely already told them, or someone at the event did, I'm sure. I wouldn't be surprised if they were already on their way to Vermont."

"I'm glad Joe and Grant offered to pack up the equipment without you," I reply, rubbing my thumb across his wrist as our laced hands sit in his lap. Thank god I have an automatic so I can hold his hand easier.

"Grant felt guilty. We can milk that for a while," Chase tells me. Turns out, Grant did buy two marijuana plants of his own, and Bennie saw them at his place and asked him about them. Grant told him, in detail, who explained all about the marijuana laws in Vermont. And that I had my own plants at home. Bennie went searching for them at the fundraiser and found them. He admitted he found out the names because he saw I had "Bert & Ernie food" written on a bottle of plant food in the shed. The only way to keep Chase from punching Bennie in that moment was to pull him to me, which led to another kiss, in front of everyone.

"If we stayed a second longer, I think that campaign guy's mustache would have burst into flames from the heat of his anger." I grin.

198

Chase laughs. It's loud and a bit wild and sexy as all hell. He sounds free. He looks it too. His shoulders are down, his head tipped back against the headrest, and his eyes are glassy like he's been drinking but he hasn't had a drop. It's crazy but it's true and it's the only reason I haven't mentioned the inheritance or the drama that will definitely play out in the next few days, or even weeks. Because he deserves to have this moment.

I turn off the car and we both open our doors and jump out. I walk around the front of the car, knowing he'll head that way, toward the room above the garage, but I hook him by the arm and press his ass to the car, and my body into his and kiss him. "My bed is much bigger and much more comfortable."

"Your bed? In your room? In your house?"

I nod and laugh softly. "Do not tell me after all you've done tonight you're scared of my family finding out? They know I'm gay. They also know you aren't the person who planted the story. I messaged them both as I made my way over to the park." I run the tip of my nose up the column of his strong neck, inhaling that clean sharp smell of his. It's slightly woodsy with notes of citrus and I've missed it so damn much I actually switched my pillow with the lumpy one in the garage room that he last slept on. "Also, Autumn is out at a game night with friends. Luke and Scott actually asked me to go too, but I have to work. Woody's room is on the other side of the house, and he sleeps so deep, he usually doesn't even wake up for his own alarm. We have to go in and physically shake him awake."

That seems to calm his nerves and he lets me pull him up the stairs. I hang my keys on the homemade wooden hooks beside the door and head straight for the stairs, bringing Chase with me. My room is at the end of the hall on the left. Across from mine is my parents' room, which stays unoccupied, and next to it is a linen closet, then the bathroom and then Autumn's room. I make it a point to show him that, so he knows he doesn't have to be worried about being overheard tonight. I want to hear him when I make him come.

The door to my room is open, and as we step inside, I feel something other than lust fluttering in my gut. I feel regret. The bed's a rumpled mess, the furniture from a secondhand shop in Colchester, my walls are a garish shade of deep purple that I somehow convinced my parents to let me paint them when I was fourteen. The throw rug on the floor is worn and faded, just like the curtains which have been on my windows as long as the hideous wall color.

But Chase isn't looking at any of that. He's looking at me.

"It's not exactly a fancy loft."

"I just gave up millions, Bowen," Chase says as he pushes the door closed and those blue eyes hold mine. "For the right to be here, with you, without hiding. And it wasn't to critique the decor."

"What was it for?"

He takes both his hands and pushes my jean jacket off my shoulders. I keep my arms straight so it slips to the floor. He steps into me, his lips landing on the side of my neck. They're warm and firm and when his tongue darts out and licks at my skin I shiver. His hands move up and under my shirt, fingertips pressing hard as they trail their way up over my abs and torso, taking my T-shirt higher and higher. I tip my head back and close my eyes, enjoying all the sensations I never thought I'd get to feel again with him. Or at all, honestly. Because no one has made me feel as alive with lust, and love, as Chase Ashton. And I realize I haven't told him. He told half the town he loved me and I haven't said it back. I pull my head up and open my mouth to speak but he's rolling his thumbs over both my pebbled nipples now and so the only sound I can make is a groan.

"You're so fucking hot," he murmurs against my neck. He pinches both my nipples until my balls tingle and then pulls away long enough to pull my shirt up over my head.

He's in just a T-shirt and jeans but it might as well be a snowsuit. It's too much. I reach for the hem of his shirt, but he's got his hands buried in my hair now and his mouth pressed to mine, his tongue crushing my thoughts to dust. Before I know it, he's got my pants and underwear at my ankles, so I step out of them.

He's still fully clothed. I break our endless kiss. The scratch of his five o'clock shadow still making my skin tingle even when I pull away. "One of these things is not like the other," I tell him, fisting my hard cock and giving it a much needed pump.

He smiles, all confidence and cockiness in the best possible way, and undoes his pants, pulling his own erection out into the open. He grabs it at the base after running his thumb over the moisture glistening on the cut tip. "Looks pretty similar to me."

"I'm going to need to take a closer look," I reply and drop to my knees.

"Bowen I—" I don't wait for the rest of that sentence, I just take him into my mouth inch by glorious inch. He's heavy and salty on my tongue as I start moving. He's panting and I can feel his balls tighten as I play with them but he grabs my hair and pulls me off him. I tilt my head and look up at him. "I don't want to come like this."

"How do you want to come?"

"With you inside me."

I open my mouth, to ask if he's sure. But he's sure. And so am I.

I get to my feet and grab his shoulders and move him toward the bed. He falls back onto it and it creaks like the old pile of wood it is. I crawl on top of him, sucking and kissing my way up his body, from the dark hair above his groin to his navel, to each of his rock hard nipples and then up his neck. "This is going to take time," I tell him softly. "And if you want to stop, at any time, just say so. I'm good with waiting. We've got all the time in the world now."

"I won't ask you to stop," Chase promises. "But I will beg you to start."

He winks. I laugh and then kiss him, positioning myself on my side, pressing into him, my cock rubbing against his hip, leaving a wet spot. My hand squeezes his thick thigh before gliding upwards, the downy dark hairs on his legs tickling my fingertips. I find my way between his legs, cupping his balls for a second, which gets me a grunt of frustration before I let my hand dip behind them. "Spread your legs. Bend your knees."

He follows my orders without hesitation. I slip my index finger between his ass cheeks. I line it up with his hole, the pad of my finger rubbing it with a gentle firmness. He doesn't flinch or tense, but his eyes pinch shut. He's nervous. I kiss him, slow and easy, and move my hand away.

"You don't have to stop."

"I do," I reply and pull open my night table drawer. "I need lube."

He reaches up and rakes his fingers through my hair while I pull out lube and a condom, dropping the condom on the pillow beside his head. His eyes move toward it. "I haven't been with anyone before."

I flip open the top of the lube and tip the bottle but stop short of squeezing it into my hand. He's suggesting we go bare. The idea sends a lightning bolt of heat directly into my groin and my cock actually jerks. "But I have," I answer simply. "So this is the safest thing."

"For now?" he asks. "Because it's just you for me and I want everything about us to be raw and real."

Fuck. Emotionally needy, sexually greedy Chase is the best Chase of all. "Let's both get tested and then these can go."

He nods and his tongue slips out and wets his bottom lip in anticipation. I close the lube and toss it on the pillow beside the condom, my eyes never leaving his face. His eyes are bright and clear. His face holds the slightest pink flush of anticipation. That perfectly puffed-up hair is splayed every which way in a tousled mess. And I've never seen a better sight in my life. Then he adds a tiny, self-conscious smile and my heart suddenly feels too big for my chest. "I told you I would beg. So do I have to?"

I shake my head, too scared to speak because the only words I want to say are I love you and right now, with so much lust between us, it might cheapen the meaning. My hand makes its way over his hip and between his ass cheeks again. Drenched in lube I put my finger back to his hole. I lift up to kiss him, and the motion moves my arm up and my finger breaches his entrance. Just one finger but as soon as it pushes past the first ring of muscle his mouth falls open and a small, deep moan escapes. I nip his chin, my teeth dragging across it. "You okay?"

"Yeah. You've done this before. And I've played with toys," he whispers. "Get to the good part."

I grin. "Bossy."

I push my finger all the way in without hesitation and when I slide out, I make sure to press it purposely against his sweet spot and he arches his back as bliss washes over his face. "More."

I kiss him and add a second finger this time. Before long I'm not finger fucking him anymore, he's fucking my fingers. Using his feet planted on the bed to rock his ass up and down on my hand. His arms are above his head, clutching two panels of wood on my slatted headboard. "Bowen."

"I know." He's ready and not a moment too soon. My dick is throbbing. "Switch spots with me."

He wants to question me, I can tell by the way his eyebrows pull together but when I remove my fingers from him, he doesn't argue. He sits up and moves over so I can lie on my back where he once was. I grab the condom, roll it on, and lube myself up while he sits beside me and watches. I'm almost quaking with need and you can hear it in my voice, which comes out uneven. "Climb on top. Straddle me."

"What?"

"I think you need to control this," I say, pressing my thumb into the base of the underside of my cock so it stands up tall and straight. "Ride me."

Chase pulls his bottom lip between his teeth. There's hesitation but he moves until he's got a knee on either side of me. I reach up with my free hand, cup the back of his neck, and pull his mouth to mine. While he's tipped forward invading my mouth with relentless sweeps of his tongue, his ass is tipped up and I take the moment to position myself at his entrance. His kiss gets less commanding, as his focus turns to our lower halves. I slowly rub the coated tip over his hole. "Go easy and slow. It's different than fingers and even toys."

"Ump," I don't know what word that is supposed to be and I don't think he does either because he's bearing down and the tip of my dick is making its way inside of him.

He doesn't stop but he pushes down so slowly I feel like he's not moving until I realize my entire head is squeezed tight, and then bit by bit the shaft follows. I am breathing in gulps that I'm holding until my lungs burn and then exhaling in a burst and gulping in more air. This is intense in ways I've never experienced. I've had first times, I've taken other people's first times before. But this is some new level heat, passion, and need.

His head is tipped back and I think his eyes are shut tight judging by the creases in the corners by his temples, which is all I can see. I watch his Adam's apple bob and his chest rise and fall. And then, everything stops when his ass comes to rest on my hips.

"Breathe." I'm not sure if I'm reminding him or me.

"I didn't think it would work."

"We work." I contract the muscles in my ass and abdomen, making my dick twitch inside him. My hands crawl up his thighs until my left one fists his cock and my right gives his ass cheek a quick, hard slap. "I need you to move, Chase."

His chin drops to his chest and his eyes land on me and oh my God, he looks as turned on as I feel and then, eyes still glued to mine, he lifts his ass just a little bit and presses back down. And he does it again and again, strokes getting longer and quicker, and I follow his lead with my hand wrapped around his length, using the milky liquid leaking from his tip to get him wet.

I want him to come so bad but I'm desperate for my own release. And the way he's looking at me, eyes never blinking, like he's studying me, is so hot. I circle my hips as he lowers down on me again and that breaks the stare because his eyes roll back in his head. "Do that again."

"Arch your back."

He does and I repeat the motion and he groans so loud it might just do the impossible and wake my brother. And I don't even care. Inside I'm battling my own release, shoving it away and clawing it back. Dancing on the edge. I want to close my eyes and let go but I won't jump without him. Plus, I want to see him come so I refuse to let my lids fall closed.

He's bouncing on me in a short, hard, erratic rhythm. Once, twice, three times. Oh god. I feel his dick throb and then shoot as he lets out a roar of a moan. He comes so hard I swear it hits the ceiling and he collapses forward onto my hand and his mess. I grip his ass with my free hand and slam up into him one last time as every muscle in my body seizes and I come so hard I feel like I'm falling.

We're a sweaty, sticky mess of limbs and with our torsos flush, our hearts are lined up, hammering against our respective rib cages with such intensity it's like they're trying to break free so they can merge. "You're the most amazing man I know," I whisper.

"And the best lay?" he whispers back and I laugh.

"That too."

Fifteen minutes later we've managed to untangle ourselves and sneak off to the bathroom to share a sensual but PG-13 shower. We emerge back into the hall, both with towels wrapped around our waist and nothing more, when Autumn appears at the top of the stairs. We freeze like deer in the beams of an eighteen wheeler on the interstate. She stumbles at the sight of us and quickly comes to a stop.

"Hey," I say casually. Like it's totally normal for her to catch me half naked in our hall with a dude. It's not. I've never bought a man home. "How was game night?"

"Great. Luke says you have to come next time so he isn't the only one who never remembers the rules." Her eyes dart to me and back to Chase "I see you two… worked things out?"

"Yeah," I reply with a nod as my damp hair drips onto my shoulders. "Chase is my boyfriend."

"I see." She looks at Chase again. Her voice is even and calm. "Treat him right or I will end you."

"I love him," Chase replies.

"Then we should get along just fine." She winks and flashes him a smile. Then, without another word, disappears into her room.

I turn and saunter back to my room and it takes a second, but Chase follows. We both drop the towels. I toss the lube and empty condom wrapper onto the night table and straighten the sheets, climbing into bed and holding back the covers for Chase. He climbs in next to me. We lie side-by-side staring up at the celling. "You okay?"

"Yeah. Of course. That was just weird," Chase explains as my eyes trace a small crack in the plaster above us. "I'm just a little dumbfounded by how simple and nice that was. And also jealous."

"She threatened to end you."

He lets out a breathy chuckle. "Yeah. I'd prefer that to what my parents will say."

We lie there in silence for a few minutes and just when I think he might be asleep he rolls onto his side and shifts lower in the bed, his head coming to rest on my chest. I pull my arm from behind my head and wrap it around his back. "How exactly did your parents react? You said it was great."

"They were champs," I tell him and fight the sadness creeping into my chest. "My dad nodded and hugged me and told me he didn't care and my mom kissed my forehead and told me she was sorry that society made gay teens feel like they owed anyone, even their parents, an announcement and explanation of their sexuality."

He tips his head up and I'm not surprised to see the shock on his face. "My mom was a rampant supporter of gay rights well before she had a gay son."

"I wish I could have met them," he finally says.

"I wish they could have met you," I tell him, moving my head to gently kiss the top of his. "They'd be so happy I've fallen in love."

"You have?"

"Yes. I have." I feel his arm tighten across my chest, holding me closer. "I'm sorry I didn't say it sooner."

"We were busy," Chase quips and we're both smiling. I don't have to look at him to know. "I'm glad you feel the same but even if you didn't, I would have been glad I told you anyway."

A heartbeat passes.

"That's a lie. It would have sucked," Chase admits.

I laugh and he pulls himself up so he's resting his head next to mine on the pillow. "I know it would've sucked. I've been there before."

"You won't be there again."

Chase gently presses his palm into the side of my face and kisses me and I know he's right. Between his family and that asshole Bennie and the election, I have no idea what happens next for us. But I do know, without a doubt, it isn't heartbreak. And that's enough.

25

CHASE

"Hey Chase!" Murphy calls out over the din of the crowd. "Can you tell your boyfriend if he wears a hole in the floor, Tanner is going to be just as pissed as he is when he breaks a glass."

I smile at the joke and then walk over and block Bowen's path so he has to stop pacing. I put my hands on his shoulders, which are covered in a very neatly pressed charcoal gray dress shirt. His hair is brushed and Autumn put some kind of product in it that keeps it flat. My fingers have been twitching all night with the need to muss it up. Our eyes meet and I can see the worry and fear in them. I'd do anything to take it away, but it's not up to me. It's up to the citizens of Burlington.

"Whatever happens, it'll be okay." He nods. I'm not buying it. "Say it. Repeat it."

"Whatever happens it will be okay." His shoulders seem to loosen a little. I pull him close for a minute and kiss his cheek. When I let go, he smiles. "Thanks."

"Anytime."

When Harrison agreed to host Woody's supporters tonight, as a possible victory party, I took care of the audio visual, bringing the sixty-inch tv from my office's conference room to the bar this afternoon and paying our tech guy overtime to set everything up. I even offered to pay for private caterers but the chef here wouldn't hear of it. Joss Matheson is very protective about his kitchen, apparently. But he offered to make a special menu. There're plates of incredible finger food everywhere. Tiny crispy flaky sausage rolls, individual prawn cocktails, and these things he calls Devils on Horseback which are dates wrapped in bacon and man, who knew that combination would be delicious? Apparently the Brits. It's heaven.

The bar is pretty packed too. Woody has a lot of supporters, which makes me think he's got a real shot at this despite the debacle with the paper. The front-page story last week was a retraction, clearing the Whitlock name and admitting the source gave false information. The lawyer, a friend of Peter's, made sure that the paper knew that was the only way to avoid a legal battle. One she made it clear they would lose.

Grant, Joe, and his wife Sarah are here. So are all the bar staff and their partners. Bowen introduced me to most of them like Tanner and his husband Jax, Auden and his husband Carter, Chef Joss and his boyfriend Kai who grinned when he met me announcing, "Good to know the hot farmer is taken."

Not really sure what that's about, but I like that he — and everyone else — knows Bowen is mine.

The polls have been closed for over two hours, which was right around the time the love of my life started pacing. I take his hand in mine. "Want a drink?"

"Yes. But no. I shouldn't," he replies.

"Waiting for the champagne. Good call," I say and he cocks his head, blinking at me.

"You're so confident I'm jealous."

"Whatever happens it will be okay," I repeat. I know he doesn't believe it, but I believe enough for both of us. "But I need a glass of red."

I give his hand a final reassuring squeeze and weave my way through the crowd to the bar. Murph leans in. "What can I get you? A Malbec? Cab? Valium for Bowen?"

"All of the above," I quip and he laughs. "I'll take a Cab. Thanks Murph."

"Have you met my boyfriend?" Murph asks, reaching for a wine glass above him and tilting his head to the occupied seat beside me. "He was straight, like you. Guess Bowen and I have superpowers."

I look at the dark-haired guy beside me who is shaking his head with a smile. "Jason. Hey. And I apologize. Murph is filterless."

"Chase. Nice to meet you." I shake his hand. "Filters are overrated."

"Thank you." Murph winks at me and slides the wine across the bar.

"Turn it up!" Autumn hollers suddenly, pointing at the television and jumping up and down.

Tanner scrambles for the remote. The local news station is ready to report some preliminary numbers, apparently, which is why Autumn is yelling. Tanner turns up the TV and the room falls silent.

"Well, I have to say Gail, I don't think there's been a closer race," the male announcer says to his colleague.

"That's true Gordon. We've had snap elections before to fill unexpected vacancies but never fought with such… gusto," she concludes.

"That's one way to put it," I grumble.

"Just give us the numbers!" I hear Autumn bark. Some people giggle.

"But now it looks like we have enough counted votes to declare…" He pauses and I swear not a single person in the room is breathing. "With sixty-nine percent of the vote, our next mayor is Woody Whitlock."

I don't actually hear the entire last name leave the anchor's mouth because the room erupts in celebration. I leave my wine and battle my way back to Bowen. Everyone around him is jumping and screaming and Woody and Autumn have arms wrapped around him but he's swiveling his head around urgently. Looking for me.

When our eyes meet, he breaks from his family and we yank each other into a bear hug. "Un-freaking-believable!"

"Hard fought," I counter. "And well earned."

He pulls back, cupping my face in his hands he lays one on me, brief but intense. Still holding my face, he says. "I know you're right and everything would have been okay if he didn't win."

I nod.

"That's a lie. It would have sucked," he replies. Same words I said two long weeks ago.

I laugh. "But you'd still have me."

"Fact."

"Bowen!" Woody calls. "The paper wants a picture of the family."

"I hate this part," Bowen whispers and turns with a fake but polite smile on his face.

I watch him make his way to his family, and I can't help but think of my own. My parents do not take my calls and they don't return them. No mention of the inheritance. No invites to events they need me to attend. Pure and utter silence. My cousin hasn't reached out and my aunt hasn't either. The only one who has, shockingly, is Colin. To tell me they know, and they do not approve. But he does.

"Look bro, you can fuck whoever you want. I don't care what parts they have."

Crass, but that's always been Colin. "I'm not just fucking him, Colin. I'm dating him. Seriously. Exclusively."

"Okay. You can do that too with whoever you want," Colin replied. "I don't exactly want to hear the details or anything."

"I didn't want to hear the details when you lost your virginity to that camp counselor at fifteen, but you insisted on telling me anyway," I reminded him.

"Because I thought I was giving you pointers you would need," Colin replied defensively. "You were still a virgin."

"Well now I'm not. In any aspect of the word," I couldn't help but add.

"Congrats," he replied so awkwardly I had to cover the phone so he didn't hear me chuckle. "And if I ever want to know how to suck a dick, I'll gladly take your advice."

"I'll gladly give it."

"Can we talk about the real problem here?" Colin had replied. "They're not going to give you that inheritance."

"I thought that might happen."

"You had less than six months to keep your mouth shut, Chase," Colin had sounded so fucking baffled and yet also impressed. "You were so close."

"I know. And I have no regrets."

It was the best conversation I ever had with my brother and I laid awake that night, with Bowen breathing softly beside me, wondering if it would have happened if I'd stayed in the closet and waited to get that money. I think in some odd way, I'd earned a respect he'd never had for me before.

"Chase!" I turn and see Bowen waving me over.

I walk over, nodding politely at the paper's photographer. Autumn leans in. "We want you in one of the pictures."

"Oh. Really?"

"Of course," Woody smiles. "We owe you a lot."

"But I get it if—" Bowen starts but I cut him off by wrapping a proud arm around his shoulder and smoothing the front of my dress shirt. He relaxes into me, looping his arm around my waist and the photographer snaps away. When he's done, the reporter interviews Woody and a news crew asks him to come outside.

I grab Bowen and pull him toward the bar, smirking. "Let's get you that champagne you've been holding out for."

At one in the morning, the last supporter wanders out the door. Most of the staff have gone home too and it's just Tanner and the clean-up crew I hired, which Joss was more than okay with. Woody and Autumn left in the family station wagon, which has its days numbered because Woody promises they're getting a hybrid now.

I walk Bowen back to my loft, his hand laced through mine. But when we get there, I'm shocked to see my Aunt Hilda standing outside. I drop his hand and pick up my pace. "What's wrong? Who died?"

Icy fear swirls in my gut, but she looks at me wide eyed and shakes her head. "Oh heavens, Chase, no one."

"It's the middle of the night," I reply and stare down at her with confusion. "Did your car break down? Are you okay?"

"Perfectly fine, thank you," she snaps and smooths her hair as a breeze picks up the ends of her silvery bob. "My word, Chase I'm old but I can be up past midnight. I'm not exactly a Gremlin."

"A what?" Bowen asks and Aunt Hilda frowns. "Sorry, ma'am. Chase, maybe I should head home."

"Whatever for? You're dating my nephew, right?" Aunt Hilda asks, and then keeps talking before he can answer. "Couples spend the night with each other all the time. How do you think my daughter had a baby seven months after her wedding?"

"I... Umm..." Bowen looks at me, completely at a loss as to what to say. To be honest I am too. That's the first time anyone has ever confirmed that my cousin got pregnant before her wedding.

I turn back to my aunt. She waves a hand as if clearing the air. "Anyway, I wanted to tell you that I didn't let Amy lose her money and I'm not going to let you lose it either."

"Aunt Hilda I appreciate your…support," I say carefully because I think it's support. Right? It's hard to tell with her frown and her clipped speech. "And I don't know how you got a doctor to fake a pregnancy timeline, but the fact is, there's nothing to hide here. I mean there was, but it's too late now. My father will never allow me to have the money. Grandfather was very clear that this would be considered immoral to him. He voted against gay marriage, remember?"

She rolls her eyes. "Yes. I remember. I hated that."

"You did?" How is this the first I'm hearing of it, I wonder.

"Are you aware that both your father and I are the trustees and we must agree on the inheritances being bestowed upon the grandchildren?" she asks, adjusting the strap of her designer bag on her shoulder. I nod and she sighs. "Are you also aware that, because of potential parental bias, if we don't agree the decision defaults to the trustee who is not the parent?"

"What?" I'm a smart boy with a degree but my brain can't compute at the moment.

"Oh, dear boy." Aunt Hilda gets annoyed. "I wanted Amy to get her inheritance. He did not. Because we were deadlocked, the will said his judgement should be considered the final decision because he wasn't the parent. So, your brother Colin found a friend he knew, some brother of a guy who he went to law school with, who would write a brief clinical report claiming that the baby was, without a doubt, a large preemie. That's the only way I could get your father to agree to give Amy her inheritance. Colin has asked me to return the favor. So, I will."

"You will?"

"I don't need a fake doctor's note or any kind of trickery," Hilda announces, her lips, still painted a perfect subtle coral color even though it's the middle of the night and she likely got out of bed to come here. "I think the whole clause was just your grandfather's way of continuing to be a bigoted asshole even in death. So your dad may say no, but I'll veto it. You'll get your inheritance."

"Aunt Hilda… I don't know what to say." Never in a million years did I expect this to happen. I was resigned. I'd made peace. But now I feel like I just won the lottery and I'm at a loss.

"Thank you usually works," Bowen whispers against my ear and I remember he's right behind me.

Hilda smiles at him. I clear my throat. "Thank you, Aunt Hilda. I would hug you if we were the type of family that did that."

"Maybe we should try it out," she replies, and I not only hug her but lift her off her feet.

"Enough!" she bellows but it's mixed with laughter.

I delicately deposit her back on her pristine Chanel slingbacks. She smooths invisible wrinkles out of her blouse, her blue eyes move to Bowen again. "Congratulation to your brother on his successful mayoral campaign."

"Thank you, ma'am."

"I'm not a fan of ma'am," she snaps and digs her keys out of her purse. "I'll have you two over for dinner some night soon and you can call me Hilda then."

"Okay. Sure." Bowen smiles, but his eyes are dazed. Yeah, my family is a trip he isn't used to taking. I get it. But I think we'll be okay navigating it together now that the familial topography seems to be changing.

I lace my fingers through his and Aunt Hilda walks away waving over her shoulder. "Ta ta for now! And remember, glassware does not go in an ice machine."

I laugh. Some things will never change.

We watch her until she's safely inside at the end of the block and her taillights disappear around the corner. And that's when it sinks in. I can sell Dauntless to Grant. I can go back to school and study music. I can start that music camp I want to start. I can…

"Are you okay?" Bowen asks.

"I love you," I say but it's garbled. I'm choking on the emotion of it all.

I crash my mouth onto his and kiss him like he's all that matters, because in the end he is. I press him into the front door, my tongue dancing with his, our bodies rubbing and grinding. Finally, he gives me a gentle shove and pulls in a ragged breath, his thumb glancing across his bottom lip and he pulls his mouth into a smile. "Can we take this inside? I really want to fuck you."

I laugh and he punches the code on the keypad to make the door buzz open. We almost run down the hall and Bowen stabs at the elevator keypad, putting in the code that allows access to my floor with the impatience of a toddler. "You're in a rush."

The doors swish open and we tumble inside. I laugh because by the time the elevator lands on my floor, he's already got both our shirts unbuttoned. "You're excited."

As if to prove my point I palm his length through his dress pants. He grins and pushes his hips forward into my hand. "I've never fucked a millionaire before."

"Ha!" I bark and shove my hands into the hair I've been dying to mess up all damn night. "You're cute."

"Just cute?' he questions, brushing our lips together, the same way that very first kiss started.

"More than cute," I reply, tugging on the hand laced through my fingers. He likes that. "You're everything. That's why I'm so calm about this, I think. Because that inheritance. It's just icing on the cake. You're the cake."

He blinks. "I love you."

"I know." I kiss him slowly and gently but I end it with a teasing tug of his bottom lip between my teeth. "Now let's go upstairs so I can have my cake… and eat it too."

"How did you manage to make my dick harder with baking innuendo?" He chuckles and I chase him up the stairs.

After he fucks me so long and so hard I see stars, he collapses onto my chest, and my legs unhook from his back and we lay there, his dick still inside me, because we don't have to worry about disposing of a condom since our tests came back four days ago. I brush his tangled golden hair back from his face so I can see his amber eyes and I say, "You know, Aunt Hilda's support might be all I need, but it might not be. This isn't a done deal."

"I know. I don't care. Do you?" he whispers back. And I shake my head.

"Nah. Like I said, icing." I drink in his lazy smile, because it's the only thing that can soothe my parched soul. "But if it happens, I would love it if you came with me to complete everything. Sign the papers and face my dad and everything."

Bowen blinks but doesn't hesitate. "Of course I'll be there."

Five months, two weeks, seventeen days and twelve hours later, I walk into Sprysky and Gentry with Bowen's hand in mine. Dad is there, but he doesn't speak a word to me. Iris explains the rules that Aunt Hilda did to me the night of the election and it plays out exactly the way Aunt Hilda predicted it would. My dad objects. Aunt Hilda overrules. Peter recites the rules of the will if an inheritance is contested by one of the trustees. Dad's face grows redder and redder but he doesn't protest or argue or call anyone names, which I know he wants to do. Especially when Aunt Hilda's smile grows smug.

As soon as his signature is on the document he storms towards the door of the conference room but pauses. "I'm not ashamed you're… what you are, Chase. It's how you embarrassed the family at that event. Making a spectacle out of it. You owe us an apology for that."

"No. I don't," I reply calmly.

"Mr. Ashton, your son told me he loved me. That's all," Bowen says, and I'm shocked he's speaking up. "If your son had told a woman that, on stage at a public event, would it have been considered a spectacle to you?"

"We don't do things like that in our family," he says, avoiding the actual question like the seasoned politician he is.

"He's right, we don't," I say and look him in the eyes for what I think may be the last time ever. And I'm okay with that if it is. "But we should. Having tried it I have to say five stars. Highly recommend."

"I don't even know who you are anymore Chase," he shakes his head in disgust and storms out.

"He's right. He doesn't know you," Bowen says quietly. "And it's his loss."

I see Aunt Hilda's face smile softly as she signs the documents Peter puts in front of her. Then I sign and Peter and Iris smile triumphantly. Being the liberal, diverse firm that they are, I'm sure this feels like a win for them too. Peter tucks the paperwork into a folder. "The funds will be wired into the account you gave us in the next twenty-four hours."

I shake both their hands. Bowen hugs every single person in the room, including Aunt Hilda who is getting much better at giving and receiving affection.

Outside I kiss him. "Let's go to Vino and Veritas for a celebratory drink."

"And then home?" he asks and wiggles his eyebrows.

"You already fucked a millionaire, remember?" I guide us down the street, leaves in vibrant oranges, reds, and yellows litter the sidewalk and a crisp fall breeze circles us.

"Yeah, but now it's official." He turns his head, leaning in so his lips brush my ear when he speaks. "And I wanna *be* fucked by a millionaire."

Arousal tears hard and fast through my veins. "Okay, so home and V and V later?"

He laughs. "You want me so bad."

"Fuck yeah I do," I reply. "More than I wanted three and a half million dollars."

And then I kiss him, right there in the middle of the sidewalk, in broad daylight.

ACKNOWLEDGMENTS

When Sarina Bowen told I'd be part of In Vino Veritas it felt like winning the lottery, for the second time. The first time was when she invited me to write in the Moo U series. Thank you Sarina for giving me this opportunity and for being such a joy to work with. You not only inspire me to be a better author, you share the wisdom, skills and tips I need to get there. Also a million thanks to Jane, Natasha and Jenn. Heart Eyes Press has the ultimate dream team. I've never worked with a better group of people in the publishing world. Full stop. And the extra bonus of working on these projects is getting to know and collaborate with so many talented authors. Birkie, Leslie, Garrett, Rachel and Lori, thank you for all the support, brainstorming, laughs and grammar discussions (to come or not to cum, that is the question.). Expect to be tackle hugged if I ever have the pleasure of meeting any of you in person. Sorry not sorry.

I'm grateful for the talented, diligent work of my editor Brandi Zelenka at Notes in the Margin and the proofing skills of Claudia Fosca Stahl, who always finds the time to fit me into her schedule. Thank you both so much. Much love to my husband Jack who kept me fed, and kept the dog alive, as I powered through this manuscript in thirty-eight days. Thank you to my agent Kimberly for the constant support, as well as her team at Brower Literary. A shout out to my dear friend Novid, who I dedicated this book to, for being a good friend and keeping Jack company while I ignored everything and everyone but my words. Thanks to my mom and my friends who have always been there to support me. And to the readers and bloggers who continue to support me and my work, thank you. You guys are the best. May Bowen and Chase bring you all the feels they brought me.